Single-Minded

Single Dads of Dragonfly Lake

Amy Knupp

Chapter One

West

My three chattery reasons for living, my daughters—Scarlet, Sienna, and Nova—were even more animated than usual this morning as they ate their breakfast.

Maybe it was because today was the first day of summer break, and their favorite babysitter, seventeen-year-old Allison, would be their full-time companion for the next two and a half months.

Maybe they were feeding off my emotional state. I tried to hide it, but this was a big day for me too. I couldn't deny I was shaky inside with exhilaration and determination.

"Can we go swimming every day, Allie?" four-year-old Nova asked.

"We'll go swimming a lot if you want to," the babysitter said, taking the fourth chair at the table.

Allison had shown up right on time at seven thirty, her eyes bright and eager for her first day of her summer job. I trusted Allison. She was the most responsible seventeen-year-old I'd ever met and loved my girls. But this was new. Full-time was a lot. My girls were a lot.

"One day at a time, Nova," I told my youngest as I filled my travel mug with coffee.

"I want to do *all...the...things!*" she said in a burst of exuberance that almost always made me grin.

"Right now the thing you need to do is eat your breakfast," I told her, dumping ice cubes into my five-gallon water cooler I took to the jobsite every day, wherever we were working.

"I'm done, but Sienna's not," Nova said.

I glanced over my shoulder. Nova's and Scarlet's plates were indeed empty. Sienna's had a half-eaten piece of toast and both her sausage links, which were pushed to the farthest side of her plate.

"What's wrong with your food, Sienna?" I asked.

"Sausage is just...ew, Daddy," Sienna said, wrinkling her nose.

"You ate it yesterday," I said.

She stared at her plate, nostrils flaring, head shaking, as her sisters looked on.

"It's just sausage, Si-Si," Nova preached.

Sienna picked up her toast instead and took a dainty bite.

"I'll take your sausage," Scarlet, Sienna's fraternal twin, offered enthusiastically.

Sienna shoved her plate to her sister and continued to eat her toast.

I shrugged and considered it settled, then glanced at the time. Twenty till eight. Time for me to boogie. I turned to Allison.

"There's plenty in the fridge for lunch for all of you. If you go to the beach, don't forget the arm floats for Nova."

"A Novel Place is having story time at eleven, so I thought I'd take them," Allison said, and I swear if I could double her wages, I would.

"They'll love it," I said. I took my wallet out and gave her a couple of bills when the girls weren't looking. "Get them each one book," I told her quietly.

Money was tight, as usual, but books were one thing I stretched to make work.

Money would be less tight if I landed Davis Morten's position at work.

My phone buzzed with a text message. I pulled it out of my pocket to see my boss's name.

Levi: Running late. Plumbing emergency at my mom's. Start without me.

West: I got it covered. Take care of your mom.

Levi: You sure? You good with this?

West: 100% sure.

"I gotta roll," I told Allison and my girls. "Love you, squirrels," I said to my daughters, rounding the kitchen table and kissing each in turn.

"Love you, Daddy!" they all said.

I grabbed my lunch from the fridge, my day's worth of beverages, and my work bag.

"Be good for Allison," I called on my way out the door. "Allison, call if you need anything."

"We'll be fine," the babysitter assured me.

I headed out into the morning sunshine. The weather was already promising to be sweltering by afternoon. I was thankful to be starting a weeks-long indoor project. A cush job, as Nick Carlisle, the lead of the other crew and my competition for Davis's job, had pointed out last week. I'd happily take it, as he was overseeing a boathouse, deck, and gazebo build.

I climbed into my SUV, my mind switching from little-girl mode to work.

Levi Dawson, the owner and head contractor, had turned things upside down at work last week, or rather Davis's retirement announcement had. Levi's method of replacing the fifty-something workhorse was smart as hell. He'd pitted me versus Nick Carlisle, as we had seniority and the most experience. For the next two to three months, we'd each lead a crew on separate projects. At the end of the summer, he'd make one of us the foreman directly under him for good.

That was going to be me if I had anything to say about it.

The project I was heading up would likely take close to two months, maybe more, depending on any supply delays. Apparently it was a big-ass project, and the homeowner was paying big-ass bucks to have it squeezed into a cancellation slot.

I checked the address for the job and noted it was on Honeysuckle Road, out by my buddy Max's house, if I wasn't mistaken. I pointed the SUV that way.

As Levi was the one to meet with potential clients and bid out projects, I didn't know much about this one other than what the plans told me. It was a main floor gut of a big house directly on the shore. That tracked with being a neighbor of Max, who'd played in the NFL a few years back and had the lakeside house to show for it.

Since Levi had planned to meet the homeowner and me

first thing this morning to go over the project in detail, I didn't even know the homeowner's first name. She was apparently new to town, obviously had some cash, and I couldn't help but picture a hoity-toity widow in her sixties. None of that mattered to me. I just hoped she was easygoing, not a clientzilla, because I intended to rock the hell out of the project.

As I drove through downtown Dragonfly Lake, a text message sounded through the SUV's Bluetooth system. My ex-wife's name popped up on the display.

"Happy fucking Monday," I muttered to myself.

I didn't hear from Flora often, which pissed me off on the girls' behalf but was a blessing as far as my peace level was concerned. There was nothing peaceful about Flora.

I had the Bluetooth system read her message to me.

Flora: We'll be in the area tomorrow. Want to take the girls to an early dinner before Gil's show. Can we pick them up at three?

"God dammit." I pounded the steering wheel. "Three isn't fucking dinner; it's the middle of the afternoon." The girls would need a fourth meal before bedtime if they ate at three.

Flora's appearances were few and far between. As much as I questioned whether she was a positive part of the girls' lives, she *was* their mother. I kept hoping she'd get her shit and her priorities together and be someone they could look up to, but that seemed to be more and more of a pipe dream.

I dictated my response.

West: Do I have a choice?

Flora: Don't be like that.

West: Honest question. Do I have a choice between three tomorrow or maybe you could fit them in the next day and spend more time with them?

Flora: We have to be in Omaha the next day.

Of course they did.

In other words, my only choice was either to let the girls spend a tiny slot of time with their mom or make them miss out altogether. It was a shitty choice, but when I'd gotten full-time custody, I'd agreed Flora could visit her daughters whenever she wanted to. Back then, I'd hoped she'd be a regular presence in their lives instead of a special event whenever she and her guitarist boyfriend happened to be close enough to stop by for a few minutes.

West: I'll be working at three.

Flora: I can get them at daycare.

West: They have a full-time babysitter at our place. Where do you plan to take them?

Flora: Gil wants Dragonfly Diner. We'll go there.

I clenched my back teeth together. She put her boyfriend's desires over our girls'. Every. Single. Time.

You'd think I'd be used to it by now, but she continually disappointed me. That was Flora though. She'd been fun when we first met in the army. She'd gotten pregnant before we'd even thought whether we could make it long-term, but did that stop us from trying? Hell no. If I had a dollar for every bad decision I'd made where relationships were concerned, I could retire.

> West: Pick them up at my place. Have them home by five.

> Flora: We'll be done before that. Gil needs to be in Nashville by six.

Fucking fantastic.

I didn't respond. I had nothing else to say, at least nothing civil or productive.

I drove by Max's house and verified his house number was two lots down from my target.

When I spotted the right numbers on a mailbox, my brows went up. Ms. Holiday's house was cottage-style, but that term was misleading because *cottage* made you think small. There was nothing small about this place.

The exterior was white siding with gray stonework. The structure was an L-shape, one side a connected three-car garage with a bonus room above it, complete with a cupola. On the garage.

Definitely seven figures, I thought as I pulled up along the curb and killed the engine. I could see why Levi claimed this was gonna be a showpiece.

As I climbed out of the truck, I got another text message.

> Flora: Tell the girls I'll see them tomorrow.

"Go to hell," I said under my breath, my irritation flooding right back in. Flora had that effect on me.

I pulled my tool belt out and put it on, catching myself in a scowl.

The bitch of it was, while Flora annoyed me with everything out of her mouth—or her fingertips in this case—I was more pissed at myself when it came to her. She was Exhibit A in the case of me rushing in with a woman.

When we'd met, we'd been all about lust and cutting loose. We'd had fun together. Just before I was discharged, we found out she was three months pregnant. Flora's discharge was two months after mine.

I'd known she wasn't ready to settle down, but I also knew everything changed when babies came into the mix. I convinced her to give us a chance and move to Dragonfly Lake with me.

Looking back, I could see she was never going to be content in a small town. She likely wouldn't be happy in a big city either. What Flora apparently preferred was roaming, living on the road, and avoiding responsibility.

I should've seen that early on. When we'd started having problems, before the twins were even born, I should've faced that and let her go. Instead we were on and off for years, long enough for Nova to be conceived. My youngest daughter was the sole reason I couldn't regret being a stubborn dumbass who didn't know when to throw in the towel.

As I walked up the driveway, I fought to shove my irritation away. This job was important. My chance to prove myself. To prove that, while I was shit at relationships, I had value when it came to my career.

I rang the doorbell and eventually heard someone approaching inside. I stood taller and forced my mind away from my ex, toward exceeding expectations on this project.

When the door opened and I laid eyes on the client, my heart skipped a beat.

Holy shit balls.

Ms. Holiday was not a sixty-year-old widow.

I'd seen this woman before. I'd noticed her at Chance and Rowan's party a couple of weeks ago before I'd had to run out for a kid emergency. How the hell could I *not* notice her?

She was beautiful, with piercing blue eyes beneath long lashes, unadorned lips that curved into a sexy-without-trying smile, and an air about her that spoke of money and class, in spite of her casual outfit of cutoff denim shorts that revealed gorgeous legs, a sleeveless top with a halter neckline that showed off sexy, delicate shoulders, and blinged-out flip-flops my daughters would drool over.

Ah, hell.

I cleared my throat and felt like an old-time cartoon character with stars dancing around my head but fuck that.

"Morning," I said. "I'm West Aldridge from Dawson Construction."

"I know." Her smile turned knowing in a way that made my blood race. She held out her delicate-looking hand and surprised me with the firmness of her shake when I took it. "I'm Presley Holiday."

My blood raced like it was *not* supposed to race on a job. Or preferably ever.

"Come on in, West."

I followed her inside, cussing inwardly and steeling myself against the effect this woman had on me in the first five seconds of meeting her.

Chapter Two

Presley

West Aldridge at close range had even more impact on me than he had across a crowded patio three weeks ago at Rowan and Chance's party.

Those stunning green eyes were kind and attentive. His square jaw was solid, strong, and made all the more masculine by his beard. When we'd shaken hands, his was large and undoubtedly powerful, yet his touch had been restrained, almost gentle. As we'd made physical contact, my heart had fluttered in my chest.

I was so not the flutters-from-a-guy type.

As I stepped back to let him into my home, I took him in as a whole. He wore a black tee that revealed biceps I wasn't going to get out of my head anytime soon. His muscular legs were thick beneath cargo pants. And that tool belt...

I hadn't realized I was into guys with beards and tool belts until now.

"Levi had an emergency," West said as he looked

around at my new home. "He might join us later, but we'll start without him."

"I'm sure you and I can handle it just fine," I said, allowing my lips to curve into a flirty smile.

"Once you show me around, I won't need to bother you." His tone wasn't unkind, just businesslike. No grin in return. Not at all flirty.

Okay. I could read a guy. Business it was then. He'd be here for who knew how many weeks. Getting along was key. Which of course meant crossing any lines into flirtation would be a bad idea.

I was down with that. This eye candy might've been part of the reason I'd called Dawson Construction in the first place but only a small part. Multiple recommendations for Levi's company from my friends and their friends weighed a lot more heavily than the instant attraction I'd had to West at that party.

That kind of reaction to a man wasn't normal for me, but then nothing in my life had been normal for the past three weeks. I'd jumped straight off the cliff of normal when I'd walked out on my career.

"I'm assuming you have the plans from Levi?" I asked.

"Yes, ma'am." He held up a thick contractor's portfolio, but I almost didn't notice as I tried to swallow the *ma'am*.

I was thirty-five years old. I'd put West close to my age, maybe a couple of years younger. There was no need for him to *ma'am* me. But maybe that was just him being polite.

"We're gutting this whole level," he said. "Opening it up. New kitchen, new master suite, powder room, utility room, new everything, plus finishing the bonus room above the garage."

"Yes." I stepped from the foyer into the hall. "There's the formal dining room." I pointed at the mostly enclosed room, then to the opposite side. "Living room, obviously." We walked down the short hall to the kitchen doorway. "Powder and utility are that way. Kitchen's here."

He glanced to the powder room, then followed me into the kitchen. "We got some eighties going on here with the walled-off rooms, huh?"

"So much eighties," I said. "I fell in love with the lot and the view. The house is okay but..."

"We'll make it better. Nice breakfast nook. We're updating the glass there, right?"

He wasn't referring to his notes, so I could tell he'd studied the plans.

"Right," I said of the sunroom-style alcove. "Make it look like today instead of yesteryear."

He eyed the kitchen, taking in relevant details, nodded, then said, "And the master?"

I led him through the living room to the empty master suite that looked out on the lake, just like the breakfast nook and the living room.

"That's quite a view," he said, glancing toward the lake before stepping in the opposite direction, past the closets, and looking into the bathroom. "Are you not living here?"

"I am. I moved in on Saturday, but knowing you guys were starting today, I have everything either on the second floor or in storage."

He nodded. "It's gonna be loud. No way around it. You don't work from home, do you?"

"I...don't work." I forced a smile, trying to cover how much that was messing with my head.

I could see him trying to puzzle that out. No job. Big house. Expensive remodeling project.

"I was an investment banker until three weeks ago," I explained.

His brows shot up. "But now you're not?"

"Now I'm not. I loved the job...until I didn't. It was long hours, high stress, starting to become toxic. My boss was a condescending, sexist jackass."

"Sounds like leaving was a good decision then," he said as he checked something in his portfolio.

"Yeah." Even I could hear the lack of conviction in my answer, but that wasn't accurate. Leaving my job *was* the right decision. I nodded and tried again. "It definitely was. I'm just trying to figure out what to do with myself."

"You don't have something lined up?" His brow furrowed as if that didn't compute.

"No." I let out a little laugh, hoping that hid how I was freaking out pretty much full-time. "This remodeling project is it."

When I'd left my job, I'd been fueled by multiple things: concerning news from my doctor, ongoing insistence by my BFF, Chloe, that my job wasn't worth the stress and lack of respect from my boss, and chronic resentment at said boss. Walking out, seeing his stunned expression, had rocketed me to a natural high that had lasted for days.

"Levi said you purchased this place earlier in the spring?" West said.

I nodded. "It's funny how things work out. I bought it on a whim when I was still working and living in Nashville. Had no idea what I'd do with it. Rent it out, use it for a weekend place... When I quit my job, all I could think about was getting away, out of the city. Far away from everything. Starting over."

Recovering.

Getting healthy.

Learning to relax.

That was turning out to be quite the challenge.

"Gonna be rough for a few weeks," West said, "with a work crew here every day, making a racket."

"I figure I'll spend time outside, floating on the lake, reading, gardening."

"You garden?" He didn't hide his surprise.

With a self-conscious grin, I admitted, "Not yet. It's supposed to be soothing. Meditative. I bought some flowers to plant."

Please, let it be meditative. Let me get swept away by it, taken out of my head.

My head wasn't a good place right now.

For the first two and a half weeks after I'd quit, I'd kept busy by getting my Nashville condo ready to sell. I moved things to storage, painted, made some minor repairs, had the flooring replaced. I hired a staging company. I put it on the market a week ago and got a good offer right away. Then this past Saturday, I made the move to Dragonfly Lake.

Once the movers had left and I was alone in my new place, I expected to feel invigorated, excited, joyful. I'd done it. I'd taken a huge step toward changing my frantic, unhealthy life.

Instead, I'd been jittery, unable to sit still, nearly panic-stricken at the emptiness that stretched out in front of me.

My single-minded purpose since grad school had been to earn a shit ton of money, then invest it and turn it into a double shit ton. Quadruple. Tenfold.

By working my fool ass off, plus having spot-on gut instincts and general good luck, I'd accomplished a bigger net worth than I'd thought possible. When most people would think, *I've made my nest egg; I'm good,* I became determined to do it again. Build it into more. Climb higher.

"I'm gonna take a closer look at the kitchen," West said,

closing his portfolio and leaving the bedroom, dragging me out of my musing.

I followed him. "I was under the impression there'd be a whole crew here. I bought a dozen donuts for you guys," I said, gesturing to the box on the counter as I reentered the kitchen.

West was eyeing the windows in the sunroom, then turned his attention to me.

"Paul, Nathan, and Fritz will be here shortly to get started with demo. Some days it'll be the four of us. Some days it'll be more. Just depends on the day and the tasks. You didn't have to get us anything, but thank you."

"I would've gotten coffee too, but I don't love the bakery's one-size-fits-all pot of java. I haven't figured out the best place to get coffee in town. What's your favorite?"

He paused as if he hadn't thought about it before. "I just make some at home. I don't know of a good coffee source in town."

"You're kidding me." This town might be small, but its people still needed good coffee.

"No, ma'am."

Ma'am again.

"Can I ask you a personal question?"

"You can ask," he said.

"How old are you?"

"Thirty-one."

I filed that away. "I'm only four years older. You don't need to call me *ma'am*."

With a tilt of his head, he said, "Are you not from the South? It's a way to be polite."

"Be less polite. Pretty please? Just call me Presley."

"Yes, ma—" He stopped himself, laughed. "Presley. I'll do my best.

"And please eat some donuts." I opened the box and held it out. "Save me from myself."

He grinned, and my God, my heart... I swear it fluttered again. It didn't make sense how much this guy's smile affected me.

"You got a sweet tooth?" he asked as he took a single glazed donut from me.

"If it's bad for me, I crave it. Sugar, wine, coffee, you name it."

"The guys'll take some of these off your hands when they get here. I'm going to poke around a little deeper, see what we're up against."

"Anything I can do to help?"

"No, ma— Dammit," he said quietly. "Presley. I'll just do my thing, and you can do yours."

"Okay," I said, as if I had any idea what my thing was. "I'm going to eat a donut out on the patio, then maybe plant flowers."

After that, I had no clue, but I needed to figure it out. It was that or lose my mind.

Chapter Three

Presley

Sunrise on the lake was a thing of beauty, and I had a front-row seat to it. Every day for the rest of my life, if I wanted it.

I'd woken up at quarter till five, even though I had no reason to be awake until West and his crew arrived. Old habits died hard.

New habits were going to take a bit.

Like sleeping. Relaxing. Plus filling my waking hours with...something.

I'd texted Chloe, my best friend since business school, and asked her if she could get away for breakfast at the Dragonfly Diner.

Breakfast was *something*. It would fill an hour.

Baby steps.

Just after I was seated at a booth along the front windows with a view of the heart of town, Chloe came in, glanced around, greeted Patrick—one of the servers—by name, and headed toward me.

I stood and hugged her.

"God, it's good to see you," I said.

Chloe laughed. "I just saw you Saturday. Because you live in town now," she said with pronounced enthusiasm.

"I'm still getting used to that," I said as we slid into opposite sides of the booth.

"Good morning, ladies." Patrick came up to our table with a coffeepot. "Do we want coffee?"

Chloe flipped her mug over. I eyed the pot, knew it would be mediocre, and turned my mug upright anyway.

"Yes, please," I said in case my face had revealed my thoughts about standard diner coffee. Normally I liked my coffee black, but that was when it was the good stuff and I wanted to savor the true flavor. "Could we get real cream too?"

"You bet, sugar. Do you need some time with the menu?" Patrick asked as he poured.

Chloe looked at me in question.

"Those waffles..." I said.

"Dragonfly Dust," Chloe said.

"Those. Please."

"That's really why you moved to town, isn't it?" Chloe said.

"Definitely a perk," I said.

"Oh, new resident?" Patrick asked. "Welcome to Dragonfly Lake. The waffles are a marvelous reason to move here. What can I get you, Chloe?"

She hesitated.

"You want the waffles," I said, knowing my friend's sugar tooth.

"We're celebrating your move. I want the waffles."

"You got it." Patrick hurried off to another table.

The place was filling up fast, despite it being barely six thirty.

I eyed my mug, knowing the java was subpar. I'd had it before. With a sigh, I glanced around for Patrick to see if the cream was on its way. The bowl of artificial creamers on the table... No.

"You're such a snob," Chloe said, laughing.

"I like good coffee."

"Bronson's spoiled you."

"I miss Bronson's."

The indie artisan coffee shop was across the street from my condo in Nashville. Chloe had lived two floors below mine until she and Holden hooked up, and Bronson's had been our daily routine for years. I'd kept it up even after she moved out. Bronson's specialized in craft-brewed coffee. Once you started drinking the high-quality stuff on the daily, it was impossible to go back to standard fare.

"Is there really not one place to get"—I lowered my voice—"even halfway decent coffee in this town? Like, even somewhere off the square? Anywhere?"

She tilted her head and shot me a look that said, *Sorry but no.* "You have money. Go online and buy the nicest home coffeemaker you can find."

"I'm on it. At least the waffles are going to be amazing."

"Nothing compares," Chloe said as Patrick delivered an individual-sized cream pitcher.

"Your waffles just came up," he said. "I'll be right back."

We thanked him, and I poured cream into my coffee.

"Where's Sutton this morning?" I asked as we waited. "I figured you'd bring her with you."

"Holden's taking her to Quincy's at her usual time. It's hard to pivot with a one-year-old. She was just waking up when I left."

"I didn't think about that when I invited you out. I'm confusing Mom Chloe with Single Chloe. Sorry about that. It's okay to tell me no."

"I didn't want to tell you no. Holden can handle it just fine today. You sounded a little...desperate in your text."

"You can't hear a text."

"You know what I mean. Something about the *please tell me you can save me from myself and meet me for breakfast.*"

"Ah," I said. "I might've felt a little desperate."

Patrick returned with our waffles, saving me from having to say more.

"You're amazing," I told the server who was probably in his late forties.

"All I do is deliver," he said dramatically. "These waffles speak for themselves."

Dragonfly Dust Waffles were thick Belgian waffles that had blue, green, and purple sprinkles in the batter. On top was a generous tower of homemade whipped cream and more sprinkles, these in the shape of tiny dragonflies in the same colors. They were a thing of culinary beauty, a treasure at this unassuming diner. Almost enough to make up for the blah brew in my cup.

Once Patrick left us, I poured pure maple syrup on my sugar-laden waffles and took my first bite. The sensory pleasure of sweetness on my tongue was instant.

"Between this and donuts from Sugar, I might become diabetic before I hit thirty-six," I said.

Chloe laughed. "They do have eggs here."

I made a face that showed my opinion of eggs, particularly as I dipped my next bite into the thick, fluffy whipped cream.

"So what's up with the desperation?" Chloe asked.

My waffle-induced endorphin rush faded. I chewed and stared at my food, organizing my thoughts.

"Things sort of caught up with me over the weekend," I said. "I finally got all the moving details and real estate stuff taken care of. I've been consumed by that for the three weeks since I quit, you know?"

"You basically overhauled everything in your life in three weeks," Chloe said empathetically, nailing the issue like only my best friend could. "And now you have time to think."

"What have I done, Chloe? Like, I threw away more than a decade's worth of career. All my life goals were tied up in that job. Now suddenly I have this blank slate, and I don't know what to do with it."

"You said you don't want to go back to investment banking, right?"

I let the idea roll around in my head while I ate another bite. The thought of starting a new position with a different company doing what I'd done since grad school... There was a part of me that missed the challenge, the thrill of success, the sense of accomplishment, but... "Honestly? It sounds exhausting."

"I've thought you were nearing burnout for the last year or two."

"You might be right. I didn't see it while I was in it. I didn't have time to see it."

"You didn't have time to do anything but work, eat carryout, and hit Bronson's every day."

"Fact. I thrived on it for so long..."

"But you're human, and that job required a super-human effort always. Plus your boss..."

I made a face. "Toad."

Rob Landers was the one part of my career I'd detested.

He was twenty years older than me, had been in the industry forever, had been good at the job in his day, but he sucked as a manager. Throw three parts barely veiled misogyny into the mix, and I'd been at a slow boil for the past few years.

From the day he'd become a partner and been put in charge of my division, my love for the job had slowly leaked out of me. The final straw came when I'd expressed interest in becoming a partner. He'd assured me I had no chance, even though I was the youngest VP in the firm's history and had the numbers to back up my competency.

Normally when someone told me I couldn't do something, I put my head down and proved them wrong, but between years of friction with Landers and other old-schoolers in the industry, the extreme demand of the career itself both in terms of time and stress, and my doctor's advice, his condescension had snapped something in me. I think I'd been working toward making changes in my life on some level for months. He merely fast-forwarded me.

"You were a badass superhuman investment banker for more than a decade. You gave it everything," Chloe said with admiration in her tone. "But I don't know how much longer you could've sustained that, even without the toad. You haven't had a life since undergrad."

She didn't lie. To succeed at that career, you had to eat, sleep, and breathe it. To succeed as a woman, you had to give up the sleep part and basically hustle for eighteen hours a day.

"It's time for you to have a life," she continued. "Maybe meet a guy, fall in love, start a family."

I scoffed. "Should I take cooking lessons first so I can be a good housewife?"

Chloe laughed. "I'm getting you an apron for your birthday."

"You know me better than that."

"I know you're not the relationship type or the 'stay at home and look at the lake all day' type."

"And I've been at home looking at the lake for two days straight now."

"Thus the desperation."

"I'm losing my mind." I dared a drink of coffee, then chased it with a bite of waffle.

"Didn't the remodelers start yesterday?"

"They did. Demolition is loud. I spent most of the day outside. I even planted flowers."

Her brows went up as if she couldn't believe it.

"Twenty pots," I told her. "I set them around the deck and along the steps going down to the water. They're gorgeous, but next time I'm hiring a landscaper."

"Gardening is supposed to be relaxing. Therapeutic."

"I'm not the right girl for that. It turns out I don't like dirt."

Chloe laughed. "That's an important thing to learn about yourself, I guess. Cross landscaper off the list of possible new careers." She took a bite, chewed, swallowed. "So demo. Remodeling. Have you seen West yet?"

I tried to hold back a smile, but the thought of him made that difficult. "Eight a.m. yesterday, he was the one at my door."

Chloe's brows rose. "Not Levi?"

"Levi had an emergency of some kind, so it was just West at first, then three of the other guys joined him with all the equipment."

"And?"

"They demoed half the main floor down to studs. The kitchen is today."

"Yay, demo," she said dryly. "You know what I really want to hear about. Or rather who."

I finished the food in my mouth. "I'm unreasonably attracted to him," I said in as unbothered a voice as I could manage. Inside, I was bothered just thinking about him. "That guy-in-a-tool-belt thing? It's for real."

"Yeah," she said, making it a two-syllable word with the tone of *du-uhh*.

"He's not my type," I said. "Just like you said at the party."

When I'd spotted West Aldridge at Rowan and Chance's gender-reveal party, something had happened to me. There was almost an actual click of lust locking into place. I'd never experienced anything like it before. Not on that level.

"And yet?" Chloe prompted.

I shook my head. "He made it clear we're business only."

She tilted her head. "Understandable. Your project is big. He'll probably be in your house for weeks."

I couldn't deny the way my blood heated at that thought. "I might've had a handyman-nailing-me fantasy or two last night," I said, grinning. "Another reason I need something to occupy my mind and my hours. In his mind, I'm his client and nothing else."

"Rowan said he's all about his little girls and doesn't do relationships."

"I wouldn't want a relationship, just a mutual relieving of tension. A satisfaction of curiosity. I doubt we have anything in common."

Chloe shrugged. "I'm sure you'll get to know more about him if he's spending eight hours a day in your home."

"Possibly," I said, though I wasn't so sure. We'd talked a few times yesterday, but it was only about the project. That and I'd given him the garage code so they could get in whether I was home or not. "Ideally I won't be sitting around at home all day every day."

"Which brings us back to, what do you want to do with the rest of your life?"

I shoved the last big bite of waffle into my mouth, hoping the sugar rush would compensate for the unpleasantness her question aroused.

"I used to like that you were so direct," I grumped once my food was gone.

"You still like that I'm direct." Chloe pointed at me with her fork. "Sitting around, planting flowers isn't doing it for you. What would? A part-time job somewhere like the boutique? A gym membership and a personal trainer?"

"No and no," I said easily, though I should definitely consider the trainer.

"What about finance stuff? Could you open a personal financial-services business?"

I had the background for that, but advising individuals on saving and investing sounded like torture. Some people were made for nurturing, hand-holding, and teaching, which would be a lot of what a small-town financial-services business would entail, but that wasn't me.

I'd gone into finance to make big money. I didn't care if people judged me for that. It was who I was, who my background had made me, and I wasn't going to apologize for it. But I was going to be honest with myself about what called to me.

I made a gagging sound as I automatically reached for my mug, then stopped myself from taking a drink.

Chloe laughed. "Okay, so we know what you don't like. What *do* you like?"

"Coffee," I said, staring at the butterscotch-colored, diluted joe in my mug. "*Good* coffee."

"So you said," she said indulgently. "Talk to Monty, the owner here. Suggest some better coffee."

My mind was off and running in a different direction. "What if I opened my own coffee shop instead?"

Anyone else might not've taken me seriously, but my business-school bestie took the baton and went. "You've got the money, the coffee knowledge, and the business background."

I sat up straighter, my sad mug forgotten, and met Chloe's gaze. Without words, we shared the understanding that this could be exactly what I did for my next career.

"Wow," she said.

"Wow. I need to think through everything, but I haven't felt sparked like this since I quit. Since before I quit."

Patrick slid the bill tray onto our table and kept on going, as if he sensed there was something big going on with our discussion, and he didn't want to interrupt.

Distractedly I pulled out my card and set it down to cover the bill.

Chloe took her purse out, but I waved her away.

"I've got this one. You can get the next time. Chloe!" Excitement zipped through me at the coffee shop prospect.

Our eyes met again, and my brows shot up. It was all I could do to sit still.

"I have to get to work, but tell me what I can do," she said. "I can help you research or taste test or whatever."

I laughed, because this was sort of crazy and yet sort of awesome.

"I'll definitely keep you posted."

By the time I walked out the diner door, I was absolutely buzzing with possibilities.

Chapter Four

West

Day two of the Holiday project was nearing an end, and I had yet to see Presley.

Which was just fine with me.

The guys and I had made good progress on the demo and hoped to finish gutting the main floor tomorrow.

Though ripping out cabinets, yanking up flooring, and pulling down drywall was damn hard work, this job, at least today, nearly felt like cheating in the battle with Nick, my competitor for the foreman position. Presley had cranked up the AC considerably yesterday when she'd noticed my guys sweating, so the temp was close to thirty degrees cooler than the other crew's outdoor project in the Tennessee sun.

Nick was also dealing with a disruptive homeowner on their jobsite. Mr. Castille, a retired teacher, was apparently questioning everything they did and how they did it. Nick had to take time out to explain every step, which had to be exhausting and would likely put the project behind schedule soon, if it hadn't already.

The job went more smoothly when the homeowner didn't interfere or, like Presley, didn't even bother to be home.

I hauled an old cabinet from the laundry room out to the truck for donation, as the cabinetry was still in usable condition. As I had every single time I'd come out here today, I glanced around for a sign of Presley.

I was jonesing for a glimpse of her. Just a glimpse. A guy couldn't get in trouble from a glimpse.

Back inside, we were pulling out the last of the old cabinets from the laundry room when my phone rang. The babysitter's name flashed on my screen, spiking my heart rate, as Allison didn't call unless there was a problem.

I hurried away from the racket and exited to the back patio so I could hear, then answered.

"What's up, Allison?"

"Hi, West. Sorry to bother you at work, but the girls' mom hasn't picked them up yet. I was wondering if you'd heard from her?"

I checked my watch. It was 3:32. She was thirty-two minutes late for her daughters. *Dammit.*

"I haven't heard from her," I growled, trying to keep my anger to myself. "How are the girls doing?"

"I've been distracting them with riddles, but Scarlet noticed the time a few minutes ago and told the others. Sienna and Nova are in tears, feeding off each other. Scarlet is marching around the house ranting."

Sounded about right. If I wasn't so pissed at my ex, I'd be amused by my oldest—by minutes—daughter.

I checked my phone to make sure I hadn't missed a call or text. "No messages on this end," I said.

Holding in a curse or twelve, I mentally spun through

my options. First priority was my girls. I'd have words with Flora later.

I couldn't leave the jobsite, not for this. There were emergencies that would warrant that, but this wasn't one of them. This was a matter of soothing my little girls.

"Put Sienna on the phone," I told Allison.

On the other end, I heard commotion, then Scarlet's voice in the distance, which sounded excited instead of mad, then Allie's muffled response.

Allie came back on. "She just got here. I'll go help them load up. Anything I need to tell their mom?"

"I'll handle her later," I muttered. "Thanks, Allie."

I disconnected and finally let out the blue streak I'd been holding in.

That woman... It was one thing to jack with *my* emotions—and she'd done that plenty back in the day—but it was an altogether different matter when you messed with my girls'.

As I stared out at the lake, I talked myself down from the ex-induced rage and frustration. As badly as I wanted to call Flora and lay into her right now, I knew the girls were with her. They'd hear everything, and I didn't want that. I hoped they'd somehow have a fun dinner with their mom and her boyfriend.

The lake was relatively peaceful at the moment. A pair of ducks floated to the right of Presley's dock, their eyes peeled for fish. Though the day was a scorcher, I stood under the pergola roof in the shade, and a light breeze blew over me. The guys' racket was barely audible out here. I could see how this view and the peace could convince someone to buy the property in spite of all the work it needed.

When I turned to go back inside, I noticed a reusable

water bottle with flowers on it and words in a script font that Presley must have left on the outdoor dining table. I stepped closer to read what the bottle said. *Drink your effing water.*

That drew the beginnings of a grin from me.

Then I noticed some kind of silky, gauzy robe thing draped over one of the chairs. It was cream-colored with a pink floral print. Feminine, delicate, sexy. I swallowed hard, trying not to imagine *the client* wearing the sheer wrap.

Looking away, I was struck by the contrast between the coarse, sassy water bottle saying and the sweet, flowery wrap. It intrigued me further. Was Presley sassy or sweet? Would she like dirty talk or sweet nothings in bed?

I groaned and shook my head at my dumbass self. That line of thinking was nothing but trouble.

When I went back into the house, it was quiet. I headed to the laundry room to find it empty of cabinets and men, but their tools were still there.

The door from the garage opened, and the guys returned.

"We got those all loaded up," Paul said. "What's next?"

"That's all we're gonna tackle here today," I said. "You guys take those out to Sorensen's and unload them. I'll clean up here."

"You going to hang around and wait for the homeowner?" Paul asked.

I shook my head. I needed to consult with Presley about her flooring choice, but I couldn't do that until she saw fit to check in with us. I didn't know when she'd be home.

"I can wait for her," Nathan said, grinning like the clueless twenty-two-year-old he was. "She's hot."

"Shut it," I snapped.

"Just stating a fact."

I advanced on him. "That's not appropriate. If you can't figure that out, you know where the door is."

"Dude, okay." His grin disappeared. He raised his hands in surrender, then bent to pick up his tools.

I turned away, scowling, trying to ignore that I was more worked up than the situation called for. It wasn't appropriate to say something like that ever, but the urge to shove the new guy as I'd advanced on him... That was just as out of line.

To Paul, I said, "Let me know if you have any problems delivering. Otherwise see you tomorrow."

"Later," Paul said, picking up his tool belt and taking out the truck keys. They went out through the garage and left me to tidy up.

Once I was done shop vaccing all the dust and debris from our day, I made sure our equipment was out of the way, then went to the patio door to lock it.

As I secured the lock, my eyes strayed to the left and landed on that sheer, feminine robe again. What had she been wearing underneath it when she'd taken it off? Pajamas? A swimsuit? Had anyone been around to see?

The door to the garage opened, and I jolted guiltily, wondering what the guys had forgotten.

When I turned around, my heart double-timed, because it wasn't the guys.

"Wow," Presley said, taking in the open space that used to be the closed-off kitchen.

There was my glimpse, and damn was it a nice one.

She wore a little white skirt with two buttons at the waist that I couldn't help imagining my large fingers undoing, a corset-style top in lime green that revealed a two-inch swath of tempting skin at her waist, and heels with a dainty strap across the front of each foot and another around her ankle.

I was sure she intended her outfit to be simple and summery, but the complications that image of her was going to cause in my head...

I stepped forward, unsure if she'd spotted me yet.

"Hey, Presley." Whereas yesterday I'd struggled to break the *ma'am* habit, today, after a night filled with wild, erotic appearances by her in my restless dreams, her first name rolled off my tongue too easily.

"West. You've been busy."

"The guys just left," I said, snapping myself out of fuck-she-*is*-hot mode and into business mode. "I was locking up."

She walked to the center of the much larger open space and spun slowly, taking in the changes, stopping when she faced the wall of windows that looked out on the lake. She smiled and nodded. "Yes," she drew out. "This is what I was hoping for."

My gaze got caught up on the bit of her middle that showed. I imagined gripping her slender waist and pulling her on my lap—

Jesus.

I turned to look at the view, yanking my thoughts out of the gutter.

"What's next?" she asked.

I cleared my throat, as I'd planned to fill her in whenever I saw her. I hadn't planned on my thoughts going spicy.

Turning my attention to the house, I pointed out the remaining demo we'd take on tomorrow, which would center on the bathrooms.

"There's been another delay with the flooring you chose for the living area and bedroom," I told her. "We can still get it, but it's going to slow everything down by at least two weeks. Do you want to wait, or would you like to pick something similar?"

"Waiting isn't my strong point. I'll choose something else."

I quietly exhaled my relief. We could deal with the floor delay if we had to, but going with a different product would make our lives easier and the project smoother.

"Levi brought samples by," I told her as I walked over to the sample boards propped against the wall.

Presley followed me, stopping next to me and watching as I spread out the four panels of samples. "Do you need my answer right now?"

"Just in the next couple of days. Check them out when it's dark outside and in the middle of the day so you can see how they look in different light."

"I'll do that." She seemed distracted as she nodded. "I have a question for you." She turned to face me, pegged me with eyes the color of the sky on a cloudless summer day.

I swallowed and bent down to straighten the sample boards unnecessarily. I needed to build up some resistance to this woman who had such an effect on me. I knew plenty of pretty girls. I'd worked with attractive homeowners before. But something about Presley Holiday put me off-kilter from the inside out.

"Whatcha got?" I asked casually, as if my thoughts weren't off the rails.

"Your crew is booked for a few months, right? Levi said he worked me in when someone else canceled?"

"That's right."

We'd been planning on a room addition for the Petersons, but now that they were divorcing, the project was off, and the house was going on the market instead.

"Do you know how far out exactly?" she asked.

"Last I heard, we were booked through October."

She pressed her lips together and looked like her thoughts were racing.

"You got another project in mind?" I asked.

She straightened and brightened in an instant. "I'm opening a coffee shop. I signed a lease on one of the spaces in the former community center this afternoon. It's one of the smaller ones, and it's already been gutted. It's like a blank canvas. I need to find someone to build out the space."

"Back up for a sec. Yesterday you said you didn't know what you were gonna do with your time. You were thinking gardening."

"It didn't take. Dirt under the fingernails..." She shook her head and made a face.

I checked out her fingernails. They were well-groomed, medium length, no sign of dirt, and painted Nova's favorite shade of lavender.

"I had breakfast at the diner with Chloe Henry," she continued. "Their coffee isn't great. I mentioned it to Chloe, and one thing led to another."

"The diner's coffee sucks so you're opening a coffee shop? This all happened in a day?"

"It's been quite a day," she said, smiling widely and brimming with so much energy she was practically vibrating. "Things just sort of lined up."

I laughed, trying to wrap my head around this force that was a five-foot-five knockout of a woman.

"You know when some things just sort of happen at the right time and seem like they're meant to be?" she continued.

I didn't really, but I nodded.

"I got the idea at breakfast. It invigorated me like

nothing else has for, God, years. Chloe had to rush off to work. I was planning on coming back here to check in with you guys, but I strolled over to the gazebo on the square first, found a bench, and did a preliminary search on my phone for coffee in Dragonfly Lake."

"Didn't find much, I'm betting."

"No coffee shops. The closest one listed is in Runner. Second closest is Nashville."

"Sounds about right."

"My mind was spinning. I started getting all kinds of ideas. Decor, menu... Pretty soon, my phone dinged with a text from Chloe. She mentioned my idea to Holden, and he told her the former community center retail spots were just listed."

I'd seen something about that on the Tattler, the town app, but hadn't thought much about it.

"So you marched across the street and signed a lease?" I teased.

"Kind of? There was some research in there. Costs of running a coffee shop, ways to market it, challenges. I read a couple dozen articles while I waited for the real estate guy to show up."

I noticed she didn't mention anything about financing. Based on the rumors that she'd bought this property with cash, my guess was she didn't need outside financing.

This girl was a damn unicorn. I'd never met anyone like her. Looks, brains, guts... Was there anything she didn't have?

She's so far out of your league that you're not even playing the same sport. She's Formula 1 racing, and you're a sumo wrestler standing in one place.

Which was neither here nor there, because I wasn't

interested in anything other than these glimpses. That was as real as my attraction to her would ever get.

"So you need a build-out," I said, taking it back to the one topic I knew anything about.

"Preferably long before October. Are there other reputable companies in town?"

"There are, but any company worth their salt is booked through the summer and beyond. That's how it is in this industry. This is our high season."

She frowned, and I could tell her thoughts were spinning again.

"What would you do if you were me?" she asked.

I laughed. "Well, if I were *me*, I'd do the work myself on the weekends. If I were *you*, I'd try to find a couple of guys who knew what they were doing to do it after hours and make it worth their while financially."

"Like your coworkers."

"Something like that." The thought of Nathan or Paul or Nick or Fritz working with her after hours didn't sit right.

"Are you interested?" she asked, pegging me with a hopeful look.

I couldn't think of a less feasible idea, what with my girls and my...*attraction*. I shook my head. "I'm a single dad. My girls don't get enough of my time as it is."

She nodded, pacing slowly with her arms crossed. "Can you give me any names of someone who could take a look and help me figure out what I need? I'm willing to do as much of the work as I can, but I'd need guidance."

"You're going to put up walls and install plumbing?"

Her shoulders sank a little. "Not by myself, obviously. Do you have anyone on your crew who doesn't have a family and might want to earn extra money?"

I gritted my teeth, imagining one of our guys spending

time with Presley. "Tell me more about what you need done."

"I don't really know. I need an expert to help me figure it out. Maybe Levi?"

I checked my watch. Flora would likely be dropping off the girls in the next half hour. The former community center was across the square from the diner. I could have her bring them to me there.

"I've got a few minutes if you can show me now," I said.

It was a bad idea, but I told myself I could use the extra money for my girls. And the hell if I was going to let Levi or any of the other thugs I worked with be her contractor knight in shining armor.

If she was going to be *invigorated*, I wanted to be the one helping her get that way.

Chapter Five

West

The whirlwind named Presley had been upgraded in my mind to a hurricane.

Hurricanes did more damage, and she had the potential to wreak absolute havoc on me.

But only if you let her, I reminded myself.

On the short drive to the former community center, I'd texted Flora the change in plans. Then I'd reined myself in. Reminded myself taking on this project would be a bad idea. I was hearing her out, and I'd give her my two cents. Then I was out.

I was far from a coffee expert, but listening to her spout her ideas and plans was starting to make *me* excited about the prospects of her shop. That's how powerful her energy and enthusiasm were.

She'd nabbed the best spot in the former city-owned building—the front corner that faced the square as well as the walkway down the side. There were a few larger spaces and three smaller ones. Hers was the best of the smaller ones and ideal for what she had in mind for her coffee shop.

"So office and storage in back, two single gender-neutral restrooms over here," I summarized, pointing. "The kitchen in that area, the counter here, and the self-serve area there?"

"What do you think of that?" she asked.

I shrugged. "I have no experience with running a coffee shop, so all I can offer is a construction viewpoint."

"Which is?"

"It's doable and not very complex. A lot depends on what kind of kitchen you want."

"I don't know what I'm going to do about food, if anything," she said, "but I'd like a full kitchen in place, with more than one oven."

"How soon do you want this?"

"Well," she said, facing me with an irresistible grin. "I suppose you can't do it by tomorrow..."

"I never said *I* could do it ever," I clarified.

When her shoulders sagged, I reassured her, "What I *can* do is ask my coworkers, see if anyone's interested."

"Really? You think you can find someone who will do it?"

I suspected there were multiple someones who'd step up for no other reason than to work with *her* specifically. Plus the money. The money would be welcome for any of us. Levi paid us fairly, but there were never enough funds when you had three little princesses.

"I'd be surprised if we can't find someone. We'll need to run it by Levi to make sure he's cool with it. He should be, as long as it's all after-hours work."

"How long do you think it would take?" she asked. "Like, if you hypothetically decided to do it, how long?"

"I'd need to think about that, put some things down on paper. A lot would depend on if I had help."

"I told you I'd help."

My brows shot up.

"I know what you're thinking," she said.

"What am I thinking?"

"That I'd be more in the way than helpful, but I can assure you, my drive is unparalleled when I decide I want something." Her eyes flared with intent. Was there a double meaning in there? Interest?

It didn't matter if there was. That was not happening, no matter how she made my blood pound.

As if sensing she hadn't convinced me, she said, "I like to be busy. I'm not good at sitting around my house. I'd rather get a hammer and help build walls between creating a business plan and deciding on beans and blends. I err toward workaholism. I'm trying to avoid that again, but there's a happy medium between overworking and planting flowers, right?"

"Sure is."

Commotion out on the sidewalk caught my eye. My daughters approached, mouths running, bodies hopping, twisting, turning, with Flora lagging behind them.

We could hear the girls even before the door opened, all excited chatter and high spirits. They waited for their mom to catch up. Nova pressed her face against the glass, peering inside and jumping up and down when she spotted me.

"Gonna need some glass cleaner," I said to Presley as I headed to the door. "Sorry about that."

"Nothing to be sorry about. Are these your daughters?" Presley asked, laughing.

"This is my circus. These are my monkeys." I opened

the door, and it was as if someone had turned the volume from two to nine in an instant.

"Daddy!" Nova threw her arms around me.

"Hi, Daddy," Sienna and Scarlet said together and gathered in for their share of a group hug, with me bending down and pulling all three of them in.

"You girls smell like sugar," I said, then pretended to nibble on their necks, eliciting an uproar of giggles that made me laugh too.

I stood and met Flora's impatient gaze.

"Everything go okay?" I asked.

"We had a fun time," she said. "We all had waffles."

"Did you get any protein in them?" I asked my ex.

"We got extra whipped cream!" Scarlet hollered.

"Of course you did," I said. They'd go for that any time they were allowed.

Between the no-protein meal and the loads of sugar, we were in for a wild evening.

"I gotta run," Flora said. "Gil's waiting at the curb. Bye, girls!" She blew a kiss and took off without even hugging them.

I would never understand that woman.

All three girls talked at once, telling me about dinner, waffles, sprinkles, and God knew what else. I noticed Presley standing across the room, watching us with a smile on her face that likely covered a base of overwhelm at the sheer volume and chaos that surrounded our family of four like a swarm of mosquitos.

"Daddy, can we go to Colorado to see the mountains and feed the chipmunks?" Nova asked, jumping up and down.

"I want to go to Chicago to the giant Ferris wheel!" Scarlet said. "And shop on the Magnificent Mile."

My brows went up as this was the first I'd heard of any of this.

"I want to see the Grand Canyon," Sienna said with less volume but equal enthusiasm.

"Chicago has a museum with a T. rex named Sue!" Scarlet argued.

Because apparently this was an argument about where we were traveling, which was, in reality, nowhere.

"Where did all this come from?" I asked them, though it was obvious Flora and Gil had put ideas into their heads.

"Mommy and Gil go all over the country," Scarlet said authoritatively. "They've been to forty-six states."

"They told us the coolest stuff," Nova said.

"The Grand Canyon is miles and miles and miles deep," Sienna related.

"It's one mile deep and miles and miles long," her twin corrected.

"Colorado has the biggest, biggest mountains," Nova said. "And you can ride a tram to the top and feed peanuts to the chipmunks."

"Girls," I said in a tone to get their attention. "Did you notice we're not alone?"

They looked around and spotted Presley, who still appeared amused and overwhelmed.

"Hi there," Presley said as she approached. "I'm Presley."

"This is Scarlet, Sienna, and Nova," I said, placing my hand on each of their heads as I introduced them. "Say hello to Miss Presley, girls."

"Hi!" Nova said. "You're pretty."

Leave it to my blunt four-year-old. She was spot-on with her assessment.

"Hi, Nova. So are you," Presley said. "You're all three adorable."

"I'm here for work," I told my daughters.

"You said you were working at a big house," Scarlet said.

"I'm working at Miss Presley's big house," I confirmed. "This is Miss Presley's business."

The three of them looked around in confusion.

"This doesn't look like a business," Sienna said.

"I went to dance camp here," Scarlet said.

"This used to be the community center," I told them. "The city built a new community center, and now this building is turning into businesses."

"I'm planning to open a coffee shop," Presley explained. "I'm going to get coffee beans from all over the world to make delicious coffee drinks."

"I don't like coffee," Nova said.

"Our mom has been all over the world," Scarlet said.

"All over the country," I clarified. "Their mom's boyfriend is a musician. He books gigs all over the US and travels to them in his van. Flora goes with him."

"Have you been to Chicago?" Scarlet asked Presley.

"I have," Presley said. "The Magnificent Mile is a fun place to shop."

"Did you see the T. rex when you were shopping?" Nova asked, looking nervous.

"The T. rex is in a museum, and it's not a real dinosaur," Sienna told her.

"It is *too* real," Scarlet said. "But it's just the bones now. Real bones."

"I didn't see the T. rex," Presley said, "but I saw the Ferris wheel on Navy Pier."

"Did you go to Colorado?" Nova asked.

"I've been to Denver, which is the capital of Colorado," Presley told her.

"Are there chipmunks there?" my youngest persisted.

"I didn't see any, but I was in a hotel," Presley said.

I was sure Presley had jet-setted all over the world as an investment banker and that her travel experiences were quite different from Flora and Gil's, where they slept in their van at odd hours due to his small-venue shows.

Time to rein in their grilling of Presley. "Okay, girls—"

"Can we please go to Chicago?" Scarlet asked.

"Or any trip," Sienna said. "We never get to go anywhere."

"It costs a lot of money to travel," I said. "Last I knew, you three liked to get new school clothes."

Their enthusiasm disappeared like the air escaping from an untied balloon. I clenched my jaw, hating that I couldn't give my girls every damn thing.

"I need to finish up with Miss Presley and get you three home. Why don't you go sit on that bench right outside." I pointed to the bench that was visible out the side window, lining the walking path. "Only that bench."

"I want to stay with you, Daddy," Sienna said as Scarlet and Nova raced for the door.

I put my arm around my quiet girl and pulled her into my side, confident she'd hang out in silence. It also meant one less personality sitting out on that single bench.

"You've got your hands full with these smart little girls," Presley said, smiling at Sienna.

"That's for sure," I said.

That right there was why I had no business taking on extra work.

"So you want this built out as soon as humanly possible," I said, getting back to our discussion. "Have you given any thought to the finishes you want? Will the walls be painted? Brick? Shelves? Cabinets? Start thinking about specifics and what you'll want help with."

"Actually..." She pulled out her phone and started swiping. "I know exactly the style I want."

Presley moved next to me and held up her phone so I could see a photo of a coffee shop. Sections of white brick mixed with contemporary slate-blue walls, silver fixtures, and pecan-colored floors.

"That's nice," I said, "and not too complex. The brick-work will slow it down a little and add to your expense, but nothing else screams out to me as being a problem."

She lowered her phone so Sienna could see too.

"It's pretty," my daughter said.

"I think so too," Presley told her, then turned back to me. "I'm okay with the expense. I don't want to cut corners. I want this shop to be my future, so I might as well do it the way I want it now, right?"

I put some space between us, because being that close, I caught her light, feminine scent, and it was doing things to me. Making me think of her as more than the decision maker in this project and the other one.

"It's cheaper long-term to do it right the first time," I agreed, but inside, I was puzzling over Presley Holiday.

Yesterday she'd been aimless, restless. I'd been able to see it on her even though I'd only just met her.

Today she'd wanted better coffee than she could find in town, and now, less than twelve hours later, she'd signed a lease on a shop and was barreling forward with opening a business.

Who did that?

Someone with the cash to back it up, for starters.

Speaking of cash...

"The saying holds true here," I said. "In any construction project, you can pick two of the three: good, fast, or cheap."

"I want good and fast," she said without hesitation. She stepped closer, facing me, as if to convey this was important. "I understand this would be a lot for anyone to do on the weekends or after hours. I'm willing to pay well for the labor. If there's any way you can do it, I'd like to work with you, West. Will you think about it?"

I felt Sienna crane her neck to look up at me. "Maybe we could use the money to go on a trip, Daddy," she pointed out quietly.

I peered down at her, took in her earnest, yearning expression. I flipped my gaze to the two outside, the other two parts of my heart.

I wanted to give these three everything their hearts desired. As a construction worker with no college degree and no other training save for the military, my earning potential would never be in the jet-set range. But maybe I could find a way to do this extra project. It'd mean sacrificing time with them for a few weeks and finding someone to stay with them, but it could also mean giving them travel memories they'd hold on to for the rest of their lives.

I let out a conflicted breath. "I'll think about it," I told Presley.

I had a feeling I'd do nothing *but* think about it until I could come to the best decision.

Chapter Six

Presley

Wednesday afternoon I was on my patio, deeply engrossed in an Ethiopian coffee grower's website, when I realized someone was standing on the other side of the table from me, and I startled.

"West," I said on an exhale. "You scared me."

"That wasn't my intent."

I glanced around, taking stock of my surroundings, realizing the construction racket from inside had stopped. The shadows of the trees on my lot were long, and though the sun was still up, it was no longer beating down on the dock directly. In fact, the dock was now in shadow.

"Mind if I sit?" he asked.

I gestured to the chair dumbly, taking in the sight of him. He wore dark gray cargo-style work pants and a black tee with the small Dawson Construction logo on the side of his chest. His thick chest with well-defined pecs was discernible through the shirt. He looked like a man who'd labored all day: dusty, a little dirty, a hint of sweat on his chest, and yet so appealing, even though he'd removed his tool belt.

I checked the time on my phone as he sat. "It's ten after five?"

"Yes, ma'am."

I narrowed my eyes at the *ma'am*, and he laughed and shrugged.

My stomach rumbled with hunger I hadn't previously noticed.

"Where were you when I came out here?" he asked. "I've never seen someone so focused in all my life."

"Ethiopia."

His brows shot up.

"They have some of the best coffee in the world," I explained. "I'm researching suppliers."

"You've been out here for hours. I'm surprised you could concentrate with the noise."

"I was locked in on my research. I guess I missed lunch."

He tilted his head at me. "Didn't you just come up with this coffee idea yesterday?"

"Yes." I picked up my extra-large Vietnamese iced coffee from Bronson's for another sip but realized it was empty. Even the ice was gone.

"Is there a hard deadline for something?" he asked.

"No, but I have so much to learn."

"You found good coffee?" He gestured to my empty cup.

"I drove in to the shop I used to live across from to meet with Renny Bronson, the owner. That woman's a wealth of information, and she generously gave me two hours to pick her brain."

"You've been busy."

"I love being busy."

He nodded, but he looked as if he was biting down on a response. "I found someone to take on your after-hours project," he said instead.

"Yeah?" I shoved down the disappointment that it wasn't him and reminded myself of my priorities—to get my shop built out and opened. Not to get sidetracked by this tower of man muscle.

"If we can make the schedule work," he said, "I'm in."

I wanted to do a fist pump, but I held on to my composure and kept it professional. "What schedule would work for you?"

I could be flexible if it meant West would do the work. Not because he looked like he did. Not because he kept popping into my head when I closed my eyes and tried to sleep. I wanted him on the project because I trusted his construction abilities.

Or maybe all three of those reasons, I thought with a private smile.

"My mom and her husband live in Nashville and will take the girls on weekends. I can get a babysitter two evenings a week, possibly three. I've got some conflicts this Saturday and next that we'll have to work around."

"I'll make it work," I said without hesitation. "You're hired."

"We haven't talked money yet."

"What's your hourly charge?"

He named a dollar amount.

"I'll pay you double that."

His brows shot up, and he studied me, as if waiting for me to change my mind.

"You're taking time away from your kids, plus paying

for extra childcare," I said. "This is important enough to me to make it worth your time."

"I appreciate that."

I clapped my hands together once, practically bouncing in my seat, eager and excited and beside myself with optimism because he'd said yes. "When can we start? Do you have any time tonight? We could go by the shop and start figuring out more specifics."

He checked his watch and frowned. "I need to relieve Allie, get my girls dinner, spend some time with them before bed."

I wilted back into my chair, belatedly realizing it wasn't realistic to think he could pivot on a dime and spend his evening working on my project. "Of course. Don't mind me. I'm just excited and hyperfocused. I can research the rest of these suppliers on my list tonight instead."

He chuckled. "Don't forget to eat."

"Right," I said, absently thinking I hadn't stocked up on groceries since moving in. I'd grabbed a lot of carryout so far and existed on that, cookies, popcorn, and wine.

The number one reason I'd just changed my entire life —address, career, goals—was to take better care of myself. I might not be a health wizard, but I knew cookies, popcorn, and wine were not doing it.

"Dammit," I bit out, disgusted with myself.

"Sorry. Guess that's not my business," West said, seeming like he was about to stand.

"That wasn't directed at you," I clarified. "Nothing to apologize for. I do need to eat. I suck at this."

"At eating? Or not working too much?"

"Ouch." This guy didn't really know me, had just met me three days ago, and was spot on with that guess. "I'm trying to get better at that but failing."

"What would happen if you waited until tomorrow to research suppliers?"

"I'd sit around tonight, antsy and nervous because I could be researching suppliers." It was an honest response, and I knew as it spilled out of me, it was the wrong answer. "I'm not so good at moderation."

"What do you do to relax?" he asked.

I gazed out at the pretty lake, where a small boat carrying a fisherman was trolling past my dock. *What do I do to relax?*

With a self-effacing grin, I said, "I have no idea. I haven't had time to relax since middle school."

"Why do I think you're serious about that?"

"Because I am. I couldn't afford to relax when I was in finance. I barely had time to sleep."

"You can't keep doing that for too long," he said.

"That's why I'm here, at least in theory."

"You moved to Dragonfly Lake to relax?"

"Right. To slow down." I picked up my tall coffee cup, then remembered it was empty.

I closed my eyes, hesitating before saying more. I hadn't told anyone this before. West seemed like a safe sounding board. Low stakes, unlike Chloe, who'd ride me daily to slow down and take a weaving class or something equally hellacious if she knew what was going on. "My mom died of a heart attack at age fifty," I started.

He let out a low whistle. "That's young."

I nodded. "Her marriage with my dad was...*bad*," I summarized, not wanting to get into how he'd hit her on the regular. "She finally left him when I was ten. She received no support, but we were safe. It's not easy to feed and clothe two kids as a single mom with no specialized skills, no degree."

"I was raised by a single mom too," he said. "She had to work two jobs for my whole childhood. She was the office manager at Skeeter's Auto Repair during the day and worked nights cleaning businesses." His love for his mom was evident in his tone.

"Mine was the manager of a chain restaurant," I said, feeling a kinship with him that surprised me. "They worked her seventy to eighty hours a week, always on her feet, always dealing with staff shortages, employees who flaked, customers who complained. She basically worked herself to death."

I felt his gaze on me.

"Yes, I was doing the same thing she was except investment banking instead of restaurant management," I said before he could point it out. "Like I told you, I'm driven, and I had goals. I didn't notice the similarities. I didn't take the time to notice."

"But you must have if you moved here to change."

"A few months ago, I started getting headaches, but mostly I worked through them. Eventually I had a couple dizzy spells, so I made an appointment with my doctor. My blood pressure was really high. Like, scary high. She put me on meds and bluntly told me I was going to end up with a heart attack or a stroke before I was fifty."

West grimaced. "She got through to you?"

"She did. I'd already bought this house, kind of on a whim, but she made me realize my job was doing the same thing to me that my mom's did to her. Before that, I had this idea that I was making the big bucks, so it was somehow different. I wasn't working myself to the bone. I wasn't on my feet all day, running around, waiting tables. I had to face up to the fact I was fooling myself."

"So you quit."

I shook my head. "I kept doing what I was doing. The only difference was I was sort of aware that I was doing it. *When* I stopped for thirty seconds and thought about it. Then one Friday afternoon, my boss was shitty to me yet again, and it hit me. Boom. I was done."

"You quit on the spot, but it'd been building up," he said, and I nodded.

"Exactly. I wasn't the type to quit, let alone with no notice. But when he blew off my career goals again, I could practically feel my blood pressure going up, and I decided fuck this. This is crazy. I need to make some changes."

"So you quit your job, sold your house, and moved to a small town. Those are pretty big changes."

"But not enough, it turns out. Because last Sunday and Monday, once I moved in, I had nothing to do *except* relax, and I was climbing the walls before eight a.m."

"And Tuesday you decided to open a coffee shop," he said, sounding more than a little amused.

"I'm my own worst enemy." I frowned as doubts flooded in. "Did I make a mistake?"

This wasn't like me. I didn't question myself. In my former career, there was no time to question myself. I'd always done my research and followed my gut. Trusted my instinct. Blazed forward with confidence.

"Sounds like maybe you need to find some balance," West said. "What if you tried working eight-hour days instead of fourteen?"

It made sense but... "So if I start at eight o'clock, quit at four, then what?"

"Then you relax."

I bit down on frustration. If I could relax, I would. "I don't know how. I can't sit around and do nothing."

"What do you like to do that isn't work?"

"What do *you* like to do that isn't work?" I countered.

"I hike, kayak, fish, curl up with the girls on the couch and watch a Disney movie."

Imagining this burly, gruff man curled up with three little girls under a fuzzy blanket, watching *Frozen*... I might pay a large sum of money to see that. Especially if he was shirtless.

"I've never done any of those things. I'm not sure I'm the nature type, and I know I'm not the movie type."

"You could take up yoga, do a painting class, learn how to knit over at Fat Cat, rent a boat..."

"Boating's relaxing?" I asked, intrigued. I didn't know the first thing about boating or boats, but I did have a boathouse, a dock, and a lake out my back door.

"It's like going for a peaceful Sunday afternoon drive in the country except better."

I'd never found driving to be peaceful, but maybe I just hadn't tried it in the country on a Sunday.

"I bet your girls take up a lot of your time," I said.

"They do, and it's not always relaxing."

I laughed. "Is it *ever* relaxing?"

"On those rare occasions when they're all three asleep before I drift off for the night." A slow smile crept across his face, and I'm pretty sure my ovaries released an egg or two.

"I thought about trying yoga," I said.

"It'd pass some time," he said.

He stood abruptly, and I suddenly felt dumb for whining about my stupid problem when he had daughters waiting for him and a babysitter to relieve.

"I better get going," he said.

"Sorry." I stood too. "When can we meet to start talking details about the shop?"

"If you can be here tomorrow at quitting time, we could head over then. I can ask Allie to stay until five thirty."

"I can do that." We walked through the house together as we talked.

"I can put in a full day on Sunday," he said. "I promised my girls I'd take them to the Honeysuckle Festival Saturday."

"I heard about that."

We reached the door to the garage, stopped, and faced each other. "You're a resident now. Better check the festival out. It'll force you to take a break from working, at any rate."

"True." He didn't need to know how everything in me detested that thought. "Tell your cuties hi."

"Yeah," he said, but something in his tone told me he wouldn't, and his openness faded slightly, like a wall went up. "Have a good night."

I thought we'd gotten to friend-like terms in the past few minutes. We'd bonded over having single moms. I'd told him something no one else knew. But his goodbye felt one hundred percent back to *you're my client*.

Because I'd mentioned his girls?

"I'll see you tomorrow," I said.

Had I said something wrong to them yesterday? Or did he just not want me around his kids?

I'd heard of people not wanting their kids to get to know the person they were dating until they were sure it was going somewhere, but we were working together, not dating.

As I watched him walk to his SUV, my eyes on his perfect ass with every step away from me, a thought popped into my head. Spending hours in bed with a guy like him was one way to get away from working all the time.

Too bad he was giving me signs he wasn't up for that.

Chapter Seven

Presley

I loved Chloe's extended family. The Henrys had kindly welcomed me into their group Saturday afternoon on the square to gorge ourselves on food truck fare while listening to live music at the Honeysuckle Festival.

They'd managed to grab a spot under one of the big trees and had spread out several blankets picnic-style in the shade. I sat on one with Chloe, Holden, and Sutton, their toddler daughter. Sutton was more interested in watching her three-month-old cousin Bronte, Cash and Ava's daughter, than in eating her hot dog.

"How's the Korean rice bowl, Presley?" Quincy asked me. "I couldn't decide between that and the chicken and waffles."

"It was delicious," I said, "but a lot of food."

"Maybe I'll go get one of those," Zane, Hayden's husband, said.

"Because barbecue and a burger aren't enough for one man's lunch," Hayden teased him.

"I shared the barbecue with our son," Zane countered. "Our little man can put down the food," he told the rest of us proudly.

"Must be a growth spurt," Chloe said. "You sure aren't packing on the pounds in a bad way, are you, Harrison?" She tickled the two-year-old's belly, drawing a laugh from him.

"Don't talk about pounds, please," Everly said from her spot resting her back against the tree trunk. "I've gained three this week alone."

"Good," Ava said. "Baby Beckham's in there growing big and strong."

Everly was seven and a half months pregnant but looked fantastic, contrary to her worries about gaining too much weight.

"Judging by the kicks, he's going to be a soccer player," Everly said, and her husband, Seth, caressed her round abdomen with so much love and tenderness it made me squirm.

I'd been feeling squirmy since we'd all sat down. Though the Henrys were one big, happy family, there were five distinct subgroups made of a couple and a kid, or in Seth and Everly's case, a baby bump in her belly.

I found it fascinating to witness the dynamics in all five couples. They seemed to have actual partnerships.

We'd never done those in the Holiday family. My dad had been controlling, domineering, and abusive, physically to my mom and emotionally to my sister and me. My sister had married a clone of our father when she was twenty. Her marriage wasn't a happy one, but she stayed with the jerk for the sake of her kids. She and I weren't very close, in part because she lived in Denver and in part because she didn't like me asking why she didn't take the boys and leave, the way our mother finally had.

I was absolutely fine with being single and had never aspired to get married. Today, though, I couldn't help noticing I was the oddball, the extra. Maybe it was because Dragonfly Lake was my home now. I wasn't a visitor anymore. I lived here just like all these people, yet *not* like these people because I existed on my own in an oversized house. A house that was going to be amazing, I reminded myself, and big enough that I could invite the whole Henry clan over at once. I might be alone, but I didn't have to be lonely.

As the five sisters-in-law discussed diaper sizes, I scanned the square, checking out the crowd of people and—okay, if I was honest with myself—maybe looking for West. Just to get a look from afar.

When I tuned in to the Henry conversation again, I realized the men were taunting Seth about how he'd handle Everly being in labor. I laughed as they turned to giving Holden a hard time about his wreck after Chloe's water broke, which had resulted in me giving them a ride to the Nashville hospital. That had been a true test of my driving skills—particularly in avoiding being pulled over for speeding—and I'd gotten them there in the nick of time.

These families were all about babies right now—having them, expecting them, probably making more. I was definitely living a different kind of life.

"I'm going to explore the booths," I told Chloe, then disappeared quietly, leaving them all to their family-centric discussions.

Earlier I'd noticed there was a boat company manning a booth, giving out info on their line of boats. Dragonfly Lake was a tourist town in the summer. Apparently festivals like this one and their Christmas parade drew people from all over the state and beyond. It was a captive audience for people who probably loved the outdoors, so it made sense to pitch boats.

It made just as much sense that I was considering buying a boat. I never in a thousand years would've dreamed I'd want one, but then again, I'd never considered I might be living on a lakeshore in a small town, in a career besides finance either. All I'd been able to see before was my all-consuming job and my drive to succeed at it.

I still wasn't sure I wanted a boat, but if it could become a hobby or a way to relax, I was all ears. Gardening was a fail, and yoga wasn't going well so far.

The two older guys at the boat booth were happy to have someone approach them willingly, it seemed. I told them I was new to town but had a dock and a boathouse. They stood up straighter as they sailed right into their pontoon pitch.

I took their brochures, my mind swimming with possibilities as I thanked them and headed for the food truck I'd spotted earlier that sold deep-fried cookie dough.

As I waited for my basket of sweetness, I took in the chaos of the festival, thinking this was my town now. I wasn't a visitor. What a self-inflicted curveball. Not necessarily in a bad way, just unexpected. I was still playing mental catch-up from all the changes.

I observed the nearby booths, most of them crowded with people. There were booths selling every imaginable use of honeysuckle—jam, infused water, body lotions and soaps, supplements, candy, tea, which I made a note to look into offering in my shop for noncoffee drinkers, and more. Several tents housed carnival games and kids' activities, and there was a section called the Market, which included the weekly farmers market stands as well as others selling handmade goods.

One of the corner tents had a long line of people coming from it. I craned my neck to read the sign and grinned—llama photo ops. Ben Holloway, the town vet and owner of the llama who frequently escaped and hoofed it to the bakery for her favorite cookies, had to be behind that.

"Only in Dragonfly Lake," I said to myself, deciding then and there that I needed a pic with the rebellious llama. It'd be a statement to myself that I belonged here now. I was a local.

As I took in the row of kids' activities, my gaze stopped abruptly. West stood in profile, his arms crossed, a grin on his face as he watched two of his girls sitting in elevated chairs, having their faces painted. One of the twins stood in front of him, watching her sisters intently.

At that moment, as if he felt my attention on him, he turned my way. Even though he was several booths away, our eyes met, and a rush of lightness swooped through my chest. The cookie-dough vendor called my name then, drawing my attention away. I stepped up to the window, took my dessert and some napkins, and made my way toward West and his daughters, telling myself I needed help eating the fried balls of dough with the chocolate frosting drizzle.

I was on a mission to be healthier, after all.

Laughing to myself, I fully acknowledged that was only a fraction of my reason for heading toward my handsome contractor.

———

West

When Presley broke eye contact and stepped up to the food truck's window, I turned my attention back to my kids.

Nova was admiring the llama on her cheek in a hand mirror as Scarlet's artist put the finishing touches on her llama. Sienna was staunchly against having anything painted on her face, holding her position even as she stood at my side and watched the whole process.

Nova hopped down, and I tipped her artist. As both girls watched the final additions to Scarlet's face, I glanced toward the food truck where I'd seen Presley.

Eventually it registered that Presley was on her way toward us, her eyes intent on me, a smile on her beautiful face. Today she was dressed in a loose, halter-style tank with the thinnest string holding it up, tying at the back of her neck, leaving no room for a bra, making me do a double-take at her tits. She must have a strapless one on, I decided after more analysis than was polite, then found I was torn between being glad she wasn't allowing that kind of view for just anyone and disappointed she wasn't for my sake. Her shorts were short, baring her perfect legs that I'd imagined wrapped around me more than once in the past week.

I cleared my throat and looked back at Scarlet as she inspected her face painting in the mirror and squealed with satisfaction. She squirmed down from the high chair and tried once again to convince her twin to get a matching llama on her cheek, but Sienna shook her head resolutely.

"Hello," Presley said, suddenly at my side.

"Hey, look who it is, girls," I said as if I was surprised to see her. In truth, I'd kept an eye out for a glimpse of her since we'd arrived. "Remember Miss Presley?"

"Miss Presley, we got face paint," Scarlet said.

"Look at you with your llamas," she said. "Super cute."

"I didn't want face paint," Sienna told her, surprising me a little because she was my shy girl who didn't usually talk to people she didn't know well.

"I think that's perfectly okay," Presley said with a warm smile. Then she sidled up next to me, pointed at her tray of sweets, and whispered in my ear, "Okay if I share these?"

My response was an affirmative growl, in part because her closeness, her sweet scent, rendered me momentarily unable to form words.

"Who wants a fried cookie dough bite?" Presley asked.

All three girls raised their hand, their eyes bright with interest.

Presley bent down and held the paper tray out. The girls swarmed her, and each grabbed a ball of battered cookie dough, paying no mind to the mess the chocolate drizzle made of their hands. My attention got caught up in Presley's shoulders from behind: narrow, feminine, and bare. I clenched my hand into a fist to prevent myself from reaching out to see if her skin felt as soft as it looked.

She straightened and offered me a sweet, but I shook my head, tamping down on the thought that the only sweet thing I wanted was her.

Damn, this woman got to me without even trying.

"Thanks for asking if it was okay to offer them one," I said so only she could hear.

"I'm afraid I learned that the hard way with Chloe's daughter," she said. "I always ask now. Sure you don't want one? They're delicious."

I shook my head again and let myself be distracted by my girls.

"These are my favorite," Nova said with conviction.

"You said funnel cakes were your favorite," Sienna told her.

Nova shook her head. "These."

"Can we have another one?" Scarlet asked Presley.

"You have to ask your daddy." Presley tapped Scarlet's nose affectionately, making my daughter laugh.

"Please, Daddy?" they all pleaded.

"One more each. Then let Miss Presley have some."

"Struggling in my pursuit of healthy," she said with an embarrassed grin.

"But at least you're not working," I said.

"Not working. Only shaking a little from withdrawal," she admitted.

We shared a private look for an instant before Nova grabbed my arm and said, "Llama pics next, Daddy! You promised."

"I promised."

"Can Miss Presley go too, Daddy?" Sienna said, quieter than Nova but with equal excitement.

"Miss Presley can be in our photo," Scarlet said confidently, having no idea the position that idea put me in.

"I was planning to get my photo with the llamas too," Presley said. "We can walk to the booth together."

My eyes widened as Nova glued herself to Presley's side and took her empty hand. I watched Presley's face for any sign she was uncomfortable with that, aware that not everyone liked it when a kid glommed onto them, but Presley's smile at my youngest seemed genuine.

"We might need to stop and wash our hands first," Presley said, laughing.

I cringed. "I imagine you just got a handful of stickiness. Sorry about that."

She shook her head as if to say there was nothing to apologize for, telling me she was a good sport.

Though Sienna held my hand as we tracked down a hand-washing station, showing me first-hand how sticky two cookie dough balls could make a little girl, the other two clamored around Presley as if she was their favorite human.

My first instinct was to worry they were too enamored with her, too easily becoming attached to her. I had to remind myself that there was no danger in Presley being nice to my girls. She and I weren't together. There was no risk of her hurting them the way their mother had. The way my ex-girlfriend, April, had. My opinion of her would, in fact, go down if she wasn't nice to my princesses. It was easy to tell when a person didn't like kids or was uncomfortable around them. I didn't get that vibe from Presley.

We eventually made it to the end of the line for llama photos, which had, thankfully, gotten shorter since the last time we'd checked.

"Who knew llamas were so popular?" Presley asked.

"Not just any llamas," I told her.

"It's Esmerelda and Betty!" Nova said in her outdoor voice.

"The cookie thieves, right?" Presley said. "Those ladies are famous."

"Rainbow sprinkles are their favorite," Scarlet said.

"One time we got to go to their barn and feed them cookies," Nova told her.

"You are lucky girls," Presley said.

"Ben's a friend of mine," I said.

"The town vet, right?" she asked. "So they're doing this to benefit who?"

"A couple is starting up an animal rescue here in town. Until now, everyone's just taken strays and unwanted animals to Ben's clinic. He's thrilled to support what they're doing."

"Sounds like a good cause then," she said.

"Do you have any pets, Miss Presley?" Sienna asked.

"I don't," she said. "I've never been able to have one because I was gone too much. What about you girls?"

"I wish we could have a dog," Sienna said.

"I want three cats," Nova proclaimed. "One for each of us."

"Our landlord won't let us have pets," Scarlet told her.

"I guess we'll all just have to settle for llama pats today then," Presley said.

"I wanna stand by Betty," Nova said of the less famous, less trouble-making llama as the line crept forward slowly. We neared the tent where the llamas were being pampered with multiple fans to keep them cool, plus, I was sure, all the cookies Ben would allow them to have. "She's the brown-and-white one."

When we finally made it to the table to pay, Presley stepped back, allowing us to go first.

"Hey, Colby," I said to the girl collecting money. "You got roped into working on a Saturday, huh?"

"I don't mind," Ben's office manager replied. "We've got shade, an endless supply of cookies, and we get to work outside."

"You get to work with the llamas," Scarlet said. "You're lucky."

"Aww, look at the puppies and kitties," Sienna said. Her attention was on a trifold poster board on Colby's table. "They're so cute!"

"Those are some of the animals available for adoption at the shelter," Colby said.

"I wish we could have one," Nova said longingly.

Presley bent over to look more closely at the photos, making me wonder if there was a pet in her future. She sure had the room for one. In that house, she had room for several.

"Hey, West," Ben said as he approached. He was in the llamas' enclosure, hovering over his four-legged darlings. His oldest daughter, Evelyn, was helping out from this side of the fence.

"How's it going?" I asked Ben.

We'd started out as a group of single dads, all of us different ages, our kids different ages, but with the common challenge of raising kids by ourselves. Now more than half our group had gotten hitched, Ben included, but our ties remained strong, and we tried to get together at least one Saturday a month.

"Great," Ben said enthusiastically. "These ladies are raking in the cash for the shelter."

"Hi, Dr. Holloway," Scarlet said.

"We're getting our picture next," Nova informed him.

"Esmerelda and Betty can't wait to see you three," Ben told them.

"There's five of us actually," Scarlet said, and Ben's gaze shot to mine, then to Presley.

"Miss Presley probably wants her own photo, girls," I said, offering her an out.

Ben's brows rose up his forehead, and I shook my head, knowing he'd jump to all the wrong conclusions because I was with a good-looking woman.

"The more the merrier," Presley said. "You get some of you four first, so your dad has some good family shots. Then you can be in my pictures too." She took out her debit card as Evelyn came our way.

"Hi, Evelyn," Scarlet said.

"Hi," Ben's daughter said to my three. She was older than my twins by a couple of years, but she and Ben and Emerson's other three played with my kids whenever the dads' group got our families together. "Come this way, and I'll show you where to stand."

As Presley looked on from her spot next to Colby and the animal photos, one of Ben's techs snapped photos of us with my phone. He stepped forward to hand it back to me.

"Wait, we need some with Miss Presley," Nova hollered.

"Use your indoor voice around the llamas," I told her, even though Ben waved it off.

Evelyn went up to Presley and said, "I'll show you where to stand."

"Why don't you make it a girls' pic?" I suggested, uncomfortable with how it would look for both Presley and me to be in it. I was her contractor, not her husband. Not even her friend, really.

"We want you in it too, Daddy," Sienna said.

I met Presley's gaze and saw the hint of a challenge there, as if she was daring me to join them.

I nodded, resigned and determined to get it over with quickly. "Where do you want me?"

"Can you pick me up so I'm taller?" Nova asked Presley.

"Nova," I said.

"Come here," Presley said and hoisted my youngest into her arms.

Soon enough, the photo shoot was over, with the tech getting shots on both my camera and Presley's.

"That's a wrap," I said, relieved she'd placed Presley and Nova on one end, the other two girls between the llamas, and me on the opposite end.

"Daddy, can we go see the fire truck next?" Nova called out as the girls bounced out of the llama tent, Presley surrounded by them, with me at the back.

As I went by, Ben came up to the fence, his brows still raised. "*That* was interesting as hell," he said so only I could hear. When he flicked a glance at Presley, I knew what he was getting at.

"That was the girls' doing," I growled quietly.

"Food for thought though," he said with a sly grin.

I should've ignored him, kept walking, but I stopped, leaned forward, and said in no uncertain terms, "You know my stance. Not going there."

He nodded, but it was smug and knowing.

Fuck that.

"Good luck with your fundraiser," I said and went to catch up with my girls.

They and Presley had stopped near the lemonade stand. All four were engaged in an animated discussion—about lemonade flavors, I realized as I got closer. I grinned, because to look at my daughters' faces, that topic was an important one in life.

Those girls... They were my everything. My reason for doing what I did. For working my ass off. For giving my all to the summer project that could get me a promotion. The raise that would come with it might enable us to move to a bigger place. The extra cash that would come from working on the coffee shop would fund the girls' first road trip. I couldn't wait to travel with them.

We were on our way to better things, the four of us. Everything would be good...as long as I could resist the pull of the enchanting woman who was currently making them smile.

Chapter Eight

West

I wasn't a religious guy, but I was pretty sure some god somewhere was laughing at me.

I'd never in my life been so captivated by a woman as I was Presley Holiday. I didn't even normally use words like *captivated*. I was consumed by thoughts of her, haunted by the desire to touch her, taste her. And I was stuck working on her construction projects for damn near all my waking hours.

It was torture. Sublime, dreadful torture.

Her home project had high stakes. My future depended on its success. Her coffee shop project would be an unexpected mini windfall for my finances. Both would make a difference in my girls' lives if I didn't fuck everything up by doing something dumb with the client.

On Sunday, I'd spent hours with Presley at her empty shop, measuring, discussing materials, drafting plans. I'd put together a timeline based on when I could get supplies in and secure childcare.

Monday I'd pulled a permit. I knew Sybil Wilson, the building inspector, well and had already had a conversation with her. She and I went way back, plus she was a coffee addict. I was optimistic she'd work with us to expedite things.

My mom and her husband, Thomas, who lived in Nashville, had agreed to take the girls for a few weekends to give me concentrated work time, which would enable Presley to open her shop sooner and me to get paid faster. Maybe I could swing a road trip with the girls before the school year started.

Today was Wednesday. The guys had gone to pick up lunch at Tripz, the convenience store where everything was guaranteed to be unhealthy and overpriced. I'd brought a sandwich from home, as I often did, and was sitting in my SUV in Presley's driveway with the window down, listening to a baseball podcast.

Presley had been gone for most of the morning, which should've made it easier for me to concentrate as we pulled electrical wires throughout the main floor. Paul was a licensed electrician, so he was in charge of the electric. Damn good thing, because I couldn't stop glancing around for the homeowner every few minutes like a puppy looking for treats.

I stuffed the last of my sandwich in my mouth and laughed at a comment the sports commentator made about the Yankees.

"Hey, West," Presley said at my open window, scaring the shit out of me. "If I needed someone to work on my boathouse, is that something your company could do?"

I swallowed my food, congratulating myself for not choking on it, and took a big swig of water. "Afternoon," I said. "Didn't hear you coming."

"Oh. Sorry about that. I parked at the end of the driveway so I'd be out of your way."

I took my keys out of the ignition, cutting off the podcast, then got out of the vehicle, getting a good look at her as she stepped back.

She wore a fitted plain-white short-sleeve shirt that wrapped to one side and had a deep V-neck, revealing a tantalizing bit of cleavage. The shirt was cropped a good inch or so above the waistband of her button-fly denim shorts. Once again, I imagined running my rough fingers over the soft skin at her waist before undoing those buttons one by one...

I shut the SUV door harder than necessary and told myself to stop with the dirty thoughts. Forcing my mind back to her question, I tried to catch up. I was learning that Presley's mind never slowed down.

"What kind of work on your boathouse?" I asked as we walked through the garage to enter the house. This was the first I'd heard of anything to do with the boathouse.

She shrugged. "The wood inside is in bad shape. I think it needs to be refinished? And that flat roof... It would make a perfect entertaining space. I think it was intended to be a patio, but there aren't stairs going up there. The previous owners didn't use it. I'm just wondering about my options."

"So you want to use your boathouse for entertaining?"

"I want to use my boathouse for a boat."

I swung my head to her. "I didn't know you were getting a boat."

"I'm not sure yet. The boathouse is part of the consideration. I'd also need to learn to drive a boat."

I chuckled. I couldn't fathom how much money she must have for learning to drive a boat to be a bigger deterrent than figuring out how to pay for it. This rich girl was so far out of my league it wasn't funny.

And yet I was dying to sample that skin at her waist.

"Are you laughing at me?" she said, grinning good-naturedly. "I've never driven a boat. Do you know how?"

"I do."

"Where did you learn?"

"I grew up good friends with Jagger McNamara. His family owns—"

"McNamara Marina," she cut in, nodding. "Got it."

"They offer boat safety courses and lessons."

"Perfect. But back to the boathouse..."

"I've got ten more minutes of lunch break. Let's go take a look."

If we could add on to this project, that would look good to Levi and maybe win me some points toward that promotion.

She led me through the house, out the patio door, and down the path to the shore. There were overgrown paver stones leading to the boathouse but no actual walkway, which had me agreeing that the previous owners must not have used it much. I made myself pay attention to the stones instead of Presley's ass, but not before noticing the tantalizing heart shape of it in those little shorts.

She unlocked the door and pushed it open with a loud, slow creak. Several steps led down to the deck level that was a couple of feet above the water line. A closed garage door on the lake side let filtered daylight in, enough so I could see from the top of the stairs that the wood was in bad shape.

"Is there electric?" I spotted a single bulb hanging from the ceiling.

"It's wired, but I need to change the bulb. The garage door is electric."

She reached back by the door we'd entered and hit the button to open it, allowing more light in. I followed her down the steps.

The boathouse was no frills with room for a decent-sized craft, the deck forming a vee similar to the shape of a hull, built on what appeared to be a permanent steel-pile dock foundation.

The wood needed more than refinishing. Between being old and not being treated correctly or regularly, the floor looked to be rotting in places.

Presley walked toward the cutout for the boat, peering at the water that lapped below. "I'd love to turn the roof into a patio directly over the water. I could add an outdoor sectional, a dining table, some tiki torches..."

"Since it's been wired, you might be able to do an outdoor kitchen," I said.

"Oh, maybe a wet bar? Could I get water out here?"

"We'd have to see if there's a water line." I bent down to inspect the decking more closely. "You'll need to replace all this wood," I said as I pushed against a section, and it gave a little. I stood, alarmed at how bad it was. "This isn't stable at all. We need to get back from the edges—"

Presley took a step toward me, then let out a yelp as the board beneath her cracked and shifted. I instinctively reached for her and pulled her into me. Fortunately the board hadn't broken all the way through; otherwise she might be in the drink right now.

As it was, she was facing me, chest to chest, because I'd instinctively dragged her up against me.

We stood there catching our breath. My heart pounded like a jackhammer, fifty percent from the scare, fifty percent because...Jesus. Presley Holiday was in my arms.

Part of my brain was screaming that I should let her go,

but when her hands rested on my chest and she peered up into my eyes with those pretty blues, that call went ignored.

When her gaze flitted down to my lips, all bets were off, and my dick went as hard as the steel piles beneath us.

All logical thought drained from my brain as I registered the slight sheen of her tempting lips and the way they were barely parted, as if in invitation. Ignoring the few brain cells that knew this was wrong, I leaned in and touched my lips to hers.

She was all softness and sweetness and femininity, smelling of flowers and lightness. She let out a little moan as she kissed me back, revving me up higher, hotter.

Presley was my opposite in every way. And yet her touch enflamed my blood like nothing I'd ever experienced before.

I deepened the kiss, running my tongue along the seam of her lips. She opened to me instantly, as if there was nothing she wanted more. Our tongues touched, swirled, tasted, tangled, the connection like an explosion that sent a throbbing need through my veins and straight down to my dick.

She pulled my head to hers, telling me she was all in. I slid my hands down her back, drawing her into my hard body, as if I could get her any closer. I wanted to devour her, consume her, lay her out on the floor and pound into her—

Shit.

I fought to pull back, put a few inches between our mouths, breathing hard, stunned at my urges. It was as if she turned me into an animal, which was fitting. Next to her, I was rough, coarse, clumsy, reduced to primitive thoughts.

Presley caught her lower lip with her teeth as her mouth curved into a half smile. She lifted her heavy lids and peered up at me, her eyes bright, alive, looking not at all regretful.

That didn't make kissing her okay.

I tried to find words, but all I could manage was a low growl as I looked down at her gorgeous face, those pink lips, wanting to do that again.

"Thanks for saving me," she whispered, still grinning.

That brought me back to reality enough to remember the floor we stood on wasn't safe. "We're lucky we didn't both fall through," I managed.

With my hands at her waist, I lifted her, pivoted, and set her on the bottom step, trying not to notice the feel of her bare skin beneath my palms. She weighed hardly anything.

"The stairs are okay?" she asked.

"I wouldn't assume that," I said, "but it looks like the slats closest to the water are the worst." I took out my phone, squatted down, and turned on the flashlight to inspect the wood more closely, trying to concentrate on the task. Trying to ignore the way my blood still pounded away from my brain instead of to it.

"It's very valiant of you to whisk me here to semisafety, but shouldn't you stay off the wood too?" she asked. "I'm guessing you weigh more than me. All muscle, of course."

I could hear her grin without looking up at her.

"I know how to swim if I fall through," I told her, creeping carefully toward the garage door, assessing the wood, coaching my heart to slow the hell down.

Thoughts were creeping in, making it difficult to focus on my inspection. Thoughts like, *What the godforsaken hell were you thinking to kiss her?*

Staying to the outer slats along the exterior walls, I made my way around where the bow would go, then to the other side, finding the same results there.

Presley moved up the stairs to the landing inside the door, her eyes on me.

When my pulse had slowed nearly back to normal range and my dick had calmed the hell down, I went to the stairs, headed up, and stopped two from the top, putting me at eye level with Presley. That landing would be tight quarters for both of us. I needed distance, not closeness.

"The floor needs to be replaced completely," I said, summoning my professional tone. "The walls probably just repainted. I'll take a look at the outside to be sure."

"Could your company do that?"

Without looking directly at her, as if she was the sun and could burn my retinas, I answered, "We could probably fit it in while we work on the rest of the house. Might take us a couple extra days is all. Look, Presley, I was out of line." I gestured over my shoulder as I dared to meet her gaze. "Kissing you was inappropriate and wrong. I'm sorry."

Her pretty features dipped in a frown. "I'm not. Please don't ruin it by apologizing. That was...too spectacular to apologize."

I swallowed, trying not to get lost in her imploring blue eyes. Trying not to be pulled in by her words. *Spectacular.* She thought that kiss was spectacular, and I sure as hell couldn't disagree.

"You're my client," I said, my voice rough.

She tilted her head, her expression lightening. "Does your company have a policy against kissing clients?"

I chuckled. "My company is a small construction business that doesn't pay lawyers to write up official policies, no. But common sense—"

"That felt like something that shouldn't be ruined by common sense if you ask me."

I studied her, tried to argue. The words I knew I should say didn't come out.

"I liked it," she said confidently. "But I don't want you to lose your job—"

"I wouldn't lose my job." Levi would have something to say about it, but he wouldn't can me.

I thought about explaining the promotion I was working toward, but I kept it to myself. A raise of a few thousand bucks a year might be life-changing to me, but that money wouldn't mean a thing to her. Not to a woman who'd paid cash for a lakeshore home.

She stepped closer, putting us mere inches apart. I held my ground. Hell, I was dying to pull her into me and do it all over again, but I was a grown damn adult. I could control my urges. Most of the time.

"I don't want to make you uncomfortable," she said, "but it seems like we could have *fun* together." Her brows shot up with the word *fun*. "Off the clock, of course. And no one would have to know."

She hit the garage door button to close it, then opened the door we'd come in through. She flicked a flirty smile at me, and it was all I could do to keep my hands at my sides and not yank her back into me.

"The decision is yours, West," she said as she headed out into the sunshine.

I stood there, stunned for a few seconds, then went up the last two steps and out the door. I knew damn well what the *right* thing to do was, and I was determined to do it—to keep my hands off her.

But I sure as hell was gonna have problems keeping my mind on the job for the rest of the day as I tried to wipe away the memory of what it felt like to kiss her.

Chapter Nine

Presley

I'd just taken out all the pieces of my assembly-required bookshelf and spread them around me in my temporary second-story home office when I heard the construction guys drive off Thursday afternoon. I glanced at the time and was surprised it was going on five p.m. I'd been assembling my new office furniture for hours.

I tried not to be disappointed that the crew hadn't checked in before leaving. Yeah, who was I kidding? West was the one I was disappointed about and not for professional reasons.

That kiss yesterday in the boathouse? It'd been more than twenty-four hours, and I still got light and fluttery inside whenever I thought about it. The feel of his strong hands on me, the way he lifted me as if I weighed nothing, and the kiss itself... It was commanding and decisive yet somehow tender at the same time. It'd been a tantalizing taste of what West could do to me.

I wanted more.

I'd left the ball in his court as we exited the boathouse, but it appeared he wasn't going to take me up on my offer. Wasn't even going to discuss the offer. There'd been a *good morning* and a project update first thing when he'd arrived but nothing personal.

We'd been business as usual ever since, with me looking hard for signs from him but seeing none. I would respect his wishes, but I could've sworn the connection between us was incendiary. I'd never had such a reaction to a man before, and all we'd done was kiss.

Maybe it was just that he was different from my usual type, which according to Chloe was more of a metrosexual, suit-wearing intellectual than a burly guy who worked with his hands. I couldn't lie. Those hands of West's intrigued me and heated up my middle-of-the-night fantasies as I imagined what he could do to my body with them.

These thoughts weren't helping anything right now, so I shut them down.

As I took inventory of the multiple mini plastic bags of screws and pieces on the floor in front of me, the inside door to the garage below shut loudly. I sat up straighter, trying to discern whether someone had come in or gone out.

"Presley?"

At the sound of West's voice, my pulse raced. He hadn't left after all.

"I'm upstairs," I called, glancing at the mess of slats, screws, and instructions between me and the door. "Come on up."

When his footsteps reached the top of the stairs, I said, "I'm in here."

He filled the doorway, his brows popping up as he took in the three pieces of furniture I'd already assembled, as well as the mess I was sitting in the middle of. "Hey."

"Come on in. Sit down if you want." I pointed at my brand-new desk chair.

He shook his head. "I'm dirty and sweaty. Don't want to ruin anything."

An image flashed into my head of taking him into the bathroom, peeling off his clothes, sticking him under the shower, and stepping in with him to slowly, thoroughly scrub him clean...

"Is this what you've been doing all afternoon?" he asked, snapping me out of my thoughts. He walked over to the L-shaped desk I'd assembled and placed in front of the small window that looked out on the driveway. "Putting furniture together?"

"Yes. I didn't realize it was so late."

"That seems to be a recurring theme with you," he said with a chuckle. "I'm surprised you didn't hire someone to do this for you."

"I love putting furniture together," I said. "Chloe thinks it's the weirdest thing, but I find it soothing. And rewarding." I gestured at the desk and the two side cabinets.

"How come you didn't get the good stuff that doesn't need to be assembled?"

I shrugged and grinned. "Maybe this is my hobby." Once I had the bags set out so I could see the labels, I stood and stepped over the piles of various-sized wood pieces until I faced him.

"And you thought you didn't have one," he said, peering down at me with those compelling green eyes, laugh lines appearing at the outer corners.

Something about the way he looked at me made me feel like he really *saw* me, saw parts of me others didn't. I wasn't sure how I felt about that.

"I'm trying to find ways to occupy my time that don't

count as working." I let my gaze flit to his lips, thinking once again I could pass a lot of time getting naked with him.

He apparently read my mind, because he shifted his weight from one leg to the other, seeming nervous. "Presley, you tempt me like I've never been tempted before, but I can't mix work with pleasure."

"You said you wouldn't lose your job over something like messing around with a client."

"It's not that simple." He paced a couple of steps away, looking as if he was searching for the right words, words I was pretty sure I wasn't going to like.

"My girls are everything," he said. "Everything I do is for them, to give them the best life I can. If I mess this up, I let them down."

Remembering how involved he'd been with his daughters, how obviously loving, I couldn't help but smile. "You're a really good dad."

"One of our guys at Dawson Construction is retiring due to a bad back," West said, ignoring my compliment. "He's been second-in-command under Levi."

"You want his position," I guessed.

He nodded once. "It's between me and another guy. This summer is our audition, I guess you could say. Nick's overseeing a big outdoor project, and I'm overseeing this one. Levi's gonna pick based on how we do."

"I have no complaints about the work you and the guys have done so far. I'll give you a glowing review whether you kiss me again or not." I shot a flirty grin at him.

"I appreciate that." He didn't smile in spite of my light tone. "No offense, but I don't think someone who can pay cash for a big house can understand what it's like to live paycheck to paycheck. I don't have a cushion or a backup. It's all me. Those girls are depending on me."

The conviction in his tone, the dedication to his girls... That was so...*hot.*

It didn't make sense to me. Nothing about my attraction to him made sense. I wasn't looking for a long-term guy, never mind one who came with kids. I just frankly wanted to have a good time. It'd been too long since I'd been with a guy.

And yet I needed to make something clear to him. "I totally understand living paycheck to paycheck," I said quietly. "We were dirt poor growing up, even before my parents split. I started working at fourteen to help my mom and sister pay for groceries and rent. My mom didn't get promoted to manager until I was seventeen, which helped a little, but we had no savings. My dad never paid a cent of support. So I get it, West. I remember."

My childhood, the financial insecurity, those were what had driven me to go into finance, to work my butt off, to make as much money as I could, invest it, be set for life. I never wanted to feel like if I called in sick when I legitimately had the flu, I wouldn't be able to pay the utility bill.

I'd sworn from the time I was a teenager I would never rely on someone else the way my mom had during her marriage. Their traditional setup—where the husband made the income, and the wife stayed home with the kids—did not work for me. I didn't judge anyone who chose that way of life, but it would never be me. I needed to be in charge of my own life, financial and otherwise.

"You had a deadbeat dad too, huh?" he said, his tone a lot gentler.

"Deadbeat, controlling, abusive, all the good stuff," I said.

An icy look entered his eyes. "Did he put his hands on you?"

I shook my head. "Only on my mom. He was more of the emotionally abusive type to me and my sister."

He growled low and shook his head.

"Did yours?" I asked carefully.

West

I scoffed. "My father, and I use that term only in the biological sense, disappeared when my mom told him she was pregnant with me. I never met him. No desire to." I looked at her intently. "Last I knew, he was in prison."

Her brows rose. "That's a lot to process."

I shrugged. "Not as much as if he'd ever been in my life. We didn't need him. My mom and I made it just fine."

She nodded. "I get that. My dad damaged my mom. There's no way to prove it, but I've often thought all the abuse and stress she went through with him shortened her life. She would've been better off if she'd never married him."

"Some men aren't worth the oxygen they breathe," I said.

"I guess we have single moms and deadbeat dads in common then," she said. "And you thought we were so different."

"We're different," I said with conviction. "I won't be buying a boat anytime in the near future."

"I haven't decided to buy a boat yet," she said stubbornly. "I understand your point, West. I'll just say it. I have a lot of money. I worked my ass off for it and sacrificed my health. I won't apologize for it or feel bad about it—"

"Hell no, you shouldn't feel bad about it," I said. "I respect the hell out of what you've done for yourself. Don't you dare apologize."

After watching my mom sacrifice sleep to work two jobs, be paid less than she was worth, and work twice as hard as everyone else, I knew how unfair the world could be because of gender. I was more than familiar with female willpower and determination. My mom had them in spades, and those qualities had gotten us through my childhood.

Presley had them as well. She was the kind of woman I wanted my girls exposed to—on an acquaintance basis, not something more personal, like the woman I was involved with. I didn't want my girls exposed to anyone I was involved with. Been there, done that, didn't like the T-shirt, and neither did my daughters.

What I wanted for my girls was for them to know in their hearts they could do whatever they set out to do, just like Presley had. Didn't matter if their mom was a flake or their dad was just a construction guy. I wanted them to believe in their unlimited potential the way Presley obviously did in hers.

"Something you should understand," Presley said. "I might've spent a lot of money lately, on this house and starting up my business, but normally I'm sort of thrifty."

I couldn't help but laugh. "Somehow I suspect your definition of thrifty and mine are different."

"I don't splurge very often," she insisted. "These big things lately? Those are important. I refuse to cut corners on my home and business, but normally the only thing I overspend on is shoes."

"Which explains why you want an entire wall in the master closet to be shoe storage," I said. "I've been meaning to ask you if that was right."

"It's right. Shoes are my weakness."

I glanced at her bare feet. "I haven't seen you wear the same pair twice."

"Follow me," she said, gesturing with her index finger.

She went out the door and took a left. The door opposite her office was open, allowing me an eyeful as we walked past what looked like fluffy, soft, rumpled bedding in pink and white. I almost missed a step when I spotted a puddle of silky-looking sky-blue lingerie on the floor on this side of the bed.

To my relief, she kept walking. I already knew the sweet, feminine bedding and the sexy-as-fuck underthings were going to appear in my dreams whether I wanted them to or not.

She turned into yet another bedroom and stopped not far into the room.

"This is why I need the shoe wall in the closet," she said, waving at stacks of shoe organizer shelves along one of the walls. She laughed and spun around, taking in the whole room, which seemed to be serving as a closet and a place for half-unpacked boxes. "I donated twenty-seven pairs before I moved too."

My brows climbed even higher on my forehead as I tried to think what to say.

"This is my vice. Shoes are my weakness. But otherwise, West, you and I aren't all that different."

I met her gaze, took in her soft, pretty features, allowed myself a glance at those lips that begged to be nipped and kissed. We were different all right. Different in all the *right* ways.

I did an internal head shake at myself. We *weren't* going there.

"I won't question the shoe wall anymore," I joked as if my pulse wasn't pounding through my veins with lust.

She grinned, then went serious. "I'll respect your decision. About us, I mean. I don't like it, but I'll honor it. The last thing I want to do is make you uncomfortable."

It was a little late for that, as my erection was making my pants damn uncomfortable.

I turned away with a nod, needing to get out of her personal space, where everything gave me ideas, most of them X-rated.

Once I was out in the hall and beyond the door to her bedroom, where I could breathe a little easier, I said, "I came up to tell you we're done for the day. Do you need me to lock anything?"

"No need," she said, following me to the stairs. "Thanks, West."

"Night, Presley. See you tomorrow morning."

As I jogged down the stairs, putting more space between us, I couldn't help but wonder, now that I'd made my stance about *us* clear to her, whether I was the dumbest man on the planet.

Chapter Ten

Presley

"The silver sofa," Chloe said.

I looked at Rowan for her opinion.

"Silver sofa, definitely," she agreed.

"With the stain guard warranty at the highest level you can buy," Chloe said.

"Silver sofa it is," I said excitedly, in full agreement that it was the right choice for the shop.

A couple of days ago, I'd bought a patio dining set from Lake Life Outfitters, on the opposite corner of the square, and put it inside in the front corner of my shop for now so there'd be a place to sit while construction was going on—or when my girlfriends and I met to choose decor. I hoped to eventually get a permit for outdoor seating.

This afternoon, I was glad I'd bought it, since Rowan was close to seven months pregnant. She looked wonderful, but she admitted her back was happy she was sitting after I'd walked them around the wide-open space, explaining where walls, counters, the kitchen, and everything else would go. West had moved in some of the supplies already, even though we were waiting on the building permit.

"It'll tie right in with the metal on the chairs and stools," Rowan said. "I love the silver, blue, and white color scheme. I'm excited for you."

"I'm excited for this town," Chloe said.

"The last furniture decision for today is the blue easy chair," I said. "Single-wide, double-wide, one-and-a-half width?"

I turned my laptop again to show them the differences.

"Not single," Rowan said.

"Says the pregnant girl." Chloe laughed, but it was empathetic instead of teasing. "I remember that third trimester feeling, like you're huge and clumsy and need all the space—even though you absolutely are not huge."

"I'm not quite to the third trimester, but I already feel that way." Rowan rested a hand on her belly. "I think the one-and-a-half-width chair. You don't want it to take up so much room that it crowds the door."

"Agree," I said, and added the extra-wide chair to my cart.

I'd spent the morning in Nashville at a furniture store with a helpful clerk. I didn't believe in buying comfortable furniture without sitting my butt on it to test it. The light-colored wood tables and metal chairs, which I'd picked out from a restaurant supplier, were one thing. Comfort wasn't the ultimate goal for them but rather frequent turnover of patrons.

The full-length sofa and easy chair for the lounging corner were a different story. I wanted them to be comfortable enough that people could curl up on them for hours to chat with a friend or hammer out work on a laptop.

I'd narrowed down my choices in person, then texted

Chloe and Rowan, hoping they could come by after work and weigh in on the final decisions. They'd come through, as girlfriends did. They loved the plans West and I had laid out.

Since there was a three- to four-week delay to get the furniture, I was ordering today. As I pulled the laptop closer so I could check out, the rain outside picked up intensity. It was a cozy, insulating sound. I couldn't wait for a rainy day once the shop was open. I imagined it as a refuge for people of all kinds regardless of what curveball Mother Nature dished out.

I hit the Place Order button with a whoop. "Thank you, girls. I love our choices," I told them.

"I can't wait to see it come together," Rowan said.

"By the time she opens, you'll be ready to pop that baby out," Chloe said.

"Which is going to happen magically and instantly with zero pain," Rowan said. "Denial is working for me at the moment."

As I checked that my order had gone through, movement out the window caught my eye. A guy in a ball cap jogged through the rain, getting soaked. He looked to be heading toward my door.

When I recognized West, my body reacted accordingly, as it did every time, against my better judgment. I apparently couldn't *think* my woman bits out of their attraction to that man.

I'd left the main door unlocked since we were right here, and West came inside, dripping with water and sex appeal.

Dammit though.

"Hello," I said, a question in my tone.

"Hey, ladies. I saw the lights on over here when I came out of the town hall." He shook water off his hands, then unzipped his contractor portfolio and took out an official-looking paper.

"The permit," I said excitedly.

"Sybil came through." He took out a roll of tape, went to the window next to the door, and posted the permit.

"So we can start?" I asked.

"I'll be here tomorrow evening." He looked over at Rowan. "Sam's staying with my girls," he said of her teenage stepdaughter who'd started a babysitting company with a friend. "Tell her to fuel up good. She'll need the energy." He grinned.

"She'll do better than I would," Rowan said, laughing and rubbing her belly again. "Thanks for hiring her. She seems to be thriving with this business and the way it's taking off. They're up to five sitters now."

"It's a lifesaver," West said. "We love Allie, but I can't have her working fifty hours a week."

"We love it too," Chloe said.

As Rowan and Chloe discussed Sam's business adventures, West closed his portfolio and turned to me. He flicked his gaze over my casual T-shirt dress, down to my boho slingback sandals. "Yet another pair of shoes," he said quietly, with what felt like a private half grin.

"You like 'em?" I asked flippantly, keeping my volume down as well. I took in the wetness of his black Dawson Construction tee and the way it clung to his solid chest.

He didn't answer, but I could swear heat flared in his eyes for a second before he glanced away.

"What are your plans tomorrow?" he asked, seeming to flip into business mode.

"I'm at your beck and call." The words came out flirtier than I intended. Oops. I needed to reel it in. I knew this, but it popped out before I could stop it.

He hesitated for the slightest instant, as if deciding what to say to that, then glanced at Rowan and Chloe. "I'm hoping to have the drywall delivered, but someone has to be here to let them in."

"I can be here whenever."

He checked his watch. "I'll see if I can catch Wayne tonight and arrange it. I gotta get home to my girls."

"Thanks for bringing the permit over," I said as we walked to the door.

"Later, ladies," he said to Rowan and Chloe, who responded in kind. To me, he said, "I'll let you know about the delivery."

He went back out into the rain, and I forced myself not to watch him walk away.

"Well, *that* was interesting," Chloe said.

I headed to the table, trying to act like that simple exchange hadn't had any effect on me whatsoever.

"That's what I'm thinking," Rowan said.

"What was interesting?" I asked, playing dumb as I sat.

"The tension between you two was practically making the air crackle," Chloe said.

I gave her a look that said there was no tension, and she was crazy.

"Are you and West..." Rowan started.

"Sleeping together?" Chloe added.

"No," I said. "And there was no tension. Really."

Rowan and Chloe exchanged a look. Then Rowan asked her, "Did you see the way he looked at her?"

"Then he talked to her with that growly, quiet voice," Chloe said. "Not an 'I'm here on official business' voice. More like an 'I'm imagining you naked' voice."

I felt suddenly overheated. "He did not look at me in any way," I attempted to argue, "nor did he use a voice."

Rowan laughed. "But he was definitely imagining you naked."

"God, you guys," I said on a flustered exhale. I popped back up off my chair and wandered to the window, hoping for one last glimpse of West. "The chemistry is insane. I've never reacted to a guy like this."

"It's those skinny city guys you were drawn to," Chloe said, making a face. "Of course you didn't react like you do to West, who earns a living with his body."

"Truth. I see the light now." I couldn't remember a single one of the skinny city guys at the moment, mainly because there hadn't been many and none of them had been important in my life.

Rowan made a sound of approval. "Now we're getting somewhere."

"Unfortunately we're not," I said. "I've made it clear to him I'm interested, but he shut me down."

"That didn't look like a shutdown," Chloe said.

"He couldn't hide his interest if he tried," Rowan added.

"He told me in no uncertain terms that *we* will not be happening," I said. "He doesn't do his clients."

"Pity," Rowan said.

"Poor decision, at least for *this* client," Chloe said. "But I suppose it's a good policy in general."

"You won't be the client forever," Rowan pointed out. "You live here now. You can hook up once your remodel is done."

I waved off the idea. "It's more of a proximity thing. Like, he's in my house, in my face, so I'm interested in a fling. I don't want any kind of relationship."

"Of course you don't," Chloe said.

"I'm fixing my life," I reminded her. "Focusing on *me*

instead of my job for once." I glanced around. "Well, trying."

We all laughed, because obviously I loved to work.

"And I haven't forgotten you're antimarriage," Chloe said.

"Only for myself. I'm happy for you two."

"You never want to get married?" Rowan asked.

I shook my head. "I'm too independent and not willing to give that up."

"Not all marriages are like your parents' or your sister's," Chloe said. "Two of us in this room are proof."

"You guys are so cute but not typical," I said. "I'm thinking about getting a dog."

"Are you being serious?" Chloe asked, looking stunned.

"They had all these photos of dogs who need homes at the Honeysuckle Festival," I said.

"A dog's a great idea," Rowan said. "Another living soul in that big house of yours. He'll keep you company. Maybe two dogs."

"Maybe start with one. Hey, is that Magnolia?" Chloe asked, her attention on two people with umbrellas walking past the side window toward the square. "It is. And Darius."

"Is she finally doing it?" Rowan asked, sounding excited.

"I haven't talked to her lately," Chloe said as she stood.

"Doing what?" I asked. I'd met Magnolia a few times but didn't know her well.

Chloe went to the door, opened it, and called out to Magnolia as she and Darius finished their conversation. "Hey, you. What's going on?"

Magnolia came over to the door, her eyes bright. "Hi, girls."

I smiled and watched as she came inside. I wasn't sure

what to think about this woman with porcelain skin and gorgeous hair. The first time I'd met her was a couple of years ago when Chloe had invited me to girls' night at the Barn Bar. Magnolia had been rude to Chloe that night and had been mean to her when they were kids, so my natural inclination was to dislike her.

Chloe, however, had forgiven Magnolia for the past. They were friendly now. Apparently Magnolia'd had some kind of shit life growing up, where her parents had controlled her with money—until her dad had cut her off cold turkey. I didn't know the whole story, but manipulation had been my own dad's game, so I could at least relate. I just hadn't decided if that would excuse how she'd acted toward my bestie.

"Am I interrupting?" Magnolia asked as she collapsed her umbrella.

"Not at all," I said, gesturing to the fourth empty chair.

"Tell us what you're doing with a real-estate agent," Rowan said.

"Are you taking the plunge?" Chloe asked.

Magnolia sat on the edge of the patio chair, placed her palms on the table, and inhaled deeply, as if she needed to calm herself. "I think I'm going to do it."

"Yes!" Rowan said.

"It's about damn time," Chloe said, grinning.

"I'm out of the loop," I said. "Are you leasing one of the spaces in this building?"

"I'm officially starting an event-planning business," Magnolia said. "I love planning parties and weddings. I'm the planner for Harper and Max's wedding next weekend."

"We'll get to see you in action," I said. I'd started to get to know Harper and Max before I moved to town. They'd invited me to the wedding, and Chloe had convinced me to go as friends with Kemp Essex, Holden's business partner, who'd also been planning to go solo.

"You already have," Chloe said. "She helped with my wedding reception and Rowan and Chance's gender-reveal party."

"The pink and blue cocktails were particularly perfect," I said, having sampled both.

"Thank you," Magnolia said. "I'm excited. And terrified. I didn't think it was possible to do this because I don't have any money to put toward it, but Seth Henry helped me get a small business loan, and then this building opened up, and that space next door is perfect for what I need."

"It's a cute space," I said. "Too small for what I wanted, but you just need an office and a meeting area, really."

"Exactly," Magnolia said. Her smile slipped. "I'm not a businessperson. I'm all about colors and decor and party games, so I'm nervous."

"You're already doing business stuff when you plan for someone," Chloe said. "You have to work within their budgets, and you've ordered supplies and billed for your services."

"Harper and Max are my first official paying clients, actually," Magnolia admitted. "I've always done it for fun. I didn't believe you when you said people would pay me."

"They should, and they will," Rowan said. "If you need a testimonial for your website or anything, let me know. I'll give you one."

Magnolia smiled in gratitude. "I'd love that. I hadn't thought about testimonials since my first official event isn't until next weekend."

"I'll give you one for my reception," Chloe said, "and you've helped with Rusty Anchor events. We've got photos."

"We could use those?" Magnolia asked.

"Of course. The photo op setup for my wedding reception was all your idea. So were the progressive tasting stations at the brewery events." Chloe picked up her phone and searched for relevant photos.

"Did you sign the lease yet?" I asked.

"I told him I want to sleep on it," Magnolia said. "It's at the top of my rent budget, but the location is so good you can't put a price on it."

"Between summer tourism and weekly farmers markets, you'll get a ton of walk-by traffic even being one layer off the square," Chloe said.

"Do you have a business name yet?" I asked her.

She bit her lip as she looked at me.

"You have an idea," I said.

"Tell us," Rowan said.

Magnolia sat back in the chair, pushing her hair out of her face. "I've been thinking about it a lot. I'll do any kind of event. Weddings, birthday parties, bachelorette parties, graduation parties, celebrations of any kind. Even business events like we've done at the Anchor. It's a wide variety of events, but what it comes down to is moments. The moments that matter to people. So I was thinking... Moments by Magnolia?"

"I like it," I said.

Chloe tilted her head, overthinking it.

"Love it," Rowan said.

Chloe nodded thoughtfully. "Yes. I could see *Moments* in bigger type and *by Magnolia* in a smaller script beneath it."

"Yes," Magnolia said. "I can totally see that."

"I think it's a great name," I said. "*Moments* says it all. *By Magnolia* makes it yours."

Chloe smacked the table. "Boom. One down. What about you, Pres? Did you come up with any ideas?"

I sat forward and leaned my elbows on the table. I'd been brainstorming possibilities since day one and kept coming back to the same idea. "What do you guys think of The Bean Counter?"

"Ha," Chloe, the queen of puns, said. "Double meaning. You know I love that."

"What's the double meaning?" Magnolia asked.

"I used to be in finance. Not an accountant, but close enough. And beans—"

"Coffee beans. I get that part. It's cute," Magnolia said.

I raised my brows at Rowan.

"Yes," she said. "It's perfect. You both have these wonderful names for your businesses, and Chance and I can't decide on a name for our baby girl."

"Ah, low stakes," I joked, waving it off.

"You've got time," Chloe told her. "Speaking of time, I need to make sure Holden's picking up Sutton." She typed in a message on her phone and asked Rowan, "Is Chance home already?"

"He's staying late to get the fall media budget finished," Rowan said.

"Do you still like working with your husband?" Magnolia asked.

"Most days," Rowan said, grinning. "It helps that it's not forever."

"You're going back to teaching next year, right?" I asked, knowing she'd wanted to find a position for this fall until her due date fell in late September.

"I hope to. It depends on whether there's a position at the high school." Rowan was one of those odd individuals who liked teenagers.

Chloe read a reply from her husband, then said, "Holden's got Sutton. Does anyone want to do a spur-of-the-moment celebratory dinner? It's a big day, with Magnolia leasing a business space and both of you deciding on names."

"I'd love to," I said easily, thinking it sounded much better than going home to an oversized, half-empty house. I really needed to look into a dog.

"Sam's got a babysitting gig this evening. I'm in," Rowan said.

"You know I'm in," Magnolia said.

"The Diner? Humble's? Henry's? The Cove? What sounds good?" Chloe asked.

"I could use some of Cash's hummingbird cake," I said. If we were celebrating, we'd need dessert.

"I'm up for a splurge," Magnolia said.

"Henry's is always good," Rowan agreed.

"I'll text Seth to get us a table if he's still there." Chloe sent another message off as we stood.

I turned off the lights and picked up my keys and cross-body bag.

"Ladies?" Magnolia said as we prepared to leave. "Thank you. This means the world to me. I'm more excited than terrified now."

We collapsed into a group hug. Once I locked the door, the four of us walked along the wet sidewalks toward Henry's, laughing and making predictions for our two new businesses, then suggesting girl names for Rowan's baby. We started out serious, but then we turned to outrageous suggestions, trying to one-up each other with bad ideas.

As we crossed Honeysuckle Road to Henry's, I thought about how I hadn't had a group of girlfriends since high school, had mainly just had Chloe, and then she'd moved here to Dragonfly Lake.

I loved this. It felt good to laugh, to be lighthearted, to think of things besides investments and finance. Things like coffee and startups and friendships that meant everything.

For the first time since I'd moved to Dragonfly Lake, I had the feeling I might be able to *belong* in this little town.

Chapter Eleven

West

Jagger McNamara and I had been friends since kindergarten, but we didn't get to hang out often anymore, thanks to work schedules and me being a dad.

He might've been a wild child growing up, but he had a good heart and a soft spot for my princesses. He made a point of taking us out on his boat at least a couple of times each summer. This evening was our first such ride of the season.

I'd finished work at Presley's and left at four to pick up a picnic dinner from Country Market's deli—cold fried chicken that Sienna would turn her nose up at, cheese cubes, dinner rolls, and grapes. Wanting to give the girls an extra treat, I'd stopped by Sugar and bought a dozen cookies. Then I'd relieved Allie a few minutes earlier than usual.

Jagger had zipped us across the lake in his bowrider to a quiet cove where we swam off the back of the boat then devoured our dinner.

I'd managed to keep the bakery box hidden until now, so as I slid it out of a Country Market bag, Scarlet gasped.

"Daddy got cookies!" she hollered.

"Yummy," Nova shouted.

"Did you get us Esmerelda's favorite kind?" Sienna asked, blessedly quieter than her sisters.

"I got something even better," I said, holding the box up, the lid still closed.

The three little piglets, who'd eaten big dinners—even Sienna had filled up on everything but the chicken—their appetites undoubtedly increased by swimming, clamored around me as if I hadn't fed them for a week.

"Go sit in your places in the bow, and I'll bring the cookies," I said, hoping to limit crumbs to that section.

I didn't have to tell them twice. All three bounced to the front, sat on the cushioned benches, and looked up at me expectantly like little birds. I bent down and flipped the lid open with fanfare so they could see.

Nova's mouth popped open.

Sienna sucked in her breath.

Scarlet squealed and said, "They're shaped like llamas!"

"I want a Betty one," Nova said, her eyes on the chocolate frosted.

"The white ones are Esmerelda," Sienna said, helping herself to one of those.

"Can we have one of each?" Scarlet asked.

"Pick one to start," I said, knowing I'd give in to seconds eventually.

Once the girls were munching on their dessert, I sat next to Jagger and held the box out. His brows rose as he surveyed the cookies and laughed.

"Whoever thought up making them llama shaped is a genius," he said. "That's a marketing coup."

He chose a chocolate one. I took a vanilla. Someone had decorated them with facial details including heart-shaped sunglasses and a rainbow-sprinkled blanket on each llama's back.

"I didn't think you liked the girls to have a lot of sugar," Jagger said so the girls, who were jabbering ninety miles an hour between them, couldn't hear.

"I wanted to give them a treat. Dad guilt lives. I'm working on that extra project in the evenings and on weekends. Just really got started on it this week, so they had a sitter Tuesday and Thursday evening. Tomorrow they're going to my mom's for the weekend."

"So you got them a dozen cookies." Jagger shrugged. "No judgment from me. These are good."

"It's a relief they like their babysitters so much. It seems like babysitters are raising my kids instead of me this summer."

"You're working your a—*butt* off to provide for them. When you're not working, you're taking them on boat rides and hikes in the woods. They're lucky to have you, West." He looked at the sky and the clock. "We've got about an hour of daylight left. Ready to make our way back? I'll take the long way."

"Sounds good."

"Who's ready to fly?" Jagger asked the girls.

All three of them raised their hands and laughed and made little-girl happy sounds. Once they were seated, we took off across the water, waving at fellow boaters. The number of boats out here had dropped to half while we were anchored in the cove.

"You think they'd like to go by the hotel?" Jagger asked.

"Not a doubt in my mind," I said.

The girls loved peering up at the sprawling veranda of

the impressive Marks and peeping at the guests of the fancy hotel.

As we neared the shore, Jagger slowed down to wake speed.

"It's the Marks!" Scarlet yelled loudly enough for every last person on that veranda to hear her.

The property was crawling with people, from the upper-level balconies to the veranda and all the way down to the docks.

"People-watching the rich folks is always a good time," Jagger muttered with a grin.

My gaze strayed down the shore, trying to make out Presley's dock.

"Speaking of rich folks, if you keep going toward Max Dawson's, I can show the girls Presley's house."

"Presley," he repeated. "How's that going?"

"Mostly smooth sailing. Weather's not a factor so we're on schedule so far."

Presley's house was about ten expansive lots down from the hotel's property. Max lived two houses farther down from her, on the side toward the marina, so we'd go by both.

"Hey, girls," I said once we were past the hotel and into the residential area. "Want to see the house I've been working on?"

"Miss Presley's house?" Nova asked.

"That's right," I said.

"Yes!" they all yelled.

"Remind me not to take them fishing," Jagger said with a chuckle. "You ladies have scared every last fish away from this end of the lake."

Sienna looked alarmed, while Scarlet laughed, and Nova eyed the water and yelled a boisterous, "Hello down there, fishies!"

As we got closer to Presley's, I noticed kayaks lying on a flat part of the grassy yard. Those hadn't been there earlier in the day. Someone had gone shopping, it appeared.

It wasn't until we were nearly even with her house that I noticed movement on the other side of her dock.

Presley herself appeared, straightening to a stand in the ankle-deep water, and I held in a swear word. I hadn't bargained for getting busted going by her house.

When I realized she was wearing a bikini top and shorts, I lost my ability to form words for a few seconds. Maybe stopped breathing as well. All my blood was headed somewhere besides my brain and lungs.

Her string bikini top was an innocent shade of soft pink. Two triangles of fabric covered her tits, which weren't all that large, but that didn't stop me from wanting my tongue on them.

"It's Miss Presley," Scarlet said.

"She has tie-dye boats!" Nova hollered.

That wasn't all she had. I couldn't take my eyes off her.

Presley turned our way, took a moment to figure out who we were, then broke out into a beautiful, welcoming smile that reached right down to my dick. I coached myself to calm the fuck down and quit acting like a teenage boy who got off to pictures of girls in swimsuits even as I knew the image of her looking like that would burn bright in my head tonight, and my hand would get another workout.

"Hey, it's my favorite smart-girl brigade," Presley called out, waving.

"Daddy, can we visit her, pretty please?" Scarlet asked.

"I want to see her kayaks," Sienna said. "They're so pretty!"

Jagger looked over at me. "We stopping?"

Hell, this had backfired. "For a minute. If you don't mind."

His brows shot up as if to say, *What in the hell is there to mind about stopping to talk to a woman who looks like that?*, which made me want to shove him overboard. He pulled the boat up alongside the dock.

"We were showing the girls where I'm working," I explained.

"You have a rainbow boat," Nova said, her voice filled with awe.

Presley laughed. "I sure do. I bought three new kayaks today. Want to come see them?" .

"Oh, they noticed," I told her.

"They're much prettier than the ones we rent from the marina," Scarlet said.

"Hey, now," Jagger said. "Don't be talking bad about our boats."

"They're all orange, Uncle Jag," Scarlet said as if the problem was evident.

"You think we need swirly pink ones?" he asked her.

"Yes! And purple and blue and green," Scarlet said.

"All the colors!" Nova shouted.

Jagger eyed me with a grin and a head shake. "We'll take that under advisement, princesses."

Presley bent and slid a purple-pink tie-dye kayak from the water onto the shore. I did my best not to watch her in action, instead turning to Jagger.

"You in a hurry?" I asked.

"Nope. This has the potential to be an interesting show." He shot me a look that was curious bordering on knowing, as if he had me figured out.

He likely fucking did.

It didn't take a genius to lay eyes on Presley Holiday

and guess that I or any heterosexual guy might have *thoughts* involving her.

Presley walked out onto her dock, talking to the girls as Jagger maneuvered the boat close enough for us to disembark.

Realizing Presley probably didn't know the first thing about mooring a boat, I moved toward the dock side and hopped off. I grabbed the line at the bow, tied it to the cleat, then did the same near the stern, acting like the task took all my concentration. In reality, I was striving to get my shit together and ignore that Presley was eighty percent bare-skinned and just a few feet away from me.

When the boat was secured, I stood and faced Presley, determined to keep my gaze on her face. "You sure it's okay to unleash them?"

She laughed. "If you mean let the girls out of the boat, absolutely. I want to show off my pretty new kayaks."

"You realize you could fit something bigger in your boathouse?" I asked as I helped my girls to the dock one by one, with Jagger pulling up the rear.

"I haven't ruled that out," she said. "I decided to start small."

"With three kayaks," I teased. "Have you figured which one is just right, Goldilocks?"

Jagger hopped onto the deck and came up next to me.

"This is Jagger McNamara," I told her. "Jagger, meet Presley Holiday."

They shook hands and exchanged niceties. I forced myself to follow my daughters off the dock and not think about the fact that Jagger was touching Presley, even if it was just a handshake.

Sienna and Scarlet climbed into the rainbow-colored

tandem kayak where it sat on the grass. Nova dashed to the blue-green one.

"Girls, Miss Presley didn't give you permission to get in her kayaks."

"They're fine," Presley said, coming up behind me.

"You've been busy since I left," I said.

"You probably passed the delivery truck on your way home."

"Lake Life Outfitters?" Jagger asked, joining us.

"Yes. They gave me a great deal on the third one."

Jagger stepped closer to the boats and looked them over.

"Sorry to drop in unexpectedly," I told her. "The girls love going by the hotel. You're on the way home."

"I was doing a test drive," Presley said.

"Did you figure out how to 'drive'?"

She laughed. "I learned how to paddle a kayak on YouTube. In theory. Work in progress."

"Miss Presley, can we go in the water?" Scarlet called out.

Presley met my gaze as if wanting me to weigh in.

"Not tonight, Scarlet. We can't just drop in on Miss Presley and expect a boat ride. Besides, the sun's going down soon, and our captain for our other boat ride might leave us."

"Uncle Jagger would never leave us," Scarlet said with every bit of faith in the world.

Jagger straightened from where he'd been inspecting something on the tandem kayak and sent me a smug look.

"You're right, Scarlet," Jagger said. "Uncle Jag would never leave you three angels. I might leave your dad though."

"Then we could have a sleepover at your house," Nova said.

"Oh, you think so, huh? I'd make you eat veggies for your bedtime snack," Jagger teased.

"I like veggies," Sienna said.

"She doesn't like meat," Scarlet informed him, and I sighed at this trend that wasn't dying down.

"You have a vegetarian?" Presley asked me.

"That's where she seems to be heading," I said. "I can respect that, but it's throwing a twist into meals."

"I can imagine," Presley said. She strode toward the twins in the tandem boat. "Ladies, how big are your muscles?"

Scarlet flexed a skinny bicep as Sienna climbed out of the back seat, apparently done with her imaginary boat ride. Nova bounced over and said, "Miss Presley, I'm the strongest."

"You are not," Sienna said. "You're too little."

"Am not."

"Girls," I said sternly.

"I have a rack for my kayaks," Presley said, pointing up at her patio, "but this double one is pretty heavy. You think you girls could get on one end and help me carry it up there?"

They each answered affirmatively, rising to Presley's challenge with differing amounts of enthusiasm and confidence.

I held myself back from jumping in and taking over for my daughters, seeing how they felt important being asked to help. They managed to lift their end and work with Presley to get that boat up the hill and onto the rack.

"Look at those muscles," I called out.

Jagger came up to me and said in a low voice, "Those boats are Kevlar. Lighter than your average kayak. Also pricey as hell."

"Sounds about right." I went over to the pink and purple boat, lifted it to my shoulder, and headed up the hill after them.

Jagger did the same with the blue-and-green one, and within a couple minutes, we had all three kayaks in their places.

"Thank you, ladies," Presley said to the girls.

"Welcome," Scarlet said.

Presley came over to Jagger and me and said, "You didn't have to do that, but thanks."

"Not a problem," Jagger said before I could.

"Watch me, Miss Presley," Nova called out.

Before any of us knew what she planned, she lay on the grass and rolled barrel style down the gradual hill.

"Stop before you get to the lake," I called out.

Within a few seconds, the other two were doing the same.

"They have so much energy," Presley said.

"Tell me about it. Bedtime will be fun tonight," I said. "Actually between the swimming and the boat ride, odds are at least one of them will pass out on the three-minute drive home from the marina."

Jagger laughed, and I was pretty sure it was at my expense. "It never gets old," he said.

"Your day will come," I told him. To Presley, I said, "We'll get out of your hair. Thanks for welcoming my three little tornadoes."

As Jagger headed down the hill, calling out a challenge to the girls to see who could get to the dock first, she flashed me a heated look and said, "Anytime. If they ever want to kayak in pretty boats, let me know."

"As many boats as you bought today," I told her, "we'd still be one short."

"I can fix that." She said it with a *challenge accepted* tone.

"Don't you dare," I said, unsure whether she was serious, but I could easily imagine her trekking back to Lake Life Outfitters tomorrow and picking up yet another kayak.

We got the kids on board and said our goodbyes. As Jagger eased the boat backward and the girls chattered in the seats at the bow, I watched Presley pick up her paddle and make her way up the hill in the waning light of dusk.

"You've been holding out on me," Jagger said. "You didn't mention your client looked like that."

"Why would I?"

"The bigger question is, why didn't you?" He said it as if that meant something.

Which, if I was honest with myself, it did, but honesty with oneself might not always be the best policy.

The thing I couldn't hide from though? The one that was maybe even more alarming than how much I was physically attracted to her?

I liked how kind she was to my daughters. I liked that she called them the smart-girl brigade. I liked that she could handle the chaos of an impromptu visit with grace and friendliness. I...

Fuck.

I just plain liked her.

It would be so much easier if I didn't.

Chapter Twelve

Presley

I'd met Kemp Essex a couple of years ago, when Chloe had moved back to town and married Holden, Kemp's business partner and best friend.

Kemp was a flirt with the goods to back it up—he was a tall drink of water to look at and had a body that probably inspired fantasies in a lot of women. I liked him a lot, but as for attraction, he was more like a brother to me. I couldn't explain it, just like I couldn't explain what it was about West Aldridge that drew me in like an ant to honey.

Kemp was my date for Harper and Max's wedding tonight, encouraged by Chloe and Holden since both Kemp and I had planned to attend solo. Now I had a dance partner for the evening, one who would hopefully keep my mind off West, who was also in attendance.

The five-p.m. wedding ceremony had taken place on the lakeside terrace at the Honeysuckle Inn. The weather had been about as good as one could expect in Tennessee in June—clear skies and hot. They'd kept the ceremony itself short. Guests had then enjoyed a cocktail hour on the upper terrace, which was shaded and slightly cooler. We'd later moved inside to the air-conditioned ballroom for a memorable sit-down dinner.

Now I stood between Chloe and Kemp, lining the dance floor with the rest of the guests, watching Max and Harper's first dance as husband and wife.

The thing that struck me about Harper and Max was the unmistakable connection between them. Some newlywed couples seemed to *perform* their first dance for the guests. These two? They were lost in their own world, oblivious to the dozens of people watching, talking intimately, as if it were just the two of them.

"They're gorgeous," Chloe said.

"They're practically sparkling with happiness," I said, my eyes on the bride and groom—until I spotted West on the opposite side of the dance floor.

I'd seen him sitting with Luke, one of the guys in the dad group, at the ceremony. At dinner, West had been on the opposite side of the large room from me, so while I'd definitely noticed him, it'd been from afar, with a side view as he sat at his table.

Now? I got my first full view of my brawny contractor in dress clothes. Once I noticed him in his light-colored dress pants, white open-collar shirt, and slightly darker jacket, I forgot the bride and groom were even dancing.

I couldn't ignore how his arm muscles bulged in his jacket sleeves or the way that open shirt made my fingers itch to trail downward, unbutton the rest, and strip it all off.

I will not ask West to dance tonight.

I repeated that to myself to the beat of Harper and Max's special song and forced my gaze back to the bride and groom, managing to only glance at West a couple dozen more times before the end of the song.

Afterward, Kemp and I went to the bar for a cocktail for me and a soda for him, as he was not only driving but on call for the fire department. Normally at weddings, I stuck to wine, but to battle the heat during the outdoor cocktail hour, I'd gone all in on the specialty frozen cocktails. I didn't usually find frozen drinks to be overly potent, and I'd downed two of them to cool off, only to discover the bartender was generous with the liquor.

Between those and the glass of wine with dinner, I was happily buzzed as we watched Danny, Max's son, dance first with Max and Harper, then with Max's mom. He was the only little kid here, and from what I understood, his grandmother would take him home soon. He seemed to be almost as smitten with Harper as Max was.

I briefly wondered what it would be like to have a man as visibly in love with me as Max was with Harper. That wasn't something I'd pursued before or even thought much about. It seemed more like fiction than real life.

As I watched the newlyweds, I had a hard time imagining ever giving myself over to love so completely, so trustingly. I wasn't sure I was wired for that.

Even as I had that thought, I couldn't deny there was a part of me that longed to be the girl on the other end of adoring, loving stares like Max showered Harper with.

"How do you feel about dancing?" I asked Kemp as the special dances ended and guests crowded onto the floor when a Beyonce song started.

"I feel good about it," Kemp said, smiling down at me with that boyish smile that I was certain won him as much female companionship as he could ever want. "You think you can keep up?" He nodded to the dance floor.

I finished the last of my drink, grinning widely. "Try me."

He turned out to be a good dancer, so we danced our fool butts off for a dozen or so songs straight, then took a break for hydration in the form of another colorful cocktail that was more potent than expected.

Word was out about my coffee shop, and I fielded a lot of questions about when I was opening, whether I was hiring, and if I planned to serve food.

"I cannot wait," Piper Elliott, the owner of Oopsie Daisies, said. "Literally two doors down from my apartment and business. You're a goddess."

"You must be my soul sister," I told her, laughing. "I can't believe no one's opened a coffee shop before now."

"We have plenty of bars, just no java," Jewel, Piper's cousin who was a manager at Humble's Pizza, said.

Kemp came up to me and said, "I promised Anna a dance. Do you mind?"

"Of course not. You're a free man," I told him.

Anton, who I'd met a few times, joined us in time to hear my response. "In that case," Anton said, "would you like to dance, Presley?"

"Sure." I finished the last of my drink and joined him, then went through a handful of dance partners that weren't my date and were not, thank you very much, West Aldridge.

West

I didn't know which made me crazier—Presley dancing

with Kemp Essex for ten songs straight or Presley dancing with six different guys in a row after Essex.

Luke and I stood near the bar with a group of guys that included my boss, Levi—who was Max's best man—shooting the shit and avoiding the dance floor. I wasn't a big dancer, didn't enjoy dancing, particularly anything upbeat, but I apparently couldn't get enough of watching Presley dance.

The way her body moved in that silky-looking peach dress with the slit up her thigh was tantalizing and teasing, becoming freer and looser the longer the night went on and the more cocktails she downed.

All of which was none of my business or concern, so why the hell couldn't I keep my eyes off her?

As I stood near the wall, I hoped to make my frequent gawking at the dance floor look more like casual glimpsing as Luke, Finn, and I discussed baseball, the Fourth of July, and how the dryer-than-normal summer was affecting their businesses.

My vantage point of the whole dance floor allowed me to notice when Kemp deserted Olivia London in the middle of a song, then interrupted Presley, who was dancing with some out-of-towner I didn't know. She excused herself and walked off the floor next to her date, listening intently as Kemp spoke to her. With a wide grin, Presley said something to him, then hugged him. The bastard put his arms around her waist and hugged her back.

In a flash, Kemp headed to the door and left without fanfare or a word to the bride and groom. I realized he must have gotten an emergency call. I couldn't imagine what other reason a guy would have for hurrying out of a date with Presley.

It wouldn't be cool for me to rush over to her now that

her date was gone. It also wouldn't be smart. I'd managed to keep my distance for nearly two hours so far. She was my client, not my friend.

I excused myself and went to the dessert table for a handful of mixed nuts and a bottled water. Rosy McNamara and Dotty Jaworski cornered me to ask for the inside scoop about Presley's coffee shop.

"I'm not feeding your gossip mill," I told the sixty-something ladies, grinning. I'd known Jagger's mom since early childhood and Ms. Dotty for nearly as long. "You'll have to ask the owner." I didn't know what was public knowledge and what wasn't.

"We would, but she's busy with all her gentleman suitors," Ms. Dotty said.

I glanced out to the dance floor, locating Presley easily. This time she was dancing with Ty Bishop, who was doing his best to dirty dance. I swallowed down a growl, reminded myself it was none of my business, and forced my attention back to the two women.

"You'll know when the shop opens," I assured them.

"But you don't know when that is?" Ms. Rosy asked.

"I don't know when that is. I'm just the contractor."

"You're no fun, West Aldridge," she said, then elbowed Ms. Dotty and laughed sloppily enough I could tell she'd had her share of drinks.

I encouraged the two seniors to have a second dessert, which sidetracked them as I'd hoped, then escaped to the restroom.

When I returned to the ballroom, my gaze went to the dance floor first, without conscious thought, seeking out Presley. She wasn't where she'd been five minutes ago, so I scanned the rest of the area, wondering who she was dancing with now.

Movement at the doors to the terrace caught my attention. I looked over in time to see Presley slipping outside by herself. I frowned, wondering if she was okay. From what I'd seen, she was content to be surrounded by people and churning through dance partners. What reason would she have for sneaking away by herself?

I casually made my way toward the windowed end of the ballroom that looked out on the terrace and the lake with the goal of spotting her through the glass, just to reassure myself she was okay. When I didn't see her, I slipped out the door.

I didn't see Presley anywhere. On the other side of the common area, several clusters of guests were gathered on private-room patios, but the only people on the terrace where the cocktail hour had taken place were two employees cleaning the area. I nodded at one of them as I walked to the steps that led down to the shore.

Presley was sitting on the bottom step a couple hundred feet below me, her fancy dress likely getting dirty from the ground, her elbows braced on her legs.

Concerned, I jogged down the steps. She didn't move as I approached.

"Presley?"

She slowly turned her head to look up at me, still bracing it on her arms.

"Are you okay?"

She groaned quietly.

I sat next to her, my leg not quite touching hers. "What's going on?"

She lifted her head, shaking it, then moaning again. "Overserved myself. Needed fresh air."

"Is it helping?"

She inhaled a deep breath through her nose. "Maybe?"

"You feel dizzy?"

She nodded shallowly. "Little bit."

She canted her head to the side and leaned it against my shoulder. I had to fight to keep my hands in my lap when what I wanted to do was take her in my arms and make her feel better.

"Did your date desert you?" I asked.

"He had a fire."

We sat without talking for a few minutes, during which Presley dragged in deep, audible breaths.

"I want to go home," she said eventually. "Where's Chloe?"

"She was slow dancing with her husband. Why don't I drive you home, and she can have her night out with Holden?"

"Sounds good." She straightened and frowned, her hair tousled. "Or you prob'ly don't wanna do that."

I couldn't help grinning at this slightly sloppy version of the rich girl who normally had it all together. What I wouldn't do to mess her up more thoroughly. But not like this. Not when she was half out of it. If she ever screamed my name, I needed her to be fully aware and willing.

I took in a shaky voice, then blew it out, releasing that idea. *Not gonna happen, dude. Not tonight or ever.*

I might not be willing to get romantically entangled with her, but I could get her home safely.

"I wouldn't offer if I didn't mean it." I stood and held out a hand for her. "Come on."

She placed her hand in mine, seemed to gather her strength, then attempted to stand. I helped her up and caught her at the waist as she swayed. She let out a quiet half laugh and said, "Oopsss. Didn't mean to get this buzzy."

I held her by the elbow, waiting for her to steady herself, which took a second or two, and *steady* was an exaggeration.

Grinning, I asked, "What did you drink? Straight moonshine?"

She seemed to think about that for a moment, then looked up toward the terrace where cocktail hour had been. "Those icy, fruity things. They looked frou-frou."

"They weren't though?"

She shook her head as she clumsily brushed her hair out of her face, peering down at her feet.

"You ready?" I asked. "Can you make it up the stairs?"

She took deep breaths, not bothering to look up.

Without letting myself think about what I was doing, I picked her up, my arms under her back and legs, princess style, which was strangely appropriate, and started up the stairs.

It didn't take more than three steps for me to understand this was a dumbass move on my part. The slit in her dress crawled up, baring her thigh under my fingers. Her light, feminine scent surrounded me in the humid night. Her arms fastened around my neck with all the trust in the world, and she nuzzled her head onto my shoulder.

You are a stupid, stupid man.

Nothing to do but play it off, get her up the stairs, and take her home. To her house. Alone.

Shit.

About halfway up, Presley let out a quiet sigh that tugged at something inside me. I did my best to ignore it, watching the steps, determined to blank my mind all the way to the upper terrace.

The employees were gone, leaving it empty. I considered our options, dismissing the idea of walking back through the reception. We could either go through the lobby or around the building.

"Can I set you down?" I asked.

"Mm-hmm."

I lowered her legs until her feet hit the ground in heels so high I had no idea how she'd been dancing for hours. She held on to my arm, finding her balance, her eyes opening, gaze focusing.

"We're gonna go through the lobby. It'll be a lot less attention grabbing as long as you can walk."

She nodded. "I can walk. But thanks for the ride."

She hooked her arm through mine and leaned heavily into me.

"Ready?"

"Mmm."

We made it through the inn's common room and lobby without running into anyone we knew, then out the main door to my SUV in the parking lot. I held her hand to help her up into the passenger seat, closed the door, walked to the back of the vehicle, and took a moment.

"Fuck," I said quietly, peering up at the starry sky, trying to recenter myself.

I was on sensual overload from the most tempting woman I'd ever met. Sleep would not be easy tonight, not with the images and scents and memories of how her flesh felt taunting me.

I climbed into the driver's seat, started the engine, and headed to Presley's house. She leaned her head against the window, her eyes closed, and silence fell between us.

As I pulled into her driveway, I watched for a sign that she was awake.

"Did you pass out?" I asked quietly.

She smiled in response, then slowly raised her head. "We're here?"

"Already," I said dryly. I hopped out, went to her door, and opened it once I was sure she wasn't leaning against it.

"Come on, princess," I said, holding my hand out.

She slid down from the seat like liquid pouring out of the SUV. Again, I caught her waist, steadied her. I shook my head, grinning, thinking this was so unlike the woman who was always in absolute control.

She swayed on her feet, even with me hanging on.

"I'm ssssorry, West. I don't normally get this hammered."

"Weddings can be dangerous," I said, thinking back on some I'd been to for my army buddies a few years back.

We got to the front door, and I realized she wasn't carrying a purse or bag of any kind.

"Where's your key?" I asked.

She dipped her fingers into her cleavage, and I swallowed hard, my eyes glued to the sight. When she took out a single key with no key chain, I held my hand out for it. The metal was warm from being nestled against her tit, the way my hand was itching to be.

I unlocked the door and entered with Presley still holding on to me. The house was dark, but there was enough moonlight coming in through the living room windows that I could see the short distance to the stairs. We reached the foot of them.

Flipping on the light over them, I said, "Can you make it up to bed?"

"Yep," she said succinctly, determinedly.

She bent over to take her stilettos off and tumbled clumsily sideways until she sat on the second step, laughing.

I shook my head. "You're a case," I told her, grinning. "Sit still...if you can."

I bent down in front of her and undid the tiny buckle on the strap around her ankle, slid the stilt off, then pulled her other foot up to do the same. Carrying the shoes in one hand, I held my other out for her, internally preparing myself for the upper floor I'd sworn not to return to.

We walked to her bedroom, and I went in with her, figuring it would be easier to pour her into bed than detach my arm at the doorway and hope she got across the room without keeling over. She collapsed onto the unmade bed, grabbing her pillow and curling up on her side on top of the mess of blankets.

Presley held out her hand, and I took it like a dumbass, unsure what she needed. When she yanked me toward the mattress, I caught myself with my other hand and laughed.

"I don't think so, princess," I said, straightening quickly before my willpower gave out. "I'm gonna get you a drink of water and some Tylenol. Then I'm leaving."

"You're sure?" she asked drowsily.

"I'm sure," I said resolutely. "Do you have cups up here?"

"Office," she said. "There's a fridge."

I found the minifridge, grabbed her a bottled water, then went to her bathroom and searched the cabinet for Tylenol. When I went back into her room, the first thing I noticed was the peach dress in a pile on the floor. I nearly groaned out loud. As I stepped closer, I spotted a smaller pile next to it of silver lace.

My gaze flipped to Presley, who'd pulled the pink comforter over her from the side. One leg stuck out, and the blanket dipped nearly low enough on her chest to reveal a nipple. Nearly. My mouth went dry with the realization she'd shed every stitch of her clothing.

"Good night, Presley," I said.

She mumbled what almost sounded like good night.

"There's a bottle of water and two Tylenol on your nightstand for when your head hurts."

"Mmm."

I couldn't help myself. I took one last look at her, then bent over and pressed a quick kiss to her forehead.

Then I hurried out of her room, made sure all her doors were locked, and got the hell out of her house.

Chapter Thirteen

Presley

Whoever said alcohol makes you sleep better was full of crap.

Granted, there were the first couple of hours after I landed in bed when I slept like the dead. I'd woken up a little after two in the morning, sweating and nauseated. I'd gotten up, thrown up everything in my stomach, felt relatively better afterward, then tossed, turned, and sweated liquor all night.

I reached for my nightstand and turned off the alarm I'd somehow remembered to set at some point in the night. West and I were starting work at the shop at eight this morning, and I wasn't going to miss it.

"You got this," I tried to convince myself.

I wasn't in the habit of drinking myself stupid. Wine was a regular part of my life, but I could count on one hand the number of times I'd gotten so drunk.

"Might as well wait until you're lusting after your contractor, then be sure to drink yourself out of control when he's nearby," I muttered as I rolled to my back amid tangles of comforter and sheet. "Oh, and strip off all your clothes while you're at it. Idiot."

I remembered everything from last night. The way I'd been having so much fun, dancing, meeting people, answering questions about The Bean Counter. To my surprise, I hadn't felt at all like an outsider but more like this town was welcoming me. Maybe because I'd be bringing them coffee, but that was okay.

Then when I was dancing with Ty, the basketball coach, the light, flying-high feeling had turned to spinning, dizziness, and a cold sweat.

I'd hoped a few minutes of fresh air would help, but instead I'd needed to be *carried up the damn stairs*.

As embarrassing as that was, I could also remember how safe and cared for I'd felt in West's arms. Those were foreign sensations for me. Normally I took care of myself.

I groaned at that moment of weakness, then sat up in bed, taking inventory.

Nausea gone. Head pounding like nobody's business.

One out of two wasn't bad.

Tylenol, coffee, and donuts. Those would get me through what promised to be a day of hellacious physical labor. I wasn't going to slack off though. We'd laid out a timeline, and there was no room for hungover laziness. I couldn't wait for opening day, but the only way to get there was, well, drywalling today, to be exact.

I rolled out of bed and stripped the sheets that smelled like a drunk girl, then tossed them in the hall to wash as soon as I showered.

While the shower heated, I popped some Tylenol and guzzled a bottle of cold water. Let the rehydrating begin. Then I set my coffee machine to brew an extra-large travel mug of a Costa Rican roast I was sampling for the shop.

I scrubbed the alcohol-heavy sweat off my skin, washed my hair, and felt halfway human by the time I stepped out of the shower. I had twenty minutes till I needed to be at the shop, and though West had a key, I didn't intend to be late.

In record time, I started the bedding in the washing machine and made the bed up fresh with clean sheets, knowing I'd be too tired when I got home tonight. I threw on soft, comfortable cotton shorts, a plain tank, and an unbuttoned chambray shirt with sneakers, and pulled my wet hair into a loose ponytail at my nape.

On the way, I made a quick stop at Sugar for a dozen donuts, intending to shove at least two down my throat in the next few minutes.

I parked in the lot behind the gym and hurried down the sidewalk to my shop, my headache milder but still there with every step. When I got closer, I spotted West inside, already working. As much as I'd wanted to beat him here, I couldn't deny the thrill that spiked through me at the sight of him. I hadn't scared him off completely last night then.

"Morning," I called out as I entered.

West was in the office area, which was framed, with electric and plumbing lines run, waiting to be closed in with drywall today. He set down a large sheet of drywall, turned around, and watched me approach, his brows up.

"Hi?" I said as I went through the doorway to the office, suddenly wondering if we *weren't* okay after my dumb moves last night.

A smile slowly crossed his face as he looked me over. Then he shook his head. "Didn't figure I'd see you until noon at the earliest."

"You said eight." I looked at the time on my phone. "It's three minutes after. I would've been on time if there wasn't someone in front of me at the bakery."

I held the box of donuts out for him to take while I set my phone and coffee out of the way. His eyes were still on me when I opened the box and took a chocolate cake donut.

He chose a maple-frosted, then set the box on the top of the nearby step ladder. "I suspected you were superhuman before. Now I have proof."

"What's that supposed to mean?"

He took a bite. Once he swallowed, he said, "You don't let anything stand in your way. If you want something, you go after it without a thought that it won't work out."

Was he talking about last night? When I'd tried to pull him into my bed?

I hid my cringe by taking another bite. I wandered to the side window and looked out at a pair of mourning doves hanging out in the grass near the bench as I ate the rest of my donut. Instead of savoring it, I was sidetracked by my thoughts, my embarrassment. I owed him an apology. He was helping me in so many ways, proving to be reliable to a fault, and how did I pay him back?

I shook my head, irritated with myself.

Once I finished my donut, I turned to West, who was leaning against the back wall. He popped in his last bite, watching me, as if he couldn't quite trust me not to flirt or make another move.

I stepped toward him. "West?"

He peered down at me as he chewed.

Meeting his gaze, I said, "I'm sorry about last night. Drinking too much, needing help up the stairs at the inn, needing a ride home." I closed my eyes momentarily, then opened them. "I'm sorry I tried to pull you into my bed."

He swallowed and studied me intensely. Seconds ticked by, my body tensed, and I stopped breathing as I waited for him to say something.

He finally said, "I'm sorry I wasn't in the position to let you pull me into your bed."

His gaze didn't waver, and my heart caught. Neither of us looked away for several seconds, our gazes locked. Was he saying he'd *wanted* to join me in bed? He *had* kissed the hell out of me in the boathouse.

He wasn't in the position. Did that mean because of his job? Because I was drunk? Or something else?

Could I possibly overthink one single sentence any further?

I yanked my gaze away first, flustered as hell but trying not to show it. "Okay then," I said. "So what's the plan for the day? We're doing the office first?"

———

West

More than twelve hours after Presley had shown up with donuts, I was ready to call it a day. The drywall was hung and the first coat of mudding done.

Presley had shocked me throughout the day with her determination and grit. I could tell the second she came in the door this morning that she was feeling last night's liquor, but she hadn't complained once. But I'd caught her taking Tylenol after lunch, and she had that morning-after disheveled, slightly off-kilter look to her.

Don't get me wrong. She looked damn good in a thrown-together, woke-up-like-this way, with no makeup on her face and stray wisps of hair coming out of her ponytail.

After a restless night filled with images of her in that pretty pink bed and regret that I couldn't join her, I ached to run my hands all over her and dishevel her more.

Drywalling was hard-ass labor, but she'd been here the whole day, contributing in spite of the hangover she'd finally admitted to. I'd rented a lift yesterday, unsure how much help she'd be. She didn't look particularly muscular, and I wouldn't do a solo job without one.

To my surprise, she'd gone all in and turned out to be a worthy partner even though it was her first time drywalling. I'd taught her to measure for cutouts, to cut large sheets, and to hang them.

Presley had fed me well, going after carryout burgers from the diner for lunch and Humble's pizza for dinner. We'd devoured a large pizza and a dessert of leftover donuts, sitting on the chairs we'd moved to the enclosed kitchen area, agreeing we didn't like the fishbowl feeling of the front room once the sun went down.

Afterward, she'd stretched out on the floor, flat on her back, to relieve the back strain of drywalling for hours straight. I'd run across the square to the public restrooms and come back to find her still on the floor, sound asleep, her phone on her stomach.

I'd let her sleep and done the first coat of mud on the drywall. Mudding took experience to be able to use just the right amount, so I was content to take care of it myself while Presley rested. She'd more than earned it.

I mudded the office, the storage room, and the restrooms, saving the kitchen for last in case I woke her up. As I worked around her, the most she stirred was turning her head from one side to the other, allowing me unlimited views, from her delectable thighs I imagined wrapping around me, to her tempting belly button that I could just barely see where her tank crawled up, to those slightly parted lips I longed to dip my tongue between again.

My thoughts were consumed by her as I mudded, the culmination of last night's dreams and working all day with her, on top of weeks of X-rated urges where she was concerned.

I'd hoped my desire for her would lessen as I got to know her, but it'd done the opposite. When I'd returned from the town square again, where I'd filled a bucket with water to clean my drywall tools, she finally stirred, sitting up drowsily, looking irre-fucking-sistible.

Maybe I just needed to give in to this incredible need pounding through me, spend a night with her, and get it out of our systems. A one-off to relieve the tension. What would it hurt if it meant I could move on with my life and stop losing sleep every damn night from erotic thoughts of her?

"Hey, Sleeping Beauty," I said, trying to block out thoughts of waking up next to her in her pink bed, naked.

Presley picked up her phone, saw the time, and said, "Oh, my God. I didn't mean to fall asleep."

"Your body had other ideas."

Shit, don't talk about her body. Don't think *about her body.*

She quickly stood, brushing off her backside. "I can't believe I slept for...two hours?"

"You must've been exhausted to sleep for any amount of time on that concrete floor."

"I'm sorry. You said mudding was next. What can I do to help?"

I let out a quiet laugh and busied myself scraping off the dry mud from my tools. "Mud's all done for tonight. It needs to dry overnight."

"So that's all for today?"

"Yes, ma'am."

She stared pointedly at me, hair mussed, clothes dusty, and still the most desirable woman I'd ever laid eyes on. "I thought we were over the *ma'am* thing."

I grinned. "Habit."

"So we're ready to clean up for the day?" She seemed drowsy, like she was still waking up.

"That's right."

Presley went to the table and picked up the trash from our pizza dinner as I finished scraping my tools.

"Ouch!" She tossed down the pizza box as if it had bitten her, then grabbed on to one of her fingers.

"What happened?"

"Paper cut." She lifted her uninjured hand to reveal a bleeding wound on her index finger.

I grabbed an unused napkin and handed it to her to staunch it. "Those things can bleed like a sucker."

She nodded, wincing.

"Is it deep?" I asked. That thick cardboard could do some damage.

"I can't tell," she said, not looking at the cut. "Too much blood."

I handed her a couple more napkins then went to my toolbox and grabbed some first aid supplies.

"Have a seat." I pointed to the chair. "I'll fix you up." I squirted hand sanitizer from the first aid kit on my hands.

She lowered herself to the chair, her hands in her lap, pressing a napkin tightly to the cut.

"Let me see," I said, squatting in front of her.

Holding out both hands, she turned her head away.

"Does blood make you squeamish?" I asked.

She sucked in a breath and said, "Only when it's my own."

"I got you." I removed the blood-spotted napkin. The cut was on the lower part of her index finger. "Cardboard cuts are wicked."

Still not looking, she nodded. "Is it bad?"

"Looks a mess, and it's gonna bleed a bit, but I don't think we'll need to amputate."

Her eyes were squeezed shut, head turned, and I put pressure back on the cut, waiting for the bleeding to slow down, trying not to notice how close we were, how much smaller her hands were than mine.

A wisp of hair floated onto her face, and she blew at it several times. Without thought, I brushed it behind her ear.

She met my gaze. "Thanks."

I slipped my attention down to her lips, just for a moment, and Presley's pupils grew as I made and held eye contact again.

I pulled myself out of the spell of her pretty eyes and moved the napkin to check the cut. "It's slowing down. You doing okay?"

She nodded. "Hurts like crazy for such a little injury."

"Paper cuts are a bitch."

"That's the truth."

"I need to clean it with an alcohol swab. You got any badass left in you? This'll hurt a little."

She bit her lip, nodded, and turned her head away again.

I opened the swab and uncovered the cut. "You ready? I'll be as quick as I can, but I gotta be thorough."

Presley pressed her lips together as she nodded. When I swiped the alcohol over the cut, she sucked in a breath, and a single tear popped up and fell from the outer corner of her eye.

"Almost done," I said in what I hoped was a soothing voice.

I swiped the cut two more times, then applied antibiotic cream. By the time I finished up with a bandage, Presley was tense as a coiled snake.

"All done," I said, brushing her hair back again as she opened her eyes and inspected the bandage.

As I rose to stand, I instinctively pressed my lips to her forehead to comfort her, lingering there as my brain caught up to what I was doing and how I shouldn't be doing it. When I pulled away, I made eye contact again to gauge whether I'd overstepped. What I saw in her expression was hunger. Interest. Heat.

I stood the rest of the way, pulling her up with me. She didn't move away, just peered up at me intently. I palmed her cheek, brushed my thumb over her bottom lip. When she turned slightly into my hand, I knew she was on the same page as me. I bent down and kissed her, intending to keep it light and tender, but when our mouths connected, fire shot through me like a flashover.

All the longing for her, the middle-of-the-night fantasies, the desperate need that had built up over the past few days exploded into that kiss. Our tongues met, dueled, danced a primitive mating dance. I slid my hand down to her perfect little ass cheek and gripped it, pulling her into my erection.

Presley drew my head to her mouth insistently, her greedy hands at my nape, chest pressing into me. I maneuvered her so she was between me and the wall, paying no heed to the newly applied mud, driven only by my body's need. Nestling my hard dick against her softness was heaven and hell at once, the friction a mind-blowing tease.

I ran my palm up from her waist, under her tank, along

her baby-soft skin until I reached her bra. I shoved it up over her tit, then filled my hand with her flesh, relishing the hard tip of her nipple, the rough pebbling, the silky softness. Holding her tank and bra out of my way, I lowered my head and took her nipple in my mouth, eliciting a sexy groan from her.

"We—" She broke off with a gasp as I swirled my tongue around her tip. "God," she drew out. "West, we— I thought we weren't supposed to do this."

I lifted my head and looked her in the eyes. "Do you want me to stop?"

She shook her head, her lids heavy, face flushed. "But you didn't want..."

I licked her nipple like a lollipop, then raised my head to kiss her lips. In a growl, I said, "I want. I've always wanted."

"Me too." Presley ran a hand over my beard. "Maybe not here?"

My place was out of the question. The girls were at my mom's until the morning, but... No. My little two-bedroom house wasn't right for a classy, rich girl.

"Where'd you park?" I asked.

"Behind the hardware store."

"Same. Let's go. I'll walk you to your SUV and meet you at your house."

Chapter Fourteen

Presley

We left the shop as it was, turned out the lights, locked up, and wasted no time getting to the parking lot. Walking side by side, we didn't speak.

At my SUV, West said, "See you there," in a rough voice, then shut my door.

Even after walking a block in the humid evening, I was shaking with need, my core throbbing with an ache to be filled.

Blowing out a big breath to steady myself, I backed out and headed toward home. I watched the headlights of West's SUV in the rearview the whole way, worried he'd come to his senses, remember his objections, and change his mind.

When I reached my driveway, he was still behind me. I pulled into the garage, hopped out, and gestured to him to park next to me.

He was out of his SUV in no time and headed toward

me at the door to the house as I made sure the outer garage door closed all the way.

He came up behind me, his front to my back, slipped his hand under the front of my tank, flattened it on my bare abdomen, then said in my ear, "You hiding me away like your dirty little secret?"

I heard his smile, then felt his breath whisper over my ear as he trailed his tongue over the lobe.

I was still trying to formulate an answer when he dipped his hand lower, beneath the waistband of my shorts, under my underwear, lower, until the tip of his finger dipped inside of me. "So wet," he growled.

I opened the door but didn't move, unsure if my legs would support me. He ensured I couldn't when he swiped his finger over my clit, circled it, then pulled his hand out of my shorts and pushed the door open the rest of the way. When I felt his lips on my neck, I turned around to face him, seeking out his mouth with mine.

Our lips met, tongues came together, and he grabbed my butt, one cheek in each of his large hands. The next thing I knew, he'd lifted me up, stepped inside, kicked the door shut behind us, and was carrying me through the dark house. I wrapped my legs around him and kept kissing him, unable to get enough.

The bottom floor was still empty of everything except equipment and construction supplies, so he carried me to the stairs. Instead of going up, he turned, sat about three steps up, and pulled me into a straddle over him, all without ending the kiss.

West plunged his hands into my shorts and underwear again, and this time he shoved them down my thighs. With his hand supporting my waist, I stood, and he peeled them the rest of the way off as I kicked off my shoes.

When I straddled him again, my knees on the step on either side of his hips, he lifted me up to a higher step, until my core hovered above his mouth. At the first swipe of his tongue, I whimpered, grabbed ahold of the railing, and held on for dear life. He licked and nibbled and sucked until I was writhing against his mouth, begging, sputtering incoherently.

In no time at all, I came apart, my body contracting, hand clinging to the railing as I arched into his mouth and gasped his name. His tongue kept at me, driving me higher when I didn't think it was physically possible to come any more, until a lifetime later I collapsed over him, gasping for air.

The next thing I noticed was him lifting my hips, placing the most delicate kisses to my inner thighs, as if I hadn't just become deadweight on top of him. I was still recovering, barely able to move, for sure not able to think straight. I was putty in his hands, in the best possible way.

Eventually I slid down his body far enough to kiss him, fully aware I was the only one who'd gotten relief. He drew my tank over my head, almost like an afterthought, making me laugh quietly. Next he unhooked my bra, and I slid it off, leaving me completely bare and him fully dressed.

"We should go upstairs and get you naked," I said between kisses.

"I'm too dirty and sweaty for that pretty bed of yours."

I frowned. "Me too. We can fix that." I moved off him and stood on shaky legs, holding out a hand.

I didn't miss how his eyes roved hungrily over my body. I felt his gaze almost like a physical touch, somehow responding to it even though he'd just served up an orgasm that was a ninety-seven on a scale of one to ten.

West stood and took my hand. I led him upstairs and

into my bathroom. I started the shower, and when I turned back around, he'd shed his shirt, giving me my first look at his bare chest. I stopped in my tracks and just...admired. He was solid and wide and cut, but not in an overdone body-builder way. Just...perfect.

He kicked his work boots off, then undid his pants and dropped them and his underwear to the floor. He removed his socks, then straightened, treating me to an eyeful I'd never forget. I knew in that moment I'd be forever doomed to compare all men to him, and none would ever measure up.

I managed to get my brain thinking enough to reach in and test the water. Then I stepped in, pulling him in with me. As soon as he shut the glass door, I was in his arms, running my hands up his incredible chest. With hot water raining down on us, we kissed hungrily, body to body, his erection pressed into my abdomen.

He filled my loofah with shower gel and spent the most titillating ten minutes scrubbing down every inch of my body, alternating the sponge with kisses and nips that had me aching for him once again.

When he was apparently done, he handed me the loofah. I filled it with more vanilla-scented shower gel and returned the favor, scrubbing every inch, kissing him, teasing him.

"You smell good enough to devour," I said as I hung the sponge on its hook behind him.

"Then maybe you should eat me up."

Those were my plans exactly, but hearing his sugges-tion? Revved me up all the more.

With my heart racing, insides pulsing with need again, I dropped to my knees and took him in my mouth. The way his head fell back and a moan escaped from him... *My God.*

I reveled in making him feel good, in my feminine power, in awe that I could have such an effect on this big, confident man.

As I worked him over with my mouth, I peered up to find him gazing down at me with an adoring, heavy-lidded expression I knew would resurface in my fantasies for years.

By the time West came, my body was on fire again, dying for his attention. Without me saying a word to him, once his breath was back to almost normal, he pulled me up to his mouth and kissed me fervently.

He trailed a hand down my body and found my opening with one finger, drawing a gasp from me, then a moan. He added a second finger, then showered both of my breasts with attention from his mouth and other hand, until the three-point assault had me clenching around him and calling out his name in a voice that sounded nothing like me.

Our lips found each other again, and I realized the water wasn't hot anymore.

"We should get out before it turns to ice," I said.

"Mmm," was his only reply.

I reached behind him and shut off the water, stepped out, and got us both clean, fluffy towels. He did a quick rubdown of himself, then fastened his around his waist and took my towel.

West dried every inch of me, gently, thoughtfully, taking care of me in a way I didn't remember ever having been taken care of. Not even as a child.

I never would've guessed this muscular, gruff man would have such a sweet side, but maybe that was from caring for his three little girls? Whatever it was, my heart swooned.

Once he was done, he wrapped the towel around my

back and used it to pull me flush with his body. He wrapped his arms around me, letting the towel fall to the floor, and kissed me. "I'm not done with you yet," he said in a low rumble of a voice that had me ready to climb him right then and there.

"Good thing we're clean enough for my 'pretty bed.'"

Once again, he lifted me and carried me from the bathroom to my bedroom, as if I weighed nothing.

West set me on the bed, then went back to the bathroom. I thought maybe he was turning off the light, but he left it on and came back with his pants in hand, removing his wallet from the pocket. He took out a condom, set the packet next to me, and laid his wallet on the nightstand.

Dropping his towel, he climbed over me, leaned in, and kissed me slowly, thoroughly, deliciously. He trapped each of my hands with his at the sides of my head, then trailed his mouth along my jawline, to my ear, neck, chest, kissing, licking, nibbling my flesh. Our initial urgency had been extinguished on the stairs and in the shower. Now he seemed to be deliberately slowing down, exploring every inch of me, savoring me, rebuilding the tension in my body.

He was hard again, his dick brushing against me here and there, teasing me, as he covered me with kisses and attention. His coarse beard added unique sensations, its roughness contrasting with sweet kisses and arousing nips, my hands still held in place by his.

"I promise you don't have to hold me down to keep me here," I said, grinning at him as he bent over my belly button, lavishing attention around it.

West growled low and slow, then rose so his mouth was even with mine again. He traced my lips with the tip of his tongue. "I want to worship every last bit of your body, Presley. Your skin is so soft and pretty, just begging me to muss it up with my rough beard."

"Muss away," I said, arching my hips in response to him pressing his body against me.

He released my hands, his attention intensifying, his lips and fingers and tongue all over me, down my inner thighs, hovering over my core, licking and suckling for a few seconds before moving up my torso, tantalizing the tips of my nipples as he brushed a fleeting finger over my clit. He was playing my body like an accomplished musician played an instrument, as if he'd been practicing on me for years, perfecting, finding my sweet spots, learning what made me hottest.

I ran my hands over him, relishing the hard ridges and dips of his pecs, biceps, back muscles, abs... Between the sensory treat my fingers and eyes were bringing me and the things he was doing to me, he had me wrapping my legs around him and arching against him hungrily, begging with my body. Needing him. Again.

He shifted to his knees, reached behind him to unfasten my legs, then bent over me, running his tongue up my inner thigh to my hollow, aching core. He dipped his tongue inside me, swirled it over my clit, eliciting a moan from me. Then he backed away, and I nearly cried out.

His hands never left me, trailing up my thighs, then guiding my hips, urging me to turn over. I rolled to my stomach, bracing on my knees as he pulled me up and ran his fingers down my belly to my sensitive nub, drawing a gasp from me.

He lowered his mouth to my butt cheek, kissing it, suckling, his fingers still making me squirm. Leaning over me, pressing his hard body against me, he banded an arm around my middle, holding me to him.

"I love your pretty ass," he said in my ear.

"I need you inside me, West," I managed, pushing against him, craving every bit of contact as long as he filled me soon.

He nibbled on my ear, then straightened. I heard him rip the condom wrapper open, felt the loss when he straightened enough to sheathe himself. Then his hand was back on my abdomen, dipping lower, between my legs, teasing me, then guiding him to my opening. He pushed inside of me gradually, giving me time to get used to his size.

As he rubbed my clit, I pushed back against him, taking more of him in, moaning at the fullness, the friction.

"Jesus, you feel like heaven," West said, sliding out, pushing back in, stretching me in the most delicious way.

With one hand holding my hip, he slid his other one up to my nipple, working it between his fingers, pinching it, kneading my breast, then tending to the other one as his thrusts intensified, driving my need incredibly higher.

"You're so fucking perfect," he said roughly as he rutted into me like I'd never been rutted into before.

Sweet mother of Mary, I'd been missing out with those sedate, suit-wearing guys.

When he touched my clit again, I gasped and seemed to lose all control of my body as I came apart into a jillion pieces, trusting him to put me back together.

As I became conscious of things like breathing again, West held me tightly to him as he continued to thrust into me, swearing with one final push as he came. I leaned back into him, contracting around him, still coming down from my own orgasm.

Both of us were panting, neither of us speaking. I couldn't form thoughts, let alone put them into words. I could only *feel* as periodic shudders continued to grip me.

I collapsed forward onto the mattress, spent, sated, mind honest-to-God blown. I'd never had sex like that before. Never felt anything close to the raw, uncontrolled coming together that had been one hundred percent primitive.

It was suddenly clear that all I'd had before today was civilized sex. Gentlemanly sex.

It turned out I was a big fan of West's ungentlemanly, uncivilized banging. Holy hell, it was an out-of-mind experience. I wanted more of that.

Eventually.

Right now I was spent. Sprawled at an awkward angle, half on my front, half on my side, boneless, like a bowl full of Jell-O.

West stretched out over me, most of his weight on the mattress, his chest to my back, our bodies damp with sweat, his hand enveloping mine as someone's heart pounded. I couldn't tell if it was mine, his, or both.

He brushed my hair off my face and kissed my cheek, such a gentle move after what we'd just shared.

"You okay?" he asked, which was a fair question as I still hadn't moved.

"I'm good," I purred. I shifted around to face him, snuggling into his chest, tucking my knee between his legs so we were twisted together like a pretzel. "You?"

He let out a low, sexy laugh. "Do you even have to ask? I physically can't get this grin off my face."

"It looks good on you."

"You look good on me."

I laughed. Then our lips met in lazy, unhurried kisses.

"I need to take care of the condom," he said eventually.

I nodded, and he rolled out of bed. The bathroom door closed, taking with it the only illumination in the room. I sat up and moved to the edge of the mattress, lowering my feet to the floor, unsure what was next.

He didn't plan to stay all night, did he?

I might be up for round two—or orgasm four, depending on how you tracked it—but I wasn't used to having a guy sleep over. I wasn't sure I was ready for that kind of closeness. Wasn't sure I'd ever be. That's just who I was—used to having my own space, not to mention the whole bed to myself.

As I was trying to figure out how to address it, West came out of the bathroom and sat next to me.

"My mom's bringing the girls home bright and early," he said, his hand on my thigh. "I'm gonna take my leave now so both of us can get some sleep."

I felt my shoulders relax as I nodded. "Of course. I'm not sure how good of a sleeping partner I'd be anyway."

He breathed out as if he'd been worried I wanted him to stay. Cradling the back of my head, he landed a kiss on my lips, picked up his pants and wallet, then went into the bathroom to get the rest of his clothes.

I grabbed my silky wrap and pulled it around me. When I looked up, West was watching me.

"I wondered what you wore under that," he said in a gravelly voice as he came back in, pulling his shirt down.

Flashing both sides open to give him a full-frontal view, I said, "Now you know," and laughed, loving the hungry look in his eyes.

"So much for me being able to get a wink of sleep," he said.

"Sorry, not sorry." A flicker of desire came to life deep inside of me, and I wondered how that was even possible.

Instead of acting on it, because if we crawled back in

that bed, I didn't know how soon we'd be coming out of it, I closed my wrap and led him out of the room.

When we got to the door to the garage, I turned to him. West pulled me into him with a hand at my waist, kissed me soundly, then said, "Sleep well, Presley. I'll see you back here in a few hours."

"Sweet dreams," I said as he went out the door.

I couldn't deny the thrill I got from his sexy, frustrated growl as he walked to his SUV.

Chapter Fifteen

West

Monday morning, I was a cliché. Getting laid sure as hell could improve a guy's mood.

After sleeping like the dead, I'd woken up early with lots of energy. I'd even caught myself humming in the shower. Humming, for fuck's sake. I barely recognized myself, but I wasn't complaining.

A few hours with Presley Holiday naked had rocked my world. After literally aching for her for weeks, I'd gotten her out of my system.

Something told me I'd be reliving the memories of last night for the foreseeable future. A devilish voice in my head wondered if memories would be enough, but I squelched it.

They'd have to be enough. Last night was a one-off.

My mom and Thomas had brought the girls back home early today as planned. It'd been damn good to hug my little princesses, nonstop chatter, bouncing energy, and all. My mom had assured me they'd had the best weekend, all of them, Thomas included. When I'd told her I felt bad that they were spending so much time without me this summer, she'd insisted that being with family was good for everyone.

Don't kid yourself. Allie and Kinsley and the other girls who watch them are like family in their minds, my mom had said. *Your girls make bonds easily and fast. That means they feel secure. That's because of you, West.*

Her words assuaged my concern, but they also served as a reality check and a warning. My daughters *did* bond fast and easily, particularly with women. They'd already started bonding with Presley. She could be a positive influence in their lives as long as I didn't screw up and give them any reason to think Miss Presley could be more than a client and a distant family friend.

A one-off, I reminded myself as I got out of my SUV at the construction office.

An unforgettable, mind-blowing one-off.

The Dawson Construction HQ was basically a giant heated garage with a full wood shop, plenty of storage for supplies and samples, and a cluttered but functional office.

Levi and Nick were already in the office, waiting for me. Today's meeting was a check-in on our projects before Nick and I met our crews at our respective worksites.

"Morning," I said as I came in from the work area.

"What's up?" Nick said.

"Hey, West," our boss said. "Let's get started so you two can get to your jobs. I'm running into Nashville to pick up the backordered bathroom cabinets for the Holiday project."

"They don't deliver anymore?" I asked.

"It'll take nearly a week for them to get them here. You're ready for those now."

"We were ready for them last week," I agreed, "but we've got plenty to keep us busy in the meantime."

"How's the kitchen cabinetry going?" Levi asked me.

"Slick. Alicia's doing a bang-up job as always." She was our in-house carpenter who built out all our custom cabinetry. "We've got about half of them in. The other side needed some adjustments due to changes Presley made on appliances. Alicia said she'd have them delivered by end of Thursday."

"How's that walnut looking with the paint color she picked out?"

"Really good. Presley loves it."

Maybe it was my imagination, but I thought Levi sized me up for an extra couple of seconds. Maybe it was my guilty conscience, even though I technically had nothing to feel guilty about.

Levi turned to my coworker. "Nick, I ran into Old Man Castille at the Country Market over the weekend." Levi shook his head disbelievingly. "He's happy as a clam with you and your crew. You're like the senior-citizen whisperer."

Nick laughed quietly. "I live with a senior citizen. That probably helps."

He'd moved in with his grandma a year or two ago. From what I knew, he was attentive, caring, and patient with her.

"Whatever you're doing, thank you," Levi continued. "Mr. Castille's not easy to deal with or to please, but you're doing both."

I wasn't surprised in the least. Nick was good. He'd been at Dawson for longer than me and had a way with the homeowners we worked for.

"Congrats, dude," I said, meaning it, even if it brought on fresh concern as to who Levi would choose as foreman in a few weeks.

"Thanks, man," Nick said. "Mr. Castille's one of those where you just gotta let him ask all his questions and watch everything. He loves learning, so I give him a lot of how-to's."

"You've got more patience than I do," Levi said. "Keep it up."

The Holiday project was going smoothly so far too, and we were running on schedule, which in our business was nothing short of a miracle. I felt good about the work I was doing, but I'd feel a lot more confident about getting promoted if Nick's was going off the rails. Not that I wished that on him. I didn't. Nick didn't have three girls to feed though.

We double-checked supplies we were waiting on for both projects, discussed how the rainy end of the week might affect Nick's outdoor project, and briefly went over the newest projects Levi had booked for the fall. We were having a record year, which explained why we had three new hires.

Forty-five minutes later, Levi said, "You can go, Nick. I'll plan to help you tomorrow to see how much we can get done before the weather turns."

Nick nodded, texted someone—probably his crew—said goodbye, and left the office.

I stayed put, curious what else we had to cover.

"How's it going with the homeowner?" Levi asked me as soon as the door shut.

"Presley?" I asked unnecessarily.

His question aroused a kernel of concern, but nobody knew about last night. I'd paid close attention before turning into her driveway. No one had been in sight, and the same was true when I left close to midnight. At that hour on a Sunday, this little town had gone to sleep.

Levi tilted his head slightly, barely enough to notice, as if he was again assessing me. "Yeah. Ms. Holiday. How are you getting along with her?"

Did he know something? He'd never asked me whether I got along with our customers. The assumption was I did. "Getting along just fine. She knows what she wants and makes it clear."

Boy howdy, did she, I thought, remembering the way she'd pulled me into the shower.

"We might not have a formal policy about getting involved with a client, but common sense says it's a bad idea."

"I'd agree with that," I said, keeping my face blank. "I have no desire to get involved with anyone, client or otherwise. You know that about me."

I made no secret of it. When April had moved out last year, my daughters had suffered the loss more than I had. Their heartbreak had fucking crushed me. It was the main reason I'd ruled out relationships for the foreseeable future. I would not be responsible for another heartbreak for Scarlet, Sienna, and Nova. The only way to guarantee that my breakups wouldn't hurt them was to not have any relationships in the first place.

"I saw you leave Max's wedding with Presley Saturday night," he said, watching me expectantly.

"Did you also see she was having trouble standing up without support? And that her date who drove her there got called out for a fire?"

"Are you telling me what I saw was innocent?"

"I sure as hell am," I said, my conscience clear because Saturday night *was* innocent. "I had to carry her up the stairs at the inn. She was in no condition for anything other than passing out in her own bed." I wasn't the type to take advantage of a woman, and he damn well knew that.

"Between the day job and your evening coffee shop gig, you two are spending a lot of time together."

"That can't be avoided."

"No, I guess it can't." His shoulders relaxed a notch. "We just don't need any talk about how we *treat* our clients, if you know what I mean."

"Understood."

One-off, I repeated in my head. I hadn't lied about anything. Everything he said was true as well.

Getting involved with Presley wouldn't just be stupid because of risking my daughters' disappointment. I got the distinct impression that, if Nick and I both excelled at our summer projects as we seemed to be, the final decision could very well come down to something arbitrary like client relations. Nick had tamed a busybody retiree who had nothing better to do than interfere with the project. That was a lot more desirable in a crew leader than a guy who had a secret fling with a hot homeowner.

"Anything else?" I asked Levi, impatient to start working for the day.

He shook his head. "Let's get to work."

Levi's unspoken message was clear as day. *Don't fuck yourself by fucking the client.*

Words of wisdom. Warning heard.

So why then, as I headed out to my SUV, was I fucking giddy at the thought of laying eyes on Presley again?

Chapter Sixteen

Presley

Monday morning, there was a distinct possibility I'd dressed for West.

I'd picked out my girly, pink-flowered dress that hit high on my thigh and dipped between my breasts in a neckline that teased without showing too much. I wore white sneakers with it and layered my cropped light-blue denim jacket over it. Then I'd actually put some effort into my hair, giving it beachy waves instead of throwing it up on my head like I did so often. I'd applied mascara and liner, then added pink lip gloss.

Sadly only Paul and Nathan had showed up to get today's work started. They said West had a meeting with their boss and would be here soon.

I was meeting Magnolia at my shop for a long work session. We planned to talk logos, websites, marketing plans, and more.

The guys were in the bonus room installing flooring. I

let them know I was leaving, then picked up my work bag and headed out the door into the garage.

At the same moment, West was walking into the garage. The second I laid eyes on him, a thrill and a dose of hormones shot through my body. I closed the door to the house and stood there on the single step, watching him as he approached, admiring the clean, prework version of him. When his lips curved into a smile, his eyes sparkling with the knowledge of what I looked like naked, I tried to downplay how much I wanted to throw my arms around him.

"Morning," he said in a low, private voice.

"Morning." My smile widened. I couldn't seem to tone it down or play it cool. "I almost missed you."

He checked behind him, as if making sure his coworkers weren't around, then said, "Glad you didn't. You leaving?"

"I'm meeting Magnolia at the shop today."

He frowned. "I'll probably get more work done that way." He moved closer, so he was facing me. Since I was still on the step, we were nearly at eye level.

"That's important," I said stupidly as my gaze dipped down to his lips, then popped back up to his alluring green eyes.

"You gonna be gone all day?" he asked.

"Probably most of it. So you'll be able to get a lot done, I guess."

"Pity." The word came out as a sexy growl that curled through me.

Without giving myself a chance to think it through, I pulled his head to mine and kissed him fervently, dipping my tongue in to his mouth, seeking out his tongue, my body lighting up at his familiar taste.

Knowing it would be a problem if anyone saw us, I ended it quickly, a little breathless as I met his heated gaze.

"So much for being able to get a lot done," he rumbled in a lust-filled voice. "You're not supposed to do that."

"Oops." Trying to collect myself and act unbothered, I smiled, wiped a spot of pink gloss from his mouth, then said, "Bye, West." I secured my bag on my shoulder and stepped around him to get in my SUV.

As I backed out, I saw him pause and rub his hands over his face before going inside, telling me he was affected by that kiss.

Good.

Because my blood was rushing through my body, pulsing into the center of me in a sharp ache of need.

To distract myself, I stopped at Sugar for donuts to share with Magnolia, then headed to my shop.

When I didn't see her waiting, I went down the walkway on the side to peek into her space, knowing she'd found somebody to build it out for her. Sure enough, she and a guy who looked to be around twenty were inside. I caught her eye and gestured that I'd be waiting in my shop.

I went to the side door of The Bean Counter and let myself in. I stopped just inside, taking in the feel of the place now that the walls were up. We didn't have the counter installed yet, but the front room for the public would be big enough for the lounging corner with the couch and armchair on one side and a counter with stools facing the window plus six tables on the other. I couldn't wait to see how the white brickwork we planned would look on the wall behind the counter and the self-serve area.

Leaving the door unlocked for Magnolia, I strolled to the back and entered my empty office. It would fit a desk and a small sofa. The window brought in lots of daylight, especially in the morning. I hadn't purchased the furniture for the office yet, but I loved the feel of it now that it was enclosed.

I went past the restrooms—empty square rooms with plumbing stems for now—and into the kitchen where the patio table was, along with the ladder and the pizza box and our trash from last night. I pressed my lips together in amusement, thinking how we'd basically dropped everything and hauled ass out of here.

Justified, I thought, breaking into a grin. *Last night was worth every second of haste.*

"Hello?" Magnolia called out as she entered.

I poked my head out of the kitchen. "Hey, Magnolia. The table's in here now. We can move it out by the windows if you want."

"We'll probably get more done in here where there're no distractions, don't you think?" she asked as she peered into the kitchen. "It's looking good so far. That's the storage room?" She pointed at the doorway in the back of the kitchen.

"Right. It feels completely different now that we have walls, doesn't it?"

"It feels like it's getting real," she said, her voice sparkling with excitement I knew was just as much about her business as mine.

"For both of us. I saw your guy showed up."

She nodded. "Finding Jonas was a stroke of luck. I met him at the Lily Pad when he was shopping with his girlfriend. He's trying to build up his handyman business. He used to build houses with his uncle in Mississippi, so he knows what he's doing."

"And you didn't have to wait months to get started."

"Exactly."

After small talk about the weekend and Harper and

Max's wedding—Magnolia and others thought I'd left when Kemp did, so maybe no one realized my real reason for going home early—we sat down to get busy.

I had several logo designs to narrow down, created by someone I'd found online. As we browsed through the options, Magnolia decided to use the same designer for her logo.

A few hours later, we'd both gotten a lot accomplished, with her contacting Kennedy Clayborne about marketing for both of us and me doing a deep dive into how to run social-media ads.

"I'm treating for lunch," Magnolia said when we realized it was nearly one and we hadn't taken a break. "What sounds good? Humble's? The diner? Bar food from the Fly?"

"The diner's club sandwich sounds good, but you don't have to treat." I knew money was tight for her.

"No arguing," she said. "You've been helping me all morning. I have no business experience and no clue."

"You have a kick-ass business plan."

"Thanks to Seth Henry. A year ago, I didn't have the money to treat someone who was so nice to me, but now I can, and I want to treat you."

It was just a sandwich, and it seemed to mean a lot to Magnolia, so I agreed.

She went to pick up our order while I finished watching another marketing how-to video for coffee-shop owners.

We took our food to the bench in the green area out the side door. There was enough shade from the tall trees that it was warm but not too hot.

"We've gotten a lot done, haven't we?" she asked as we dug into our lunch.

"I've checked several items off my list."

"Same. Thanks for helping me create my list. It's sort of terrifying to start a business."

"What made you decide to do it then?"

She pulled her long, thin legs up and crossed them under her. "That's a long story."

"I love stories."

She glanced around as she chewed a bite. "Everyone who's lived here for a while knows my story anyway, but it's not one I'm proud of."

I knew just enough of it to be curious.

"My dad controlled me for most of my life with money. Long story short, he cut me off and disowned me when I broke my engagement to the creep he wanted me to marry for business reasons. *His* business reasons."

I frowned. I knew Chloe had found Magnolia the night she'd dumped the creep and that whatever had happened between Chloe and Magnolia had made Chloe more sympathetic toward her childhood enemy.

"Your dad wanted you to get married for *his* business goals?" I asked, unable to understand how someone could think that was okay.

"Yep," she said. "Business is the only thing that matters to him, and as he constantly threw in my face, his all-important business bought me everything I could ever want." Her tone was steady and almost nonchalant, but there was a flash of an expression on her face that told me she was anything but nonchalant. "It turns out, I'm much happier without all those things and without him in my life."

"Nobody needs a blackmailing, bribing asshole trying to run their life," I said.

"Amen, sister. My dad let me keep my car and the clothes I could fit into a trash bag. Then he locked my bank accounts, changed the locks to his house and the one he'd bought for me, and wrote me off. All in one night."

"I'm sorry. What a piece of shit."

"That's an insult to pieces of shit everywhere," she said, her lips flirting with a smile. "He was counting on me to fail, to come begging him to take me back in, to say I'd marry the cheating piece of scum he'd chosen for me—"

"An insult to pieces of scum everywhere," I said.

"That's true too." She held out a hand for a high five, and I obliged her. "Anyway, I'm determined to succeed."

"To prove him wrong."

"You got it. Fuck him."

"Fuck him indeed. He can fuck right off along with my dad, who was also controlling and manipulative, as well as a wife-beater."

"Insecure men are such a pain in the ass," she said with conviction, and something about it made me laugh. Because it was absolutely true and yet seemed out of character for this pretty girl who I'd never heard swear before.

Magnolia laughed with me. "For real though," she insisted. "They're likely trying to compensate for small penises."

"I'm not arguing in the least." I was starting to understand her better, and in spite of the mean person she'd apparently been as a child, I was beginning to feel a kinship with her, between our asshole bully fathers and our new business aspirations. "You're going to succeed. *We* are going to succeed. Which reminds me, I'm going to need someone to plan my grand-opening event. You know anyone?"

She let out a restrained squeal. "Oh, my goodness. I'd love to do it. Tell me what you have in mind."

The day passed quickly, with both of us getting a lot accomplished, including the beginning ideas for my grand opening. I was just finishing up ordering furniture for my office when I heard the front door of the shop open. I stood, alarmed because we hadn't unlocked that door, and went out to the front room.

My heart raced for a reason other than alarm as soon as I saw West, the dirty postwork version that I liked as much as the clean prework one.

"Hey," I said, "what are you doing here?"

"Told you I was gonna do the second coat of mud after I finished at your house today."

"Right. You're already done for the day?"

"It's four thirty," he said. "Let me guess. You forgot to eat lunch?"

I laughed as Magnolia appeared in the doorway to the kitchen. "Thanks to Magnolia, I did have lunch at an appropriate lunch time."

"Hey, Magnolia," West said.

"Hi, West. I need to get to the inn for my evening shift. I still need that job while I build up my empire."

She'd told me she only had four shifts left at the Lily Pad, as she'd finally found the courage to give Dotty her notice. She'd explained how Dotty had taken her in when she had nothing, given her a job and a place to live, and how bad she felt, but Dotty, being the sweet woman she was, was totally supportive of Magnolia's ambitions.

Magnolia packed up her things, and I shut down my laptop as West sauntered into the kitchen with his impossible-to-ignore presence.

"I'll run home and change and come back and help you," I told him.

"Have a good evening, both of you," Magnolia said. Then she gave me a one-armed hug. "Thank you for all your help."

"Thank you for lunch," I told her. "I'll see you soon."

"We'll talk later this week about your event. Bye, West."

"Later," he said as he gathered the tools he'd left out last night when we took off in a hurry.

Once she was gone, he said, "Sorry to leave my tools all over. That's not my usual MO."

Unable to keep in my smile, I said, "No need to apologize. I guess we had better things to do than put tools away."

He peered down at me with a knowing smirk. "I guess we did." He dropped the smirk and said, "You don't need to help me tonight. I'll be halfway done with the mud before you can get back here."

"Is there anything else we can work on after that?" I was anxious to get my shop finished so I could open, but I was also craving time with West and maybe a repeat of last night.

"Sorry, but I've got plans with three little princesses."

Of course he did. It was Monday. He was doing a quick coat of mud before relieving his babysitter.

"What do those lucky girls have planned for the evening?" I asked, trying to tamp down on my disappointment.

He chuckled. "We're taking a picnic dinner to the marina, then renting some kayaks."

"Ugly orange ones?" I asked, acting scandalized.

"Ugly orange ones that float just fine. I better get started." He turned to his tools and got busy.

What had I even been thinking?

I'd been thinking I wanted round two with West. Like, wanted it a lot.

But we weren't a thing. We weren't going to be a thing. We were fun and no strings and a one-nighter.

I'd obsessed about him during the night after he'd left,

then woken up to thoughts of him this morning. Throughout the day, I'd caught myself thinking about him, remembering last night, wondering what he was doing at my house at that moment.

Rein it in, girlfriend, I thought. *You might have all kinds of ideas and dirty thoughts, but the fact is, he's a dad of three. His girls come first. As they should.*

Somehow in less than twenty-four hours, I'd lost my damn mind and turned *us* into an ongoing fling when we weren't one. I'd do well to remember that.

"Have a wonderful evening with your princesses." I forced nonchalance into my voice. "I'll see you tomorrow morning."

"Night, Presley. See you tomorrow."

Chapter Seventeen

West

By Thursday evening, I was ninety-five percent sure Presley was avoiding me.

After a quick dinner with my girls, I headed to her shop to get a few hours' work in while Sam Cordova, Chance's daughter, babysat.

I parked at Bergman Hardware, grabbed my tools, and hoofed it toward the shop in the rain.

I'd only seen Presley in passing since finding her and Magnolia at her shop Monday afternoon. A *good morning* on her way out of her house, an impersonal wave as she passed through our work zone, a brief response to my text on Tuesday, in which I'd explained I'd be sanding that evening at the shop and that it was a dusty, dirty, one-person job she'd be better off staying away from.

As I neared her shop, I noticed two things. One, she'd papered over all the windows so no one could see in. Two, the lights were on, telling me she was inside.

That made me way too fucking happy.

The main door was unlocked, so I went in, anticipating laying eyes on her. The first sign of her was the open, brightly colored umbrella lying on the concrete floor to dry.

When she appeared in the doorway of the kitchen, I nearly swallowed my tongue as I drank in the sight. She wasn't dressed up, wasn't wearing anything sexy, just a simple cami and some cotton shorts. Plain as plain could be.

The truth was, Presley did not look plain no matter what she wore or didn't wear.

"We're painting today?" she asked, her eyes lit with excitement. About paint.

No matter how much I tried to build my resistance to her, it was pointless. It crumbled with one glance at her, one eager question out of her mouth.

"Painting today," I said, shooting for professional but unable to keep the dumbass grin off my face as I walked toward her. "Are you here to help?"

"Am I allowed?" She moved out of the doorway to let me by, but I still managed to catch her light, sweet scent.

"You're the boss."

"That's not what you said Tuesday. You were bossy."

"Drywall dust is nasty." I set my tools down and tried to gather my thoughts about how to split up the work tonight. This woman had a way of scrambling my brain. I hadn't been sure she would show up. "I was starting to think you were avoiding me."

"I was," she said, surprising me with her bluntness.

"Why?" So much for staying professional.

"I might be slow, but the message finally got through to me."

"What message was that?"

"That we were a one and done, emphasis on the done." She shrugged. I tried to discern whether she was really that carefree about what she was saying, but I couldn't tell. "Sorry about the kiss in my garage Monday morning."

I busied myself opening the paint, putting on gloves, and crouching to prep a strainer to run it through. "You don't have to apologize," I finally said. "I liked it. But we were supposed to be a one and done."

She moved in close, watching me pour the slate-blue paint into the strainer bucket as if it was the most interesting thing she'd ever seen. "Supposed to be?"

I watched the paint flow too, trying to figure out what to say. How much to admit to. "I gave in to our...chemistry, we'll call it, against my better judgment by convincing myself it would mean getting you out of my system. Seems that was a misfire."

She crouched down next to me. "I'm not out of your system?" Her blue eyes were intense, focused. Curious. So damn enticing. And definitely not carefree. "Is that even a thing?" she asked, raising her brows in question. "Getting someone out of your system by sleeping with them?"

"Maybe," I hedged. I stood and squeezed the paint out of the strainer, then took the gloves off.

Presley stood too.

"But apparently not for me when it comes to you," I admitted.

The slow smile that lit up her face made me wonder if being honest was a mistake. That smile was so pretty though; drawing one out of her couldn't be a mistake.

"Maybe you just need a second dose," she said, stepping closer, peering up at me.

"A second dose of Presley?" I tried to resist the urge to move a fallen strand of hair off her cheek but couldn't do it. I gently brushed it away with the backs of my fingers.

Turning her cheek toward my hand, she said, "Mm-hmm," her lids fluttering shut.

I let out a quiet growl, my blood pounding with desire, teeth clenching with frustration at this weakness for her. "It wouldn't be smart."

"Because of your job?"

I studied her beautiful face, working to get my mind to focus on the question instead of the little bow of her upper lip. In that moment, I admitted to myself, as important as my job was, it wasn't what had me fighting myself so hard.

"We proved we could keep it a secret," I said. "What Levi doesn't know can't hurt me." His main concern seemed to be the optics anyway. I kept it to myself that he'd seen us Saturday, knowing it would only embarrass her.

"We did prove we could keep it a secret." She looked at me expectantly. Hopefully?

"The thing is, I can't give you anything, Presley."

"You proved you can give me a hell of an orgasm...or three."

This woman...

I loved the way she could be so proper and put together one moment, then throw out a blunt comment the next. The contrasts in her fascinated me and made me want to know her inside and out.

As she watched my reaction, desire was clear in her eyes. I ached to make her come apart right here, right now.

I put some space between us. Inhaled deeply, trying to get a grip on myself and this need for her that was more out of control than a runaway train.

"When my last relationship ended," I said, unfolding the large cloth tarp and spreading it over the patio table to protect it from the paint sprayer, "my daughters suffered a profound loss. The second mother figure in their life left just like their mom did."

"Oh, those sweet girls." She pressed a hand to her chest and frowned.

"There's nothing worse than watching my children's hearts break—except knowing I caused it. I vowed to myself not to get involved with anyone while they're at such vulnerable ages and so readily latching on to any woman who's kind to them."

Presley closed the space between us again and touched my chest. "Such a good heart in here," she said quietly. She met my gaze. "They're so lucky to have you, West."

I swallowed. "That wasn't true when April left. That was my fault. My careless decision to invite her into their lives got them hurt."

"You couldn't have known how it would end."

"I should've known it *would* end sooner rather than later."

"Your daughters seem like well-adjusted, happy little girls."

"I can't risk them getting hurt again because of my inability to make a relationship work."

She nodded. "That's a noble decision."

I narrowed my eyes, trying to figure out whether that was a sincere comment. I didn't give a shit about being noble. I just didn't want anything to hurt my girls again, especially not something I brought upon them. I couldn't spot any hint that she didn't mean it.

"The thing is," she continued, "I'm not a relationship girl myself. I'm not looking for anything permanent, West. I wouldn't know what to do with a real relationship if it smacked me upside the head." Her lips flickered into a vulnerable smile. "I like what I know of your daughters, but

I'm not asking you to take me home to them. I happen to love what you do to me when they're *not* around."

I had a hard enough time resisting her when she wasn't saying things like that. "We're supposed to be working on your coffee shop."

"You haven't started working yet," she said, her tone dripping with flirtation. She stepped closer, facing me, leaving inches between us, like a dare.

As if I needed to be dared.

I cradled her cheek in my palm and kissed her, aiming to be gentle and civilized instead of crazed, but at the first taste of her sweet, tempting lips, need shot through me. Presley seemed right there with me, gripping my upper arms as if she wouldn't let me go if I wanted to.

As I kissed the hell out of her, I wound my arms around her, trailed them down to her sweet ass, and gripped her to me, pulling her against my erection, aching for release. Our moans and sighs filled the new room, bringing me out of myself enough to remember the door was unlocked. I carried her to the table and set her on the edge of it.

"Hold that thought," I said, dipping my hand into my pants pocket for my keys. I held them up and headed for the door.

I took long strides out to the public room, fumbled the key with shaking hands, and managed to shove it in the hole and lock the door.

When I returned to the kitchen, Presley leaned against the table with not a stitch of clothing on her gorgeous body.

"Jesus, Pres." I froze for a second in the doorway, drinking in all that perfection, then moved toward her.

I lifted her to the table and laid her back on it, leaning over her to feast on her perky tits. As I laved my tongue over her and teased her nipple, she wound her legs around my waist and rubbed her soft core against my rock-hard dick, still covered by my pants. I was dying to strip down and thrust inside of her, but I wanted this to last more than three minutes.

Still standing, supporting my weight with one hand on the table, I used the other—along with my mouth—to drive her wild. Her gasps and sighs and pleas were the sexiest guide to what she loved most—a combination of tongue and teeth. I worshipped one nipple then the other, then stretched over her to her mouth. She arched up to me hungrily, grasped my head, and kissed me till I forgot my name.

Someday I'd like to kiss her for hours, as if it was its own sport, but not when she was bare naked and begging me, her legs hooked tightly around my ass as she ground her hot center against me. I was a mere mortal, unable to resist her for much longer.

"West," she cried, pulling our mouths apart. "Why do you still have your pants on?"

I grinned into her, kissed her some more, loving how hot and needy she was, not confessing to how ready to come apart I was myself.

"Not done playing yet," I eventually managed, then suckled her tit into my mouth again, drawing out another gasp. Taking my time, I swirled my tongue around her, scraped my teeth over her tip.

"Please," she said on a pant. "Need you."

I uncrossed her legs from behind me, braced her feet on the edge of the table, and drew my finger over her slick folds. She arched upward, seeking out my finger, so I buried it in her, then added another. Presley bucked her hips, gripping both my shoulders and taking what she needed.

I watched her come apart around my fingers, looking

like a fucking goddess. I groaned, my own need pounding harder at the sight I'd carry with me till the day I died. Eventually her body went lax, so I kissed her, nipping at her lips, then dipping my tongue into her mouth. The kiss was slow and molten as Presley curled one leg around my thigh until her foot rested on the back of it.

"Once again," she said between kisses, "you're still dressed."

"Did it to yourself this time. And I fucking loved it."

I straightened, pulling her up to sit on the edge of the table. I pressed another kiss to her mouth, then trailed my lips lower, taking my time to relish as much of her glistening skin as I could in spite of my desire making it hard to slow down, impossible to think straight.

Eventually I went to my knees, swirling my tongue over her center with a mind to revving her up again. Based on the way she moaned and opened to me immediately, I got the message she didn't need more revving, but I continued to tease and lave her while I reached to my back pocket for my wallet. As I pulled it out, I kissed a path along Presley's inner thigh, then stood.

Presley unzipped me and pulled out my dick, her touch making me suck my breath in, close my eyes, and run through dimensional lumber sizes from a one-by-two up to a two-by-twelve and back down again to avoid embarrassing myself.

My eyes popped open when she pressed a sweet kiss to my tip. Before I could mention how fast this would be over if she kept that up, she ripped open the condom and rolled it on me.

Without any finesse, I entered her as if this were my first time ever, roughly, urgently.

"Sorry," I said on an exhale as I stilled, went back to lumber sizes. "Give me a minute."

When I eased myself back from the edge, I opened my eyes to find her peering up at me with a sexy, smug expression.

"This is what you do to me." My voice came out ragged.

"My pleasure, big guy," she said as flirtatious as I'd ever heard her.

I slid partway out and quickly thrust in, eliciting a gasp and wiping that flirty look right off her face, morphing it into lustful.

"You think I'm big?" I asked.

"You know you're big. Ahh, yessss. God."

With a grin, I managed, "Now you think I'm God?"

She laughed. "Add ego to the 'big' list."

I growled and kissed her as our bodies found a rhythm, and she locked her legs behind me again, arching into every thrust.

This. This heaven was what I'd been craving since I walked out of her house Sunday night. A few hours with her weren't enough. That was like savoring a single bite of the best, most decadent seven-layer chocolate cake and having to leave the rest. It went against the laws of nature.

As our intensity climbed, the patio table rattled and felt like it might collapse at any minute.

"This table is shit," I gritted out.

Presley laughed again. "Not sure this...is the intended use."

I worked my hands down to her cheeks and picked her up. With my pants stuck around my thighs, I managed to move us the short distance to one of our newly sanded, thankfully unpainted walls, pressing her back against it.

The paint thought was my last coherent one for the next

indefinable block of time as I lost all track of everything except how this woman felt. How she made me feel. How I never wanted this to end and yet how fucking badly I needed to explode.

Presley's grasp on me tightened, her arms around my neck as she held on with everything in her and keened her way through her climax. Her body contracted around me, squeezing me in the hottest fucking way, and I followed her over, pressing her hard against the wall, trying to keep us both upright as I came so hard I hoped the walls could hold us.

We stood there, locked together, frozen, possibly in another dimension for a few stupendous seconds of absolute bliss. I kept my body pressed into hers, our heartbeats thundering together as we tried to catch our breath.

As I came back to reality, I slid Presley down so her feet reached the floor, our bodies still flush, the wall still supporting us. I tipped her chin up and kissed her.

"That?" she said, her lids half lowered, her cheeks pink, hair falling out of whatever had been keeping it on top of her head. "Was hot."

All I could get out was a growl of agreement.

When I thought my arms could function, I pulled my pants up to my waist so they wouldn't drop all the way to my work boots.

"You covered those windows just in time," I said, drawing a quiet laugh from her.

"I didn't do it so you could bang me against the wall, but it worked out." She ran her finger along my lower lip.

"Sure did work out," I said with a lazy, satiated grin.

I tore off a paper towel from the roll and took care of the condom, then zipped and buttoned my pants. Presley put on her sky-blue thong, then pulled those little shorts up as I considered how *not* to fixate on the fact that all I had to do to touch those luscious cheeks was run my hand up her leg and under the cotton of her shorts. We'd get a lot more done if we worked in separate rooms this evening.

As she put her bra on, I picked up her tank and held it out for her, then kissed her again.

"Now maybe I'll be able to focus on work tonight," I said.

"Because I'm out of your system?"

"Until the next time."

Her brows shot up, and she sent me a spicy look of promise.

I imagined taking my time with her, spending a full night with her, waking up and making pancakes with her, maybe taking the kayaks out at dawn.

And there it was, exactly what I'd been afraid of. The predisposition to rush in. To want too much. To imagine a relationship in something that was intended to be just a good time.

Either I needed to rein myself in and remember this was a no-strings-attached, physical-only arrangement, or I needed to retreat and save myself a whole lotta trouble.

Chapter Eighteen

West

Our dads' group used to be a bunch of lonely, confused single dads. Now two-thirds of them had defected by falling prey to some admittedly pretty ladies and going the ball-and-chain route.

In the past, we met just about every Saturday evening. The more suckers we had fall victim to love, the less we were able to coordinate schedules and carve out a few hours of guy time.

The last Saturday of June was our only get-together of the month, and we were down a guy even then. Max was still on his honeymoon, so that left Ben, Knox, Chance, Luke, and me.

Ben had offered to host, as Emerson had taken the kids swimming and then to a concert on the square. The five of us had broken in the new basketball goal Ben had bought with a high-stakes game of H-O-R-S-E. Now we sat on camp chairs in the shade of Ben's house, devouring classic burgers from the grill, corn on the cob, skillet potatoes with bacon and onions, beer from Rusty Anchor, and fresh lemonade. Luke had brought strawberries from his farm, the last of the year's crop, and had picked up shortcakes and whipped cream at Country Market for dessert.

"Doesn't get much better than this," I said, holding up my half-eaten cob and gesturing to my meal. "You make a mean burger, Ben."

"As long as we're not secretly eating llama meat," Chance said with a grin.

"The ladies are right there in sight," Ben said, nodding toward the corral where his horses and llamas grazed together.

I'd spotted the horses earlier, but at the moment, only the white llama was visible. I assumed the others were blocked from our view by the barn.

"If Esmerelda isn't begging, I don't know what she's doing," Luke said.

I turned to look. Sure enough, the long-haired llama was at the fence closest to us, staring a hole in my back.

"She's fine," Ben insisted. "She just likes attention."

"Attention or cookies?" Knox asked.

"Well, both. As long as she's in my sight, I can be sure she hasn't escaped. Every drama-free night is a win in my book."

"I wonder how llama tastes," Luke said, keeping an eye on the animal as he lifted his beer to his mouth.

"Probably tastes like chicken," Knox said.

"Don't let the hens hear that," Ben said, grinning.

"Isn't that Emerson's SUV?" Chance asked, nodding toward the intersection of Ben's long driveway and the county road.

"It is." Ben frowned as he watched his wife drive in our direction. When she stopped near us, he stood. "Is something wrong?" he asked when Emerson rolled her window down.

At the same time, the back door on the passenger side opened, and Ruby ran toward the house, wearing her swimsuit and flip-flops. "Hi, Daddy!"

"She forgot clothes to change into," Emerson said. "Hi, guys." She waved at the rest of us, and we called out greetings.

The backseat window lowered, and Xavier hollered, "Hi, Dad! Hi, everybody!"

We said hello to Ben and Emerson's only boy, whose attention was diverted to one or both of their other girls in the vehicle.

"Sorry to interrupt," Emerson said. "We'll be out of your way as soon as Ruby changes."

Ben set his plate on a side table, went to the driver's window, and planted a kiss on his wife as we discussed the concert they were heading to by a local group.

Ruby zipped out of the house and ran straight to her dad, who caught her in a hug. "Esmerelda wants her cookie, Daddy!"

"Esmerelda has become spoiled rotten," Ben told her. "It's not even Tuesday."

"She likes cookies on any day," Ruby, who was one year behind my twins in school, informed him.

"She'll have to wait," Ben said. "You're going to be late for the concert. Let's get you buckled in."

He walked her around the vehicle and helped her in as we dads made jokes about Ben's llama devotion.

Once Ben's wife and kids had left, relative quiet settled around us, save for the periodic clucking of a hen or two. Discussion turned to the book Knox and Ava were releasing in a few months, the third in their first trilogy together.

"How's that partnership going since Bronte's birth?" Ben asked. "Self-employment doesn't always allow for maternity leave."

"Not officially. Ava took a few weeks off, but she's slowly getting back into the swing of it, working part-time for now. We finished the manuscript a week before Bronte arrived, and I've been handling the editing. Quincy takes care of Bronte three days a week now."

"How's Quincy handling that?" I asked.

Knox had confessed to us a few months back that he and Quincy had been trying to get pregnant since day one of their marriage nearly a year ago with no luck. Quincy was the most natural nurturer I'd ever met. She thrived on caring for kids and did childcare in their home for a handful of rugrats. It didn't seem fair she was having trouble conceiving her own babies.

"She loves her niece to pieces," Knox said. "Caring for Bronte's the next best thing to having our own."

"It'll happen soon, man," Ben said.

"Keep on soldiering on and trying," I said.

"You better believe I will," he said with a grin.

As I stuffed the last of my burger in my mouth, a strange sound reached my ears, like a high-pitched humming noise, too high to be coming from the men. I met Chance's gaze, confusion on his face too.

Knox laughed.

"What the hell is that?" I asked, looking between Knox and Ben, who didn't appear concerned either.

"It's Esmerelda telling me she wants to eat," Ben said with a sigh.

I swung my head toward the llama. Sure enough, she still stared our way with her big, falsely woeful eyes, though

I couldn't see her mouth moving. The sound was a drawn-out moan that sounded as if she'd been wronged.

"Do you need to go feed her?" Luke asked.

Ben shook his head as he finished chewing, then said, "I fed everyone before you all got here."

"Did she not get the message?" Chance asked.

"Oh, she was right there as I fed her, chomping her hay as fast as I could get it in her feeder."

"So she's lying," I said.

Knox shot a look of amusement at Ben. "She wants dessert, doesn't she?"

Ben shook his head and muttered, "Fucking spoiled llama."

The rest of us laughed, knowing exactly who'd spoiled the animal.

"You got any cookies?" Luke asked.

"I bought a dozen before I knew you were bringing fresh berries," Ben said. "I don't know how she knows that."

"Smart llama," Knox said.

"Spoiled." Ben acted annoyed with his animals, but we all knew he loved them almost as much as he loved his new wife and four kids.

"You want me to get a cookie and take it to her?" Luke asked.

Ben laughed. "If we don't want to listen to her whining for the next hour, she's going to need a cookie."

"On it." Luke set his empty plate aside and headed into the house.

"Guess we know who wears the pants in this family," Chance said.

"Esmerelda then Emerson," Knox said.

"Spot on," Ben admitted. "And I consider myself a damn lucky man."

Luke came out of the house with a box of cookies from Sugar. He set it on one of the side tables. "Come on, West, let's go spoil this llama like a grandparent."

I got up and headed to the fence with him.

"How many grown men does it take to give a llama a cookie?" Knox hollered.

Luke flipped him off as we all laughed.

"Knox, you should write a book about giving a llama a cookie," Chance said.

"Would that be a parody of the mouse version or a how-to book?" Knox asked.

"If you give a llama a cookie, she's probably going to want one every damn day," Ben said.

Still humming, Esmerelda eyed us suspiciously as we approached, until Luke held out the cookie. Her eyes locked on the llama-shaped goodie.

"Isn't that some kind of cannibalism?" I asked, standing back so I wouldn't get llama drool on me.

"This one could be your uncle," Luke said to Esmerelda as he held out the cookie.

The llama didn't bat an eye, chomping the cookie before we could say another word.

"Wash your hands," I told Luke as we went back to the group.

Someone's phone rang as Luke headed inside, and I sat back down.

"That's me," Knox said, digging his phone out of his pocket. "Quincy's FaceTiming." He frowned. "Hey, Quince, what's up?"

"She said her first sentence, Knox!" The words burst from Quincy for all of us to hear. "Can you say it again, sweet girl?"

"Hey, Junie," Knox said to his daughter on the screen.

"Dada!" came the reply.

"What did you tell me before, sweet pea?" Quincy asked the two-year-old.

"Dada, Dada, Dada."

Luke came back out with the makings for strawberry shortcake as we all listened to Knox's conversation, keeping quiet, waiting to see if Juniper would say whatever it was she'd said to excite Quincy.

Knox stood and wandered away from the group as we all helped ourselves to shortcake, bright red strawberries, and whipped cream, filling Luke in on Juniper's milestone that she apparently wouldn't repeat for her dad.

Knox wandered back, grinning like a man in love. "Sorry about that."

"Did she do it again so you could hear it?" Chance asked.

"Nah. Apparently she said, 'Where my dada?' Once she saw me on the screen, there was no reason to ask again," he explained, laughing.

As we all settled in with our dessert, Chance said, "Things have sure changed since we first started getting together. Not only is it harder to meet, but once we do, our families can't seem to do without us, whether it was Sam not being where she was supposed to be a few months ago or Juniper hitting a milestone today."

"Or a llama protecting an injured cat," Luke said of a few weeks ago.

"A kid forgetting her clothes," Ben added.

We took turns bringing up other interruptions over the past few months, laughing more as the list grew longer.

"You get married, and it just gets worse," Ben said, grinning. He couldn't hide how stinking happy he was since getting together with Emerson.

"Rub it in, asshole," Luke said lightly. He didn't make it a secret that he wanted to find a wife and pop out more kids, but the dude worked so much on his farm I didn't see how he'd ever meet the right woman.

"Speak for yourself," I said, drawing laughter because Luke and I had this disagreement frequently.

He was all about finding a wife. I was all about staying the hell single.

"You two are overdue," Chance said. "The rest of us dropped like flies."

"Lucky flies," Knox said smugly.

I growled as Presley came to mind. Actually, if I was honest with myself, Presley hadn't been very far from my thoughts since last weekend, no matter how I tried to get her out of my head.

"I got zero prospects," Luke said matter-of-factly. "How 'bout you, West?"

I shoved a bite of shortcake in my mouth and didn't make eye contact with anyone.

"I don't think West has ever been this quiet before," Knox said.

Chance, who probably knew me best out of these guys, narrowed his eyes at me, not laughing like everyone else. "Do you have a secret, Aldridge?"

I finished my bite of dessert.

"He's not denying it, is he?" Ben said.

What I'd learned about these guys was, they would give you all kinds of hell as long as you kept secrets. If you leveled with them, they could be supportive and sometimes even offered up passable advice.

I leaned forward, setting my plate aside and resting my elbows on my knees.

"Dude, you do have a secret," Luke said.

I wasn't about to out Presley, but I could give them something. "I might be hooking up with someone."

Howls erupted around the circle as I knew they would. I waited for them to calm the hell down.

"You're worse than a bunch of twelve-year-old boys," I said. "I'm not saying a word about who it is, but it's supposed to be no-strings."

"Supposed to be?" Ben asked.

"Is," I corrected. "Neither of us wants a relationship. Just some fun."

"That's better than a yearslong dry spell," Luke said.

"It's not easy to find the opportunity to fill your own needs as a single dad," Chance said sympathetically. Then he grinned. "The one night I took for myself landed me my wife though."

"And your soon-to-be-born baby," Ben said. "That was a big night, huh?"

"That's what she said," Chance quipped.

I laughed with the rest of them but sobered faster. "I want the no-strings," I said when they quieted.

"So take the no-strings and run with it," Knox said. "Don't pay attention to what Luke says. You don't have to marry anybody."

"I've never been any good at no-strings," I admitted. "Maybe I'm missing one of the man genes, but I seem to get my heart involved prematurely whether I want to or not."

"Is your heart involved?" Luke asked. "With this mysterious hookup woman?"

I didn't immediately reply, because this was embarrassing. But I trusted these guys. They were the brothers I'd never had. Instead of answering directly, I said, "I've never figured out how to do meaningless sex. This was supposed to be exactly that. One and done."

"It's not though?" Knox asked.

"It's happened more than once," I admitted. "And I want it to happen again. But my history will tell you this is what I do. I get with a lady, and I rush in, get feelings too fast, want more. And then..." I made an explosion sound.

"I remember you moved April in pretty fast," Luke said.

"Hindsight says way too fucking fast," I agreed. "And Flora..." I shook my head. "We went from a secret relationship while we were still enlisted to pregnant to discharged to still getting to know each other to married with kids in, well, ten months flat, I guess."

Chance laughed. "I haven't known my wife for ten months yet, so I'm no help."

"Emerson and I have known each other since we were kids, but from the time we got together until we were married was, shit, just over a month," Ben said.

Knox laughed. "Six weeks for Quincy and me. When you know, you just know."

"You fuckers are no help," I said, shaking my head.

"What do you want help with?" Chance asked. "We're definitely no help when it comes to not falling fast. Are you falling for this woman?"

"No," I said quickly. "I'm just having fun."

"If you're afraid of falling, maybe play the field," Luke suggested.

That was the worst idea ever.

"So none of you have a single tip for how to hook up with someone without trying to make it into more?" I asked.

As soon as I glanced around at their faces, I realized this was the wrong group for the question. They'd all fallen fast and hard. The thing was, I believed they'd all picked wisely.

Ben and Emerson? Meant to be.

Chance and Rowan? It was like fate matched them up.

Knox might be older than Quincy by a lot, but there was no denying they were perfect together.

And we'd all witnessed how goofy in love Max and Harper were at their wedding.

These guys had all found their person. I'd proven I couldn't tell my person from a bad decision.

"I've got nothing," Knox said. "Maybe just go with the flow and see where it ends up?"

"What do you have to lose?" Ben asked.

"If my girls get attached…" I scowled.

"Your girls don't know about this hookup, do they?" Knox asked.

I shook my head.

"Then you're fine," Chance said. "Have some fun. Get your rocks off to your heart's content. See where it goes."

"If you leave me as the only single dad, I'll kick your damn ass though," Luke said.

I understood where he was coming from. "I have no intention of getting hitched, my friend. We singles'll stick together." I lifted my beer, and Luke tapped his bottle to mine. "Here's to being single and carefree."

"Keep telling yourselves that," Chance said.

Luke snarled at him and looked back at me. "Your girls are in Nashville for the weekend?"

"They'll be home tomorrow before bedtime," I said.

"After these old married farts go home to their old ladies, let's hit the bars."

I laughed, but honestly that sounded a hell of a lot better than heading home to my hand and thoughts of Presley.

"You're on."

Chapter Nineteen

Presley

When I moved to Dragonfly Lake, I'd never expected *this*.

Today was my thirty-sixth birthday, and I was spending it surrounded by girlfriends, more girlfriends than I'd had all at once since I was a kid.

Rowan and Chloe had organized dinner at The Cove, the restaurant at the Marks Hotel. As dusk approached, I sat with the two of them plus Maeve, Anna, Olivia, and Magnolia at the table with the best lake view in the covered patio dining section.

"Chloe, you did a fine job with this hotel," I said as we enjoyed our cocktails and waited for the dessert course. She'd brought me here when the property was still under construction, back when she'd been a VP at Marks International. I hadn't been inside since.

Chloe laughed. "I can't take much credit, really. Angelica worked on it through the planning stages and early construction. I oversaw it for a few months is all. But I agree, it's wonderful."

"Don't tell Cash," Olivia said, "but the food was excellent."

"My brother-in-law would be the first to agree with you," Chloe said, then emphasized, "*now*. Back when Henry's was competing with The Cove for that TV show..." She shook her head, grinning. "Enemies. He and Nola, the chef here, have made peace and have a good, if competitive, relationship."

"So we don't have to keep it a secret that we ate here," Magnolia said.

"As if anyone can keep secrets in this town," Anna said, laughing.

"That's the truth," Maeve said. "Sometimes I wonder if Loretta Lawson has hidden cams throughout town."

I laughed with them and kept it to myself that I had a secret named West Aldridge.

Since Thursday evening when we'd had the hot wall-sex hookup in the shop, he and I had snuck in some private, steamy looks and secret touches Friday when he and his crew were working at my house. Then today we'd worked all day at the shop together, until I'd had to leave for this, and he'd had to get ready for his dads' group.

We'd started the brickwork on the walls, which meant dealing with wet mortar that we couldn't allow to dry out before the bricks were in place, which meant no time for frisky business, but it'd been a great day anyway. We'd talked a lot, flirted a lot, stolen kisses.

It would have to tide me over until the next time.

I was impatient for the next time, but I knew that was just because it was new and forbidden, not to mention I'd gone without sex for too long before West.

A large sailboat with a pink and orange sail pulled up to the Marks's dock as the sun fell lower in the sky.

"What a gorgeous boat," Magnolia said as we watched it.

"It belongs to the Barringtons who live in the development on the southeast side of the lake," Anna said. "They're a sweet retired couple. They love to sail over here for drinks."

"How do you know all of this?" Rowan asked.

"She managed that development before she became the manager at the Honeysuckle Inn," Olivia explained.

"West's little girls would absolutely love this," I said, thinking maybe someday I would bring them here for dinner. Would that be weird? It would probably be weird.

"West's little girls?" Chloe asked, her head tilted with nosiness.

"Yeah, what am I missing?" Olivia asked.

Oops. I needed to be more careful with what I said. This part of the story was pretty innocent though, so I explained, "One evening a week or two ago, right after I got my kayaks, I was testing one out, and along comes this boat with three little princesses in the front."

"West's little girls," Anna guessed.

"And West and Jagger McNamara," I told them.

"That must've been a boatful of swoon," Olivia said.

"Jagger had taken them out for a boat ride," I continued, ignoring the swoon comment, "and one of their favorite things to do is go by the hotel mined gawk up at all the 'rich people.' I heard all about it because they stopped by my dock directly after the hotel drive-by."

I saw Rowan and Chloe exchange a look, but no one else appeared to, and I was able to ignore it when Maeve said, "Those girls come into the bookstore for story time.

They are adorable. Almost cute enough to make me find a sperm donor."

"Your clock is ticking loudly, huh?" Olivia said.

"Nope," Maeve insisted, though it was obvious by her mannerisms the opposite was true, and she was trying not to give in to it.

"I wasn't quite ready for parenthood," Rowan said, laughing. "Surprise!"

"A baby and a teenager in six months flat," I said.

"Do you girls want kids?" Rowan asked.

"Not if it means going it alone," Anna said.

"I support that," Chloe said, shaking her head. "They're a lot. Worth it, of course, but I don't think I'm cut out for single parenting."

"I don't know how West manages three," I said.

"What about you, Presley?" Olivia asked. "Do you want kids?"

I picked up my wineglass and sipped, reeling more than a little from the question. Without setting the glass down, I said, "Believe it or not, I haven't thought a lot about it."

"Whaaat?" Olivia said in disbelief.

"Pretty sure she speaks the truth," Chloe said. "She's been married to her job since the dawn of time."

I wrinkled my nose. "It's true. I worked so much I barely had time for meals."

"You mostly ate while you worked." Chloe knew well what she was talking about, as she'd been by my side either literally or figuratively for a lot of it.

"How many serious relationships have you had?" Anna asked.

I held my hands up in a zero sign. "Goose egg."

"None?" Olivia asked.

"Not a one. It wouldn't have worked if I had," I said. "I

wouldn't have put much time or effort into it. My job took everything."

"That's how it went when I was caring for my gram," Rowan said. "No bandwidth for a guy."

"She was so lucky to have you," Anna said.

"She was," Chloe said. "I hope someone takes such good care of me if I ever need it."

"I hope to never need it," Maeve said.

"Amen." Olivia turned back to me. "So, Presley, now that you've liberated yourself from that awful career, do you want a relationship? Kids?"

My brows shot up as I considered it. "I feel like I'm still recovering from being a robot for more than a decade, to be honest. A relationship?" I blew out my breath. "I don't know how to do that," I admitted. "My parents were dysfunctional until my mom took my sister and me and left my dad, thank God. My sister married young, and her husband is a controlling jackass. I don't even know what a healthy relationship looks like."

"You've got these two," Olivia said, pointing at Rowan and Chloe.

"Yeah. It's weird." I laughed and shrugged at Chloe. "Chloe was my fellow workaholic. My enabler. My partner in misery. Look at her now."

"She's so happy I'd slap her if I didn't like her so much," Olivia said.

"We're not getting any younger," Maeve said. "My eggs are getting tired and lonely."

"Fertility declines after age thirty-five," Anna said matter-of-factly, "and here we all are."

I sat up straighter. "I'm thirty-six and haven't thought seriously about kids. Now suddenly I'm feeling a little panicked." Mostly I was joking, but there was a thread of truth there.

"Sperm donor," Maeve said again. She grinned, but I wasn't altogether sure she was kidding.

"Sure would be faster and lower drama," Olivia said.

"But not cheap," Maeve said.

"Have you researched it?" Magnolia asked her.

"Yes, I have," Maeve answered.

Olivia made a face. "The thought of having some stranger's spooge up in there..." She shook her head and shuddered, making all of us laugh.

"So really though," I said, my mind going full speed, "they're still saying fertility goes down at thirty-five? I thought for sure that number was higher now."

"Still saying it. But lots of people have babies later in life," Maeve said.

"I need some me time before I even think about relationships and babies," I said, even as my traitorous mind conjured up an image of West. That was *not* a relationship, I reminded myself.

"I think that's smart," Rowan said. "It's what I was shooting for too. I'm not complaining," she added quickly. "Not in the least bit." Her wide smile and her hand rubbing her seven-month-pregnant belly revealed that she was in a very good place in her life. "But I can relate to needing recovery time after being so all-in on something."

"Yeah, you've got time to figure you out," Magnolia said.

"And open a coffee shop," Chloe added, laughing. "You know, while you relax and recover."

Another round of laughter arose, mine included.

As it faded, Rowan said, "We love you just the way you are."

"We love you extra for opening a coffee shop," Anna said.

"To Presley, for saving us from mediocre coffee." Magnolia lifted her glass, and everyone followed with whatever they were drinking, alcoholic or not.

As we drank to that, our server arrived with a tray full of the gorgeous desserts we'd ordered, including my seven-layer chocolate mousse cake.

"Hi, Nola," Chloe said as the chef appeared at the head of the table and set my cake in front of me.

"Hello, ladies. Chloe, good to see you. Thanks for coming out tonight, and happy birthday to you," Nola said.

"Thanks," I said. "Dinner was fantastic."

"Better than Henry's, am I right?" Nola said, making everyone laugh.

"Those are fighting words," Chloe said.

Nola's shoulders sagged with exaggeration. "I'd hoped you'd defected to my side."

"I like being married," Chloe told her. "But you're a close second for this Henry girl."

"Aww." Nola patted her heart, then turned her attention to me. "I don't think we've met, birthday girl."

I introduced myself and shook her hand.

"She's new to town," Chloe said. Then the others told her my coffee shop plans.

"I'll definitely be seeing a lot more of you then," the chef said.

"I love to hear that," I told her.

"Well, I need to get back to the kitchen," Nola said, "but I wanted to say hello and thank you ladies for choosing the best restaurant in town for your celebration."

Our conversation went in a dozen different directions as

we ate our stupendously tasty desserts and finished our drinks.

"Is anyone up for turning this into an official girls' night out?" Anna asked. "We could give them their table back here and move to the Barn Bar or the Fly."

"I'd be up for that," Maeve said. "I've got tomorrow off."

"It sounds fun," Magnolia said. "We should absolutely keep celebrating."

"I'm open," I said.

"You guys go," Chloe said. "I need to get home to relieve Holden. He took Sutton to Mimi and Papa's in Nashville all day. I promised I'd do bath time and bedtime."

"Aww," Maeve said. "You two really are cute."

"And nauseating," Olivia joked. "But I need to go home too. I have the early shift at the bakery tomorrow."

"Ouch," Anna said. "What about you, Rowan?"

She frowned. "I'd love to, but this girl is exhausted."

"You're going with the 'brewing a baby is hard work' excuse, huh?" Anna teased.

"Ab. So. Lutely," Rowan said. "I'm sorry, but my bedtime is thundering toward us."

"Will that be for sleep or for a roll in the hay with your handsome hubby?" Magnolia asked.

"There might be some debate if he wasn't with his dads' group," Rowan said. "He said he wouldn't be out very late, but it's past booty call time for me."

"You two old married ladies and one baker will miss a rocking good time," Anna said. "But we understand."

We finished our dessert and paid our bill. Once we were in the parking lot, Magnolia volunteered as designated driver, so the four of us single girls hugged the others, then piled into her old BMW.

My life might have taken a surprise turn a few weeks

ago, but it felt like it was a positive one. Not only did I have my first adult girlfriend birthday dinner, but now I was going to girls' night out with women who felt like they were becoming my close friends.

As we rode the short distance to the Fly with our windows down and music turned up, I leaned back in the seat, let the summer air blow over me, and savored the feeling of being carefree and unfettered by a job, a baby, or a boyfriend.

Chapter Twenty

Presley

When we walked into the Fly, several people in the half-full bar called out to Anna and Maeve as if they were town celebrities. A few came up to them for hugs before we could get to a table. Anna introduced me to everyone as Chloe's Nashville friend who moved to town to open a coffee shop, and I wasn't sure which was better: meeting people or the free publicity.

I noticed the reception for Magnolia was cooler, but she seemed to smile and ignore it. Then Kemp came toward us from the back half of the bar with no small amount of noise.

"Delfico is in the house," he roared and gave Anna a big hug. "Hey, Maeve-y."

"Someone's been overserved," Maeve said with a grin.

"Nah," Kemp said. "It's been a good baseball day. Hey, wedding date," he said to me with a warm smile and a wink.

"Hey, wedding date," I said back and bumped fists with

him, deciding Maeve had nailed it. Kemp was less than sober.

"Mags," he said. "I was just wondering where you were. There're a couple wankers from out of town who want to play doubles. I need my pool shark partner. You up for it?"

Magnolia looked at us girls. "Do you mind?"

"Of course not," Anna said. "Go save Kemp's ass."

"Hey," Kemp said jovially, "my ass doesn't need saving. We're a team." He pulled Magnolia into his side. "Tell her, Mags."

"Some nights I carry us," Magnolia said, grinning, eliciting a shocked expression from Kemp, "and some nights he does. Partners."

Kemp laughed, apparently appeased. "You need a cocktail?" he asked her.

Magnolia shook her head. "DD tonight. I'll find you girls when we're done wiping the floor with these *wankers*."

"We're going to get a table," Anna told her.

"I never thought I'd hear Magnolia say *wankers*," Maeve said, laughing.

The three of us found one of the last available tables as the pool partners headed to the back, where I could see a row of pool tables, all of them in use.

"This place is bigger than it looks from the front," I said as we settled into the booth, Maeve and Anna on one side, me on the other.

"This is your first time here?" Anna asked me.

"It is. I need to get out more. This is exactly what I needed but didn't know it."

"A little chaos every once in a while is a good thing," Maeve said.

"It's one of those Dragonfly Lake milestones," Anna

said. "You're an official resident now that you've been to the Fly on a Saturday night."

"Plus the llama. I've met Esmerelda," I said.

"Have you ordered Dragonfly Dust waffles?" Maeve asked.

I waved her off like that one was the easiest. "Before I even moved here. That might be partly *why* I moved here."

Before we could say more, a server arrived with three drinks—a glass of wine for me and hard seltzers for Maeve and Anna.

"Hey, Isabel," Anna said. "We didn't—"

"Kemp did," the blond server said, gesturing toward the back once she unloaded our bounty.

"He's too much," Anna said. "Thanks, Iz."

"Of course." The server hurried off to the next table.

"Do you like wine, Presley?" Anna asked.

"I do." I'd told Kemp that at Harper and Max's wedding, probably more than once as I went for the supposedly frou-frou drinks instead. "And seltzer's your thing, and Kemp knows it?"

"That's Kemp," Maeve said.

"Nice of him," I said.

"He's got ulterior motives," Maeve said, eyeing Anna.

"Stop," Anna said. "Kemp and I are just friends. Always have been. Always will be."

"I'm not debating that," Maeve said. She turned to me. "He's had a thing for Anna for years. Like, since school."

"I'll be right back," Anna said, waving at someone across the room.

"And there she goes," Maeve said with an affectionate grin and a head shake. "The social butterfly has been set free."

"Everyone loves Anna, huh?"

"More literally than you think."

"She's impossible not to like."

"Agree."

"Hey, pretty girls." Ty, who I'd danced with at the wedding reception, slid into the booth next to me.

"Hello, Ty," Maeve said, her tone of voice sounding like an eye roll.

"Hi, Ty," I said.

"To what do we owe the privilege of your presence tonight?" he asked.

"Girls' night out," Maeve said. "We're celebrating Presley's birthday." As soon as she said it, she cringed and mouthed the word *sorry* to me.

I laughed it off, unbothered. Then Ty leaned closer.

"Can I buy you a birthday drink?" he asked.

"I'm good right now, but thanks," I said, lifting my full wineglass.

"We should go out sometime," he said, directing it to me. "Belated birthday celebration?"

I glanced at Maeve, who didn't look surprised in the least. Was he actually asking me out? With an audience? Blazes of hell, this just got awkward.

"I'm...focused on opening my coffee shop right now. I don't really have time for much social life. Tonight's a fluke," I told him. "But thank you."

"Ahh, you're breaking my heart, new girl," he said. "I'll check in with you once your shop is open. You have a happy birthday."

He stood and went on his way as quickly as he'd appeared. I stared at Maeve with my mouth open.

"What was that?" I asked.

Maeve shook her head. "Ty's got a good heart, but if he's

breathing, he's flirting with someone. We just shrug him off."

Anna returned to our table and was about to sit down when someone called her name from the other direction. She hurried over to someone behind me, out of my sight.

Laughing, I said, "You weren't kidding about butterfly."

"This is how it is," Maeve said simply, with no hard feelings toward her friend. "Everyone loves Anna. Anna loves everyone."

"The opposite of Magnolia, it seems," I said carefully.

"Magnolia... She's got a long, sordid history in this town."

"She told me some of it. About her dad and her childhood and how money was used for control. And how he disowned her. I don't know her well yet, but she seems...sort of humble now? Maybe even repentant?"

Maeve looked thoughtful as she sipped her seltzer. "I think she is. But it takes a long time to outgrow a bad reputation in a small town."

"I'm beginning to understand that."

"If Chloe can forgive her, others should be able to eventually."

"I hope so. She seems to have changed."

An hour later, the Fly was packed. We'd given up our table to watch Magnolia and Kemp's pool battles. I'd met dozens of locals whose names I'd be hard-pressed to remember later, but I kept my smile pasted on and answered questions about The Bean Counter mixed in with being hit on. Maeve informed me I was "fresh meat" in a town where the dating pool was small.

"You're getting it too though," I said, because she—and Anna too—had plenty of male attention.

"Hope springs eternal for these clueless boys." She laughed.

I moved in close and said quietly, "There's no baby daddy here for you? No one you're interested in?"

She made a face. "When you live in a small town, you end up knowing too much about everyone."

I nodded. "That makes sense."

Anna rejoined us, her eyes sparkling, obviously thriving on the social scene.

"How many new friends have you made?" Maeve asked her.

"There's a lot of tourists here tonight," Anna said, "but mostly I've been catching up with locals."

"I think I've met every last one of them," I said.

"Tourists or locals?" Maeve asked.

"Both," I laughed. "I might need to do the names-on-the-cup thing at the shop so I can learn who's who because I'm definitely not retaining it tonight."

Girls' night out had been novel and lots of fun at first. When the crowd quadrupled, the noise level exploded, and the needy guys came out of the woodwork, it was flattering for the first three or so pickup lines, but then the parade of guys, most of them younger than us by more than a year or two, lost its luster. I didn't want to develop a reputation as the grumpy new girl, but my "too busy opening a business" excuse was getting a lot of wear and tear tonight.

"Hey, ladies," a pretty woman with dark skin and a wide smile said as she came up to us.

"Tansy! Hi!" Anna replied. "Have you met Presley?"

"No, ma'am," Tansy said, holding her hand out.

"Presley Holiday," I told her as I shook her hand. "I just moved to town a few weeks ago."

"You're the coffee lady," Tansy said. "I've heard about you. I'm Tansy Harrelson. It's nice to meet you."

"You too."

"Tansy works at Oopsie Daisies," Maeve said.

"So I'll be seeing you often when you open," Tansy said.

"I'll look forward to it," I said.

"Hey, Reggie," Anna said to the tall guy behind Tansy. "I haven't seen you out for ages."

"What's up, Anna?" he said.

My friends introduced me to Tansy's husband. Then Tansy said, "It's date night, and we got some crazy idea that it'd be fun to hit the Fly." She leaned into her husband and peered up at him. "Then we remembered why we stay home most nights."

"Did it used to be this loud and chaotic?" Reggie asked, grinning as if he knew he sounded sixty years old.

Hooking her arm through Reggie's, Tansy said, "We decided to use the rest of our babysitter time tonight for a stroll across the square and maybe one drink on the Rusty Anchor patio. That sounds so much saner."

"There's zero sanity here," Maeve said.

"You two have a nice rest of your evening," Anna said. "It was good to see you."

"You too. Nice to meet you, Presley." Tansy touched my upper arm as she and her husband went by, and I wished them a good evening.

"Who's up for another round?" Anna asked.

"The more I drink, the longer I can handle the noise level," Maeve said.

"I'm in." I glanced behind me and saw Tansy and Reggie go out the side door. He put his arm around her, and something inside me twinged. I'd just met them, but they seemed so close. Like a team. Them against the world.

Them against the raucous Fly crowd. While the rest of us came out to meet people and not be alone, their refuge was at home with each other.

An unfamiliar longing for that kind of partnership reared up in me, taking me by surprise. I blew it off as Anna verified my drink request and left to order at the bar.

Magnolia and Kemp, at the nearest pool table, high-fived as they apparently beat another opponent. There were groans around the table, with some people complaining that the duo was undefeated tonight.

"Woo, keep schooling 'em, Mags," Maeve called out.

Jewel and Piper came up to us then.

"Hey, pretty girls," Piper said. "This place is packed."

"Hi, pretty girls," I said back.

"Hey, you two," Maeve said. "Did you just get here?"

Jewel nodded. "I just got off work. We came out for one drink."

"Was Humble's busy tonight?" Maeve asked Jewel.

"Crazy busy." Jewel held up her cocktail. "Hence the drink."

"And the flower shop?" I asked Piper. "You must get loads of shoppers during tourist season."

Piper nodded. "Today rocked, and I have the sore feet to prove it."

Anna rejoined us, distributing our drinks. "Hey, ladies!"

We stood in a tight circle a few feet from the end pool table, our conversation gliding from one shallow topic to another. Piper and Jewel eventually wandered away to see who was in the front half of the bar. As I watched them walk away and listened to Anna comment on how cute Piper looked particularly for a last-minute drink, my heart lurched.

West and Luke were here, making their way to the counter just a few feet away from me.

Chapter Twenty-One

West

I'd had second thoughts about going out for a drink a dozen times between Ben's house and downtown. I'd told Luke I'd meet him at the Fly though.

I parked on a side street and met Luke on the sidewalk in front of the bar, coming from the other direction.

As we walked into the bar, a wave of noise and chaos rolled over us. One glance told me the place was near capacity. I braced myself against it, then told myself to lighten up and have some fun.

"What the hell are we doing, man?" Luke asked me, grinning, as we reached the edge of the crowd.

"Living the life," I said. "You sure you want to commit?"

He shrugged. "Might as well get all the bang for my buck with the babysitter. Kinsley said she could stay till midnight. I've got almost two hours to avoid my overly quiet house."

"I hear that." I wasn't a fan of my empty house either. With the girls gone for the weekend again, it was almost a shock to come home to nobody. When they were asleep in their bedroom, the house might be quiet, but it wasn't empty. "Drink first?"

He nodded, and we headed to the long counter, angling toward the back half of it where there were fewer people.

Once we had a beer, we turned toward the back section, where the pool tables and dartboards were.

"There's Kemp," Luke said and headed toward him.

I nearly stumbled when I realized Kemp was standing with Anna, Magnolia, Maeve, and Presley.

In the seconds it took to follow Luke to their cluster, I worked to wipe my blatant desire off my face and play it cool. Like a contractor running into his client and nothing more. At the same time, I drank in the sight of Presley before she spotted me.

Tonight she wore a camisole top with lace trim and a cropped hemline that gave me yet another tantalizing glimpse of the skin at her waist. Instead of her usual short skirt or shorts, she wore a long, flowy skirt with a side slit that reached her upper thigh. I was struck stupid by the idea of ducking under that skirt and burying my head between her thighs.

Cut it out, dumbass.

"What's up, Essex?" Luke said to Kemp as Anna and Maeve excused themselves to the restroom.

"Hey, guys," Kemp said.

I nodded at him and flicked my gaze to Magnolia and Presley, who seemed to be having their own conversation. When Magnolia glanced toward us, her expression changed as she saw Luke. I was guessing her frown was mirrored on his face, as I knew those two didn't care for each other. Something long in the past I either couldn't remember or didn't know.

Presley took forever to look at me, and when she finally did, her attention skipped immediately back to Magnolia, who said something privately to her, then walked away.

And then there were four.

Luke and Kemp dove into a business conversation about hard cider and Rusty Anchor that I knew nothing about, so I sidled closer to Presley and said, "Evening," in a tone I hoped sounded more like I was talking to a professional contact than a lover.

"Hi, West." When she smiled up at me, there was an instant of connection that went far beyond being the dude who was installing flooring at her house. It was so brief that I was pretty sure no one else noticed. "What happened to dads' night?"

"The single dads of us"—I gestured between Luke and me—"decided to embrace the single life by hitting the bars."

"What a coincidence," Presley said. "The single girls from dinner decided to do the same, and here we are."

"Here we are." I dug my hands into my pockets to avoid touching her the way I was dying to. I leaned closer, ever mindful of still appearing like I barely knew her. "It's loud in here."

Presley laughed and said, "Really loud."

"How was your dinner?" I asked.

"Oh, my God, so good. I had chicken fried steak and seven-layer chocolate cake."

"Cake, huh?"

"It was my birthday dinner. I felt cake was called for," she said, grinning, but I was caught up on the first part of that.

"It's your birthday?"

She nodded. "Number thirty-six. Apparently I'm suddenly too old to have kids."

"Do you want kids?" I asked her casually, as if just making conversation with my client in a random bar run-in. In truth I imagined making babies with her, and damn if the temperature in this place didn't suddenly shoot up to inferno level.

Presley shrugged. "I'm not against kids, but I don't see it happening any time soon."

"You've got the bedrooms for when you're ready," I said. I immediately realized that was a dumb thing to say when I remembered being in one of those bedrooms with her. I took a drink of my cold beer, but it didn't do much to cool me down.

"That's true," she said. "Three bedrooms once I move downstairs. I guess I better get busy fast to pop them out before I age out."

"Just do like I did and have a couple in one go."

"You're a smart man, West Aldridge," she said, laughing.

I liked it too much when she complimented me, even if it was teasing. I cleared my throat and excused myself to go to the restroom. Maybe I'd stick my head under the faucet to cool the hell off while I was there.

When I came back from the restroom, Presley, Luke, and Kemp were gone from their spot. I glanced around for them and found the three of them with Anna, Maeve, and Ty Bishop at one of the dartboards. I knew it would be smarter to wander off and see who else was here, but Bishop was standing too damn close to Presley.

I made my way through the crowd to Presley's other side and taunted Luke as he finished his turn, acting as if all the nerves in the side of my body by Presley weren't on edge, begging for me to brush up against her.

Luke bombed his last throw. As he collected his darts, he said, "Bishop, you're up."

"Are you playing?" I asked Presley.

She nodded. "My first time ever and it shows."

I noted the scoreboard and saw there were three scores. "Teams?" I asked.

Presley nodded. "I'm with Ty."

A growl rumbled deep inside me, though it didn't seem to be audible above the crowd. Just as well. I didn't have the right to growl about who she was paired up with, for darts or otherwise.

Maybe her being paired up with Bishop was what spurred my next poor decision. Whatever the cause, I didn't stop and think about it before I leaned closer to her ear and said, so no one else could hear, "Any chance we could get together later? I feel like I should give you a little something for your birthday."

I straightened and acted as if I'd just given her a benign tip for throwing a dart instead of angling for a hookup. I felt her glance up at me, but I watched Bishop, the motherfucker, throw a bull's-eye.

Presley leaned against me and pulled me down so she could say something in my ear. "As I recall, it's not a *little* something, but I'd be very interested in it."

I couldn't wipe the grin off my face as I straightened again.

Bishop could have all the bull's-eyes with the dartboard he wanted. I'd be the one lucky dude hitting the best target of all later tonight.

———

I managed to hang out for another forty minutes at the Fly before I couldn't play it cool for another second. Through some inconspicuous text exchanges, Presley and I pulled off a ruse that she had a headache and wanted to go home, and I happened to be leaving at the same time and would give her a ride.

I'd give her a ride, all right. And then I'd give her another ride.

We walked down the sidewalk toward the side street where I'd parked with a foot or two between us, making small talk the way two almost-strangers would.

I opened the passenger door for her, then went around to the driver's side, scanning the area as I did, reassuring myself there was no one out and about on this sleepy street. After I climbed in and shut the door, I leaned across the console, angled her chin up, and kissed the hell out of her. I kept it short but intense, then broke contact.

"I've been dying to do that for the past hour. Maybe five," I said as I started the engine. No sense wasting time here when we could be in her bedroom in five minutes.

"Your girls are in Nashville?" she asked, her voice sounding a little breathy.

I nodded as I pulled away from the curb.

"Can we go to your place?"

I stopped at the stop sign and didn't start up again as I looked over at her. "Why my place?"

She shrugged. "You've seen my place, way down to the innards of it, and I don't even know where you live."

"My house isn't much to see. Just a little place I rent."

Presley put her hand on my forearm. "I don't care if it's a shed in someone's backyard. I'm just curious."

I studied her, wondering how she'd react to the two-bedroom house that would fit in her living room. I wasn't embarrassed by my modest house, but it was far from the luxury she was used to, even if she *had* grown up poor.

"West." Her tone said I was being an idiot. "Do you have a decent bed?"

I laughed. "My place it is."

This was a hookup, not a marriage proposal.

Minutes later, I pulled into my one-car garage, noting that the neighbor's house on this side was dark, telling me Mrs. Lansing had gone to bed.

Presley and I made our way out of the narrow unattached garage. I punched in the code to close it, then put my hand at her waist to usher her into the house.

We entered the kitchen, and I flipped a light on, glancing around to see what state I'd left it in. It was pretty tidy, save for my breakfast dishes in the sink.

"This is cute," Presley said.

Laughing, I said, "The cabinets are from the early sixties, the linoleum on the floor probably has asbestos in the lining, and your laundry room is twice as big."

"But it's clean and cozy, and look how cute these place-mats are."

The placemats at each of the four spots at the table had rainbows and sparkles and were personalized with the girls' names. Mine said *Daddy* as the girls had insisted.

"I think you'll like my bedroom better," I said, pulling her closer.

"There's only one way to find out."

I laced our fingers together and led her through the living room to my bedroom, which was less than twenty steps.

My door was across from the girls' bedroom, with the single bathroom in between.

"I'm going to stop in here," she said, pointing at the bathroom.

"I'll be waiting," I told her and went into my room.

It too was clean. I'd made the bed as I always did, and my dirty clothes were all in the hamper in the closet. The sheets were relatively clean but not nearly the thread count she was used to. Nothing to do about that except give her so much pleasure she didn't give a single thought to what the sheets felt like.

Skipping the overhead light, I went to the nightstand and switched the lamp on low. I opened the drawer a few inches, dug to the back, and located the box of condoms as I heard the toilet flush and the bathroom sink run.

I slipped my shoes off, put them in the closet, then closed it. It was neat, but a woman like Presley would be appalled at how small it was.

When she didn't immediately appear in my room, I glanced out to see she'd flipped the girls' light on and was looking at their room from the hallway. She turned the light off and pivoted toward me as I approached.

"That's the coolest little-girl room I've ever seen," she said. "Where did you get that bed set?"

I peered down at her with a grin.

"You made it, didn't you?" she asked.

"I made it."

It was a custom full-over-full-size bunk bed shaped like a playhouse with a slide and stairs to the upper level. The window cutouts had curtains hanging in them, and there was a partial pitched roof over the top level.

"That's every kid's dream, West. And I love the glow-in-the-dark stars on the ceiling."

"Couldn't forget the stars," I said.

I tugged her away from the girls' doorway into my room and closed the door, then pulled her into my arms.

"You're kind of amazing, you know that?" she said, peering up at me. "There's so much care and love in this house. That's a hundred times more important than the size of it."

"That's not what she said," I joked.

Presley laughed as I'd hoped she would because I loved the sound of it. "You and I both know good dads are hard to come by. Scarlet, Sienna, and Nova are lucky to have you."

I leaned down to kiss her, my reply a grunt because I didn't know what to say to that. Her reaction to our little house made me like her all the more. Too much.

At that uncomfortable thought, I opted for distracting myself with something a lot more enjoyable.

"Slip your panties off for me, Presley."

Her brows shot up, but after a heartbeat, she toed her sandals off, lifted her skirt, slid her fingers under the sides of her underwear, and shoved it down her legs. As her skirt fell back in place, she stepped out of her panties, leaving a delicate pile of the softest, most feminine shade of pink lace and silk.

My blood pounded hard to my dick. "Good girl. Now sit on the edge of the bed."

She took a single step to the bed and did as I said.

Her cheeks were flushed as she lifted her gaze to me. Then I did what I'd been fantasizing about all night. I dropped to the floor, crawled between her legs, and ducked my head under her skirt, settling right between her legs.

———

Hours later, I woke up disoriented.

Presley was curled into my side, naked, sound asleep. In my bed.

As I rolled to check the time on my phone, the past few hours refilled my head. I'd made her fly apart no less than three times before sinking into her gorgeous body and finding my own release. Afterward we'd lain there, talking quietly about a wide range of topics until apparently both of us had drifted off.

That was crossing a line I knew better than to cross.

It was going on four thirty, and the sky was starting to lighten. I sat up, alarmed.

Presley rolled to her back. "What's wrong?"

I rotated to the side and stood. "I need to get you home before the sun comes up."

She sat up, and I could see her just enough that I could make out her pushing her mane of hair out of her face as she glanced around, as if getting her bearings.

"Right," she said eventually, but I wasn't sure she was on the same page as me.

"If we don't want people to know..."

"Yeah." Her voice was sleepy and so sexy I froze for a second, wondering if I was the dumbest man alive. Presley Holiday was naked in my bed, and I was going to have her get dressed so I could sneak her out?

I shook my head, clamping down on my imagination. The second the world found out we were sleeping together, everything would change. I liked things just the way they were. Secret. Sexy as fuck. Safe.

I dressed quickly, pulling on athletic shorts and a T-shirt.

Presley threw the covers off, then stretched from head to toe. Even though the light was poor, I could see just enough to go rock-hard.

"Are you trying to get me back in that bed?" I asked.

She grinned. "I wouldn't be opposed."

Seconds ticked by as I fought with myself. How long would a quickie take?

Fuck. I wanted more than a quickie with Presley. I wanted hours with her. More.

An alarm went off in my head at that single word: more.

This was what I did. I rushed in. Wanted too much too fast.

This thing with Presley was not *that*.

"If I get you home now, you have time to sleep some more before we get started at the shop," I said.

She rolled out of bed, planted a kiss on my lips, picked up her clothes from the floor, and disappeared to the bathroom.

I blew out a breath and reminded myself I was fine. This was fine. I was a goddamn grown-up, and while my pattern was to rush in, this time I was taking meticulous care not to.

Chapter Twenty-Two

Presley

Kayaking with three little girls was a lot different from kayaking alone at dawn.

Paddling by myself right after the sun rose was peaceful, centering, almost meditative. Watching nature come alive for a new day was a different adventure each time. A way to relax that kept me busy and involved at the same time.

Taking three girls out near sundown was loud, chaotic, and at times hilarious.

I wasn't complaining. In fact, I seemed to have invited chaos into my life in multiple ways lately.

Like adopting three kittens, for example.

Told you. Chaos.

I'd been planning on a dog. When I'd visited the shelter yesterday, I'd filled out paperwork for a dog. And then I'd seen one of the volunteers holding the cutest little kitten, and something about its eyes had stolen my heart.

The mostly white kitten had a few dark spots and hints

of gray tabby marks on its head. The volunteer took me back to visit its two littermates, and I was a goner. The second one was mostly white too but had more and bigger spots, as well as more gray tabby markings on its head. The third one looked as if it'd been left in the color bucket even longer, with a white underbelly but gray tabby marks on its top half. They'd just been cleared for adoption a few hours before, and now they were my roommates: Mocha, Latte, and Chai.

Today was Friday, and I'd invited West and his daughters over to see the kittens and go kayaking after the workday—and yes, I'd bought one more kayak, this one teal and royal blue.

Nova and I were in the tandem boat. The girls had insisted West use the pink and purple kayak, and he was helping Sienna and Scarlet, in their individual boats, whenever they needed it.

As we made our way back toward my dock, Nova's paddling was slowing, as West had warned me it would.

"Miss Presley, look!" Nova said.

I looked where she was pointing on the shore and spotted a small animal, maybe raccoon size, but it wasn't a raccoon. "I see it," I said in a loud whisper, not wanting to scare it as it crawled over a large rock at the shore two lots down from mine.

"Daddy!" Nova whisper-shouted and pointed.

West nodded and pointed out the animal to Scarlet as Sienna said, "It's a groundhog."

"Hi, Hoggy," Nova said, forgetting to whisper.

"Nova, are you helping Miss Presley paddle?" West asked gently.

She took her time pivoting to face the front of the boat, then dipped her paddle in just enough to have a braking effect instead, making me laugh as the boat turned at an angle toward the shore.

"Oops, sorry," Nova said when she realized what she'd done.

"It's okay," I said. "We got this, Nova. Two more docks and we can visit Mocha, Latte, and Chai."

"Oooh," she squealed. "I can't wait."

We'd spent nearly an hour playing with the little beasts before heading out in the kayaks. I was sure the girls were getting hungry in spite of the string cheese they'd snacked on. West had promised them pizza from Humble's after our boating adventure. Since my kitchen was empty as usual, and it would look odd if I joined the four of them in public, I planned to get a pie for carry-out.

A lot had changed in the two weeks since my birthday. My home construction project was entering the last stages, with the main floor mostly done, just in need of a final detail here and there. West and his crew had a day or so of work in the bonus room above the garage, and they hoped to finish the boathouse and my new entertainment patio on the boathouse roof within the next week, weather permitting.

Since that first night at West's house, he and I had managed to steal time together in secret as often as possible. He was like an addiction. I couldn't get enough of him. It wasn't just the sex, though that continued to be superlatively, mind-blowingly good. We got along well even with our clothes on. When we worked at the shop together, time flew by even though I was doing the most physical labor I'd ever done in my life and had the chronically sore muscles to show for it.

My shop was coming together, and I waffled between sheer excitement and utter terror that I'd fail at this venture. What business did I have opening a coffee shop in this small town I'd only just moved to? I might know financing and accounting, but I had no experience in retail or marketing.

I'd find a way to make it work soon enough, I supposed. West estimated we could finish by the end of next weekend.

Nova chattered nonstop about groundhogs and kittens and fish and turtles and I wasn't sure what else the rest of the way to my dock. She went a mile a minute, and before I could respond to one thing, she was on to the next, so I mostly laughed and inserted a comment here and there between gentle reminders for her to paddle when she could.

"We're coming, kitties!" she shouted as we rounded the dock, and I guided the boat toward the shore.

"Stay seated while I get out and pull us farther in, okay?" I said to her.

Nova sang her affirmative answer, pulling yet another grin from me.

As I carefully climbed out, West and the twins were just passing the dock right before mine because Scarlet had tried to paddle closer to the groundhog—in spite of Sienna pleading with her to give the "poor baby" some space—then had trouble turning her boat around.

I pulled the nose of the kayak as far up onto the shore as I could get it, then helped Nova out into the ankle-deep water.

She was off like a shot as I worked to pull the long boat all the way out of the lake.

Nova galloped out onto the dock, ushering in the other three kayakers. "Daddy! Hurry up! The kitties are—"

A shriek rang out, and then a sickening thud sounded as Nova's head hit the dock.

I sprinted to the spot where she lay on her back, crying for all she was worth.

"I've got her," I called to West, who swore and paddled the last few feet to the shore in high gear.

I kneeled beside Nova, who rolled onto her side toward me, howling in pain.

"I'm here, sweetie," I said. "I've got you."

As I pulled her into my arms, I noticed the blood on the dock. Lots of blood.

"West!" I yelled, then asked in what I hoped was a more soothing, less panicked voice, "Where do you hurt, Nova?"

She wrapped herself around me and clung to me, sobbing too hard to reply. I found my answer when I cradled her head to me and felt the blood coming from the back, her hair soaked with it in one spot.

West hollered to the twins to paddle in and wait for him to help them out, then came up beside us and crouched down.

"I think she hit her head on the cleat," I said as I pieced it together.

"Oh, Nova, girl," he said, his tone full of love and concern as he checked out the wound I couldn't see.

I met his eyes over her head, my heart pounding. There was so much blood.

He inspected the wound. "That's a big one, baby girl," he said. "Come here, princess." He shifted so he could take her from me.

Nova clung harder to me, still sobbing, her head burrowed into my shoulder as she shook it just enough for me to discern.

"I've got her," I said, holding on tightly, wishing I could make her pain go away. "Do we need to take her to the ER in Nashville?"

"I suspect she needs stitches," he said. "Doc Julian can do it in his office here in town."

"Daddy, we need to get out," Scarlet called out. "Is Nova okay?"

"She's gonna be okay," he said, which made Nova cry harder. "Just give me a couple more minutes, girls. Nova, did you hurt anything besides your head?"

He had to coax an answer out of her, but she eventually shook her head.

"Let's get you standing up," he said to me. "You sure you won't come to Daddy, princess?"

Nova continued to sob but snuggled in closer to me. I lifted my brows at West, feeling a little bad that she wouldn't go to him, but not because I didn't want to comfort her. That she trusted me so completely was weirdly gratifying. I just wanted to help her feel better.

With a lot of help from West, standing behind me with his hands under my elbows, I stood with his daughter wrapped around me. Still behind me, he leaned over my shoulder and kissed his daughter and whispered comforting words to her, his hand on my back.

"Let's get her up to the house and get her life jacket off," he said.

The twins appeared at the end of the dock, their big eyes filled with concern. Their kayaks were pulled halfway onto the shore.

"Thanks for moving your kayaks up, girls," I said to them. "That's so helpful."

"Even if I told you to wait for me," West said, planting a kiss on Scarlet's head as he reached her, then doing the same to Sienna.

"I held Si-Si's boat. Then she held mine," Scarlet reported. "Then we both pulled them up as far as we could."

"You did good," West said. "Take off your life jackets,

head up to the house, and open the door for Miss Presley while I get the boats all the way out of the lake."

With Nova in my arms, I made my careful way up the path toward the house. The twins raced by me, giving us a wide berth.

"Are we going to Dr. Julian's office?" Sienna asked.

"I think so," I said.

Scarlet reached the house first and slid the door open.

"Can you go in the kitchen and grab a bunch of paper towels?" I asked her, hoping to clean some of the blood and staunch the flow.

Both twins raced inside.

As I reached the patio, West came up behind me and put his hand on my back.

"How are we doing, princess?" he cooed to his youngest, whose cries had lessened slightly in intensity.

"It...hurts...Daddy," Nova said between shaky inhales. "It hurrrrts." She cried harder into my shoulder.

West said into my ear, "I'm going to call the doctor's office so he and his nurse can meet us."

Scarlet brought us a handful of paper towels. West thanked her, pulled out his phone, dialed the doctor, and then gently dabbed at Nova's head as the call rang on speaker.

Eight minutes later, he helped me out of the back seat of his SUV, Nova still in my arms, the twins emerging from the other side.

"Do you want to take my keys and go home?" West asked me.

I shook my head. "I'm good. Let's get this little girl some relief."

With his hand on my waist as he stood behind me, he said into my ear, "Thank you. You're incredible."

To be honest, I was more than a little shaken, but I wasn't about to desert him. He had his hands full, and he had to be freaking out, even if he hid it.

He had a lot to handle all the time with these three but particularly so when something awful like this happened. But West didn't waver. He was the pillar of strength and comfort his daughters needed.

I couldn't help but wonder who was there for him when he needed a backup or extra reassurance.

Chapter Twenty-Three

West

Dr. Julian's nurse let us in the closed clinic and had us all wait in the lobby for the doctor to arrive. I sat next to Presley, feeling bad that she still carried Nova, but my daughter was glued to her, and Presley insisted she was doing okay.

Sienna and Scarlet scampered over to the kids' corner and played with the giant bead roller coaster even though they were probably too old for it. They were being calm and patient so far, which wasn't always the case.

"So this guy is always on call?" Presley asked in a hushed voice.

"I guess he is. Has been since I was a kid." I leaned over to look at my daughter's head yet again. The bleeding had slowed, and her sobs were down to an occasional hiccup.

There was nothing worse than your kid hurting, whether it was physical or emotional. I pressed a kiss to her head, far from the wound, and checked the time, as if that would get the doctor here faster.

Presley met my gaze and took her hand off Nova for long enough to rub my upper arm briefly. It didn't solve a thing, but that little gesture made it seem like, for once, I wasn't on my own with one of my daughters' challenges, even as I worried about keeping Presley here for too long when she might've had other plans.

"Whenever you need to go, let me know," I told her. "I can handle these princesses."

"I'm up for whatever I can do to help. If that means being a human bean bag chair, I'm on it," she joked, then kissed Nova's forehead.

Something in my chest dipped at that sight, but I didn't let myself think too hard about it.

"Daddy, are we gonna be here for a long time?" Scarlet asked across the room.

"It's gonna take a bit for Doc Julian to look Nova over and mend her up."

"I'm hungry," Scarlet said.

"Me too," Sienna chimed in.

That's when the time registered. It was going on seven o'clock. String cheese didn't go that far.

"We'll get you some dinner soon," I told them.

"Pizza!" Scarlet jumped up and down.

"Shh. We'll see what time we get out of here."

"Why don't I take the twins to get carryout?" Presley said. "I can take them to your house until you're done here. If it gets late, they can put their pajamas on."

I studied her face for any reservations, because what she was offering was a lot.

Scarlet skipped over to us. "Please, Daddy? We can show her our house and our bed you made us."

I was used to doing everything for my girls by myself,

but tonight was tricky. My instinct was to question Presley again, but I saw nothing but sincerity on her face.

"Let me help," she said, as if she could read my mind and knew my doubts.

Not even their own mother would go out of her way so much.

I knew the longer this took, the more impatient Sienna and Scarlet would become, and who could blame them? There weren't many worse places to spend your Friday night than in the doctor's office.

I nodded once, hoping I wouldn't regret this, but it was for the twins' good to accept. "If you really don't mind, that'd help a lot. The squirrels get restless when they're hungry. Nova, it's time for Daddy to get his hugs now so Miss Presley can take care of your sisters."

Nova slowly turned her head toward me, her eyes red and tear filled, cheeks pink. She started to sit up, and I reached over to take her from Presley. It wasn't until I had my girl in my arms that I could see the red stain of blood on Presley's shirt.

Presley noticed it the same time I did. "Oh," she said. "That's a problem."

I angled Nova so I could dig in my pocket for my keys. "There's a sweatshirt in the back of my truck you can pull over that. The girls can show you how to get to our place," I said, pretending she hadn't been there overnight two weeks ago. I told her our usual order—no meat on Sienna's—and went for my wallet.

"Dinner's on me," Presley said. "I've been wanting to treat these pretty girls to some pizza."

"I'll pay you back later," I said.

"We'll discuss it later. How will you get home though?"

"I'll figure that out. If Jagger's around, he'll drop us off."

"Text me if you need anything or think of anything I can do to help," she said as she stood.

The twins raced over to her as if she were a magnet.

As Nova settled her head onto my shoulder, I met Presley's gaze and hoped she read the gratitude in my eyes. "Thank you. Girls, Miss Presley's in charge. Do what she says."

Presley leaned down close, close enough I caught her sweet scent, and kissed Nova's cheek. "You're a brave girl, sweetie. We'll save you some pizza and see you soon."

"Bye." Nova's voice was weak, as if she was exhausted, which I was sure she was.

I watched two thirds of my trio head for the door, one on either side of Presley, just as the nurse appeared and called us back.

Nine stitches and an hour and a half later, I carried Nova into our house. The good news was she didn't have a concussion, and Doc Julian had given her pain meds so she was more comfortable.

The kitchen was clean, with no sign of pizza or dirty dishes. I could barely make out female voices coming from the girls' room, so I headed that way with Nova still in my arms.

The sight I came upon in their bedroom tugged at me, but I tamped that down, refusing to acknowledge it. The lights were off except for the girls' two reading lights in the full-size top bunk. Stretched out in their bed between them was Presley, all of them on their backs, so wrapped up in the book Sienna was reading out loud that they didn't notice we were home.

"Hey, ladies," I said quietly.

Scarlet sat right up. "Hi, Daddy. Hey, Nova. How are you feeling?"

She slid down the slide from the top bunk, the serenity of thirty seconds ago gone.

"Okay," Nova said, not lifting her head from my shoulder.

"Are you hungry?" I asked her. She hadn't complained about it, understandably.

"Mm-hmm."

Sienna zipped down the slide and came up to my side. "Hey, little sister. Welcome home."

"Did you get stitches?" Scarlet asked.

I lowered Nova to the floor, trusting the twins to be gentle with her, as Presley moved to the top of the slide.

"You can use the stairs if you want," I told her.

"Who would want to use stairs when you can slide?" she said, making the girls giggle.

Presley slid down and stood gracefully.

"Why don't you girls take Nova to the kitchen and get her some pizza." As they headed off, I told Presley, "Jagger's waiting to give you a ride home."

"Perfect. You won't have to take the girls out again. What did the doctor say?"

I told her there was no concussion and nothing except one whopper of a cut. "We got lucky."

"So lucky. I'm so sorry the evening ended that way, West."

"Me too, but they had a great time until then."

"I did too. I'll let you get to the rest of your night. I don't want to keep Jagger waiting."

"Presley." I grabbed her hand as she went past me to the living room.

She stopped and faced me.

"Thank you. I'm used to handling everything by myself. You did more for them tonight than their mother has done for them in months."

"You don't need to thank me. I'm glad I could help."

Our eyes met and locked. I wanted to kiss her so fucking bad, but the girls' voices in the kitchen reined me in.

Presley lifted our hands, still entwined, and kissed the back of mine. "Good night, West. I hope you all sleep extra well. And if you can't make it to the shop tomorrow, it's okay. Take care of your girls."

"We should be okay. My mom will give her as much TLC as I would. Probably more."

She dropped my hand and headed for the front door. I followed her, closed the door after her, then turned to find Sienna standing in the doorway to the kitchen, watching me.

"Are you gonna marry Miss Presley, Daddy?" she asked in a quiet voice.

The question had the effect of another emergency, pumping adrenaline through me in an instant.

"No, Si-Si," I answered, rallying my brain cells to head this off gently. "Miss Presley is a friend and a customer and that's all. Did Nova get some pizza?"

"Scarlet's helping her."

"Let's go keep her company while she eats," I said, holding out my arm.

Sienna and I went into the kitchen, where Scarlet was pouring Nova a glass of milk as Nova answered her questions. I wouldn't be able to recall what they said if you paid me, as my brain was in alert mode.

I was getting too comfortable with Presley. Our secret fling was spreading into real life, into my girls' lives, and that was a nonnegotiable no, regardless of how much I liked her.

Her construction projects would both be finished in less than two weeks. I wasn't ready to walk away cold turkey right now, but I'd make sure to be by the time the work was done. Hard stop.

Chapter Twenty-Four

Presley

Hair day in Dragonfly Lake was a different experience for me.

Going to the salon here was a social event, where you could gather advice from well-meaning women and catch up on the latest around town. Posh, Emerson's salon, was one of those rare places where a sisterhood could be formed with near strangers over the course of a couple of hours.

In Nashville, I'd gone to the same stylist for several years, but I barely knew her and vice versa, because I'd generally worked while I was in the chair.

I couldn't fathom doing that here. Burying my head in work and missing out on the wide range of conversations at Posh would be a sacrilege.

It was Wednesday, just after five p.m. Chloe and I had appointments together, with Emerson doing her cut and highlight and Willow doing mine in the next chair over. Gradually the other stylists had finished their workdays, told everyone goodbye, and taken off for the evening, leaving just the four of us.

Willow was sharing tales of her eleven-year-old daughter's crush on the boy who lived next door to them, which prompted us to share our own embarrassing pre-adolescent crushes.

"Mine was Holden," Chloe said.

"Really?" Emerson met Chloe's eyes in the mirror, pausing in the middle of foiling a section of hair.

"I wouldn't lie about that," Chloe said, laughing. "Have I never told you that before?"

"You've mentioned you had feelings for him in high school, but I didn't know they went back *that* far. And you're not sick of him yet?"

We all laughed.

"I didn't tell a soul back then," Chloe said. "I wouldn't dream of admitting that to my mom. Just goes to show how much your daughter trusts you, Willow."

Willow grimaced as she sectioned off another chunk of my hair. "I hope that can somehow continue once hormones turn her into a teenage monster."

"I hear you," Emerson said. "That's getting closer for us too with Evelyn."

"You both seem to have built a solid foundation with your daughters," I said. "Obviously I know nothing about parenting, but logic says that's the first step."

"Yeah, except logic goes out the window with kids," Willow said.

"Amen," Emerson said.

"You make me want to run right out and have six of them," I joked.

My phone buzzed with a text, so I pulled it out to

check. My heart did a little dance step when I saw West's name.

> West: The fixtures and railings for the rooftop patio were just delivered.

He must still be at my house, finishing up.

> Presley: How do they look?

He sent a wide-eyed, nonsmiling emoji that I'd always interpreted as WTF.

I frowned, waiting for him to say more.

> West: Did you order these?

A photo appeared of a heavy, bronze, medieval-looking light fixture that made me think of Conan the Barbarian or some other masculine grunter who drank mead in steins.

> Presley: That would be a no.

Levi had been the one to order the fixtures I'd picked out for the top of the boathouse two or three weeks ago since I added that to the project after the fact. Apparently West hadn't seen the order.

> West: I didn't think so. These and some similarly chunky railings are what we got. These aren't your style at all.

I laughed.

> Presley: What is my style?

West: You love silver fixtures, but I'm betting for outside, with your gray and white house, you went with a sleek black something or other.

I couldn't help grinning because he'd nailed it.

Presley: Yes and yes. Do you know all your clients this well?

He sent an emoji of a disturbed face.

West: No, ma'am. You're special. I'm going to see if I can track down what happened and get the right products here. Probably not till tomorrow since it's after five.

Presley: My hero.

West: I'll show you hero.

I grinned hard. I *loved* that he knew me so well. And called me special. And sent a veiled, suggestive message.

"Who are you texting with?" Chloe asked.

Meeting her gaze in the mirror, I realized she was raising a brow at me.

"My contractor."

Chloe repeated, "Your *contractor?* You mean the big, burly, hot guy you have a mad crush on?"

I wasn't much of a blusher, but I felt my face go hot, and I couldn't wipe my smile away.

"West, I assume?" Emerson asked.

I fake-glared at Chloe. "Thanks for outing me, friend."

"Is this West Aldridge?" Willow asked.

I made eye contact with my stylist, who I'd just met an hour ago, and pressing my lips together, nodded.

"I can see why you'd crush on him," Emerson said.

"He's got the tool belt thing going on," Chloe explained, and the other two nodded knowingly.

"I was apparently the last woman alive to understand the tool belt thing," I said.

"But you get it now," Willow stated rather than asked.

"Oh, I totally get it now." I noticed Chloe looking at me curiously. "What?" I asked her.

"Has it progressed to more than a crush?" she asked.

I glanced around even though I knew we four were alone. "This is one of those 'what's shared at the salon stays at the salon' moments, right?"

Emerson made a zipping-her-lips motion.

Willow said, "Mum's the word."

"Really, it has to stay secret because of his kids," I said.

"Oh, that's interesting," Chloe said knowingly. "We won't tell anyone you slept with him."

Sounds of approval arose from the two stylists, making me smile harder.

"Sleep*ing*. And *not* sleeping," I clarified.

"I knew it," Chloe said. "You've been quieter lately."

"I *have* been busy building a coffee shop," I pointed out.

"With your hot builder sex toy."

"Don't objectify him like that," I teasingly scolded.

"He's more than just a handsome face?" Willow asked.

Everyone went quiet as I got caught up in thinking about the question.

"He's a lot more than just a handsome face." I said it in all seriousness, trying to sort through my thoughts. My... feelings. "It was supposed to be a one-time thing."

"It's more?" Willow asked, her tone telling me she understood.

I nodded. "He's... Oh, God. I just like him. A lot. He's just...good."

All three of them howled and made suggestive comments, which made me laugh.

"Absolutely that, but also he's a good human. A kind person. A badass on the outside and a marshmallow when it comes to his girls. But he's a wonderful father, not a pushover."

I told them about Nova's injury and how West had been so in control even though I could tell by looking at him he was worried to his core.

"Wait," Chloe said, "he and his daughters were at your house on a social visit?"

"To see the kittens," I explained, because how could I adopt three kittens and not invite those little girls over?

"And go kayaking," Emerson added.

"They were so taken by my colorful kayaks. I promised them we'd take them out." I grinned. "They decided my tie-dye ones are superior to Jagger's 'ugly orange ones' at the marina."

"There are definite feelings involved here," Emerson said.

"And not just about boat colors," Chloe added.

"I was just thinking this doesn't sound like your average hookup guy," Willow said.

I felt Chloe staring at me through the mirror again. I dared to meet her gaze. She narrowed her eyes, assessing. Making me squirm.

"What?" I said.

"I've never seen you like this. You're, like...bubbly."

"Bubbly?" I asked in disbelief.

She tilted her head, and Emerson gently guided her back to where she needed her.

"Sorry," Chloe said to Emerson. Then she came back to me. "Is this getting serious, Presley?"

Serious. What did that mean, exactly? I'd never had a serious relationship before, but... "I don't know. We started out as a fling."

"It sounds more like a relationship," Willow said, "when you spend time with his kiddos."

"And get bubbly when you talk about him," Emerson added.

"I'm not bubbly," I said. "I don't even know what that means."

"Like...lovesick," Willow said.

I laughed at her word choice.

"Are you falling in love?" Chloe asked in an incredulous tone.

"I..." I'd been about to deny that in a knee-jerk reaction. Presley Holiday didn't fall in love. "I wouldn't know the first thing about it. Lust? Yes. Love?" I made a face. "How do you even know when you fall in love?"

"You just...know," Emerson said.

The other two nodded.

"Not helpful," I said.

"Are you planning to end the fling when West finishes your projects?" Chloe asked.

"I hope not, but we haven't talked about what happens afterward. I see him seven days a week right now, for hours on end sometimes."

"Love is...feeling connected. Like partners in certain aspects," Emerson said.

I thought about how we'd teamed up when Nova got hurt.

"It's passion," Willow said. "Not only wanting to *F* his

brains out on the daily but feeling strongly about him as a whole person."

"It's showing interest in his interests and vice versa," Chloe said. "Like running a brewery because he likes beer."

We all laughed. "You always were more of a wine girl than a beer one," I said. And then she and Holden had hooked up and opened Rusty Anchor.

I thought about kayaking. I'd started that because West had mentioned boating. And he seemed more interested in coffee now, sampling different beans and blends I made with my home coffee machine, listening when I explained where it was from and what the flavor highlights were supposed to be.

"Ben makes me feel good about myself," Emerson said. "Like, in my head, I'm just a hot-mess hairstylist trying to hold things together and support my kids. He goes on about me being a kick-ass business owner, a rock star mom, that kind of thing. He makes me feel like I'm a better me, if that makes sense." Emerson shrugged, seeming embarrassed as she picked up another foil strip.

"Yes," Chloe said. "Holden does that too. Like, the things we don't give ourselves enough credit for, they point out how we're nailing it."

"West makes comments about how I don't let anything stand in my way. I'll do something because it's what I need to get done, but he points out that I 'do the hell out of it.'" I melted the way I did every time he complimented me like that.

"None of that sounds like *just* lust, my friend," Willow said.

"I don't know what to do with that," I said, feeling slightly panicky. "Love? Seriously. Foreign concept."

Willow laughed. "That's how it is the first time."

"And the second," Emerson said. "Maybe even more so the second time."

I looked to Chloe, because she knew me better than anyone, and in fact, she'd been so similar to me. Until Holden.

"Any idea how he feels?" Chloe asked.

I grinned. "Pretty sure he likes when I'm naked."

Everyone laughed and made indecent comments, which made us laugh harder.

That. That was the sisterhood. It felt amazing, even if the topic was freaking me the hell out.

"It sounds like you and West need to have a heart-to-heart," Emerson said when we calmed down.

"You want me to just blurt out to my contractor that I might love him?" I asked, trying to make light of this scary topic.

"I know what's going on in your head," Chloe said. "You're all about controlling as much as you can in your life. Emotions aren't always in our control."

"Especially not the *L* word," Emerson added.

"I don't know how to do love," I told them. "I don't know what happy looks like."

"Hello." Chloe waved as if to say *right here.*

Emerson waved too with the biggest smile, which spoke of her blissful, first-year-of-marriage state.

"And Rowan," Chloe said.

"She and Chance are so cute," Emerson said. "I can't wait to see him with a newborn."

"Your parents screwed you up in your head," Chloe said matter-of-factly, "but there are healthy relationships all around."

I thought about that day at the Honeysuckle Festival with all the crazy-in-love Henry siblings and nodded.

"So say I figure out I'm in love with him. How do I tell him? When do I tell him?" I asked, wondering who could draw me a diagram.

"If he says it first, it's pretty easy," Willow said.

"And if he doesn't?" I asked.

Chloe met Emerson's gaze in her mirror, looked at Willow, then shrugged. "You're smart," Chloe said. "You'll know when it feels right."

I wasn't sure what I felt for West was love, but I had a sneaking suspicion it might be.

He made me feel protected, cherished, and cared for. Even though we were different in some ways, I could be myself with him. We just meshed well whether we were installing flooring, entertaining his kids, or getting naked. I liked nearly everything about him. Loved?

Maybe loved.

I sure as hell didn't like the amorphous phrase *when it feels right.*

I was a numbers girl at heart. Black-and-white. Definable. Profitable versus in the red. High-quality coffee versus crap.

When it feels right?

I couldn't begin to wrap my head around that nonspecific concept. And honestly? I wasn't sure if it would *ever* feel right to tell West I'd broken the unspoken rules of our secret fling and fallen in love.

Chapter Twenty-Five

West

We dudes had a reputation for falling asleep right after sex. With my quirky Presley though, she was the one who drifted off.

Correction: not *my* quirky Presley.

I figured it was because the only time she ever slowed down was post orgasm.

We were at her house post orgasm, having broken in her new living room sectional, late Saturday night. Our last Saturday night.

I came down from bliss a little faster than normal, a heaviness in my chest, as Presley lay between me and the back cushion, her breaths coming slowly, evenly. She'd put her kittens to bed in the utility room, which was their headquarters until they got bigger, so it was just me and my heavy thoughts as she dozed.

After nearly seven weeks, her home construction project was basically finished. The fixture order had been mixed up with another local order, so we were able to get the right pieces in the next day. All that was left was whatever punch list Presley came up with over the next couple of weeks.

Her shop was nearly done as well, at least regarding my part of the project. We planned to finish the fixtures, cabinet pulls, and last items tomorrow. She'd be receiving the furnishings and supplies over the next week or two, and then she'd be ready to open.

The fact was, she was done with my construction services.

It was time for us to be done with...*us*.

Since Nova's injury, my daughters had talked nonstop about her—Miss Presley this and Miss Presley that. After only a few hours with her, they were getting attached, as my mom had pointed out they were apt to do.

My body tensed every time I thought about it, until I reminded myself no damage had been done. Yet.

I'd reassured them, after Sienna's marriage question Friday night, that Miss Presley was just being friendly while I worked for her. That we'd probably see her around town from time to time, but she was just a casual acquaintance.

"Hey, you," Presley said drowsily, her eyes opening halfway. The wall of windows facing the lake let in full moonlight tonight, allowing me to see her beautiful face. "Why don't you stay over? We can move to my bed."

Shit.

There was a part of me that wanted nothing more than to spend the night in her bed, wake up with her in my arms, go down on her before her eyes were open. That's what I did...I rushed in. When my dick was involved, my brain took a back seat.

"We should probably talk," I said in a quiet voice, as if

maybe it would only suck half as much if I said what I had to say quietly.

"Yeah?" Her lips stretched into a sleepy smile, telling me she wasn't reading me right.

I closed my eyes for a moment and inhaled the scent of her hair that brushed over me, as if I could stock up on her softness. Then I forced myself to sit up and settle near her feet. I tossed the ridiculously soft throw blanket her way in case she wanted to cover up and pulled on my boxer briefs.

Presley sat up and pulled the blanket around her. "What's going on, West?"

"We haven't talked about what happens now that my work here is done."

"Right. I was thinking about that earlier," she said.

"We need to cut ties, Presley. I'm not in the position to test-drive a real relationship."

She frowned. "I didn't know this was fake."

Hell, two sentences in and it was already coming out wrong.

"It's not fake. But it's secret, and there's a reason for that," I said.

"Your kids," she said, frowning. "I like your daughters, West. I thought we got along pretty well last Friday. Did they not—"

"My daughters are big fans of you, which is the problem."

"You're breaking it off with me because your daughters like me?"

"I've explained why, Presley."

"You don't want them to get hurt in your breakups. So if they like me and you're getting rid of me, won't they be upset?"

"They know you as my client and friend. They haven't

moved you into the mother figure slot yet." They'd been headed down that path though. After basically one evening with her.

Wrapping the blanket more tightly around her, Presley moved closer to me on the sectional, facing me. "What if I told you..."

I met her gaze in the moonlight, her pretty eyes reflecting earnestness and insecurity at once as I waited for her to finish her thought.

"I'm pretty sure I'm in love with you, West."

Ah, fuck.

I'd known this was going to suck, but the thought of hurting Presley wrenched my gut. My lids lowered as I tried not to think too hard about her declaration or what it *could* mean if I were in a different situation.

"I can tell you don't feel the same," she said, straightening, then tilting her head back.

"I'm not in the position where I can go there, not with anyone. I explained why—"

"You're protecting your daughters," she said, her voice hardened. "From a family."

"That's not what I'm protecting them from, and you know it. I'm protecting my family from more heartbreak. More painful transitions."

"So you don't feel anything for me?" she asked, her eyes glistening.

"I feel all kinds of things for you, but I can't let myself fall in love." I stood, because looking into her eyes was killing me. "That was never the plan."

I wanted her, but when you were a father, your wants weren't the priority.

"My girls are everything," I said. "You and I... The only

reason I gave in to our chemistry was because we agreed it was temporary."

"I don't have a lot of experience with relationships," she said, her voice husky with emotion. "Obviously I'm naive, because I thought maybe you'd change your mind if we developed feelings."

"I've learned that feelings early on don't equal the same feelings a few months later. That's where my girls get their hearts crushed."

"So you're planning to be alone until...what? Nova graduates from high school? They're all grown up and don't know how to handle it when a guy breaks their heart because they've been so protected all their lives?"

That stopped me for several seconds. "I hope they never have their hearts broken by a guy, but if they do, it's because of their decisions, not mine. That's different. I can't prevent that, short of locking them in the house for twenty years, but I can prevent my relationships from hurting them."

"By not having any relationships." She shook her head. "What about your *happiness*? What if you could be happier because of a relationship? Wouldn't that in theory make you an even better dad?"

"I don't have that luxury," I told her, thinking back on April, my ex.

She'd made me happy at first, but by the end, I'd barely blinked an eye on my own behalf when she left me. It had occurred to me after the fact that she hadn't made me very happy once the newness wore off.

I couldn't keep speeding into relationships, crossing my fingers that none of us would get hurt. I'd proven we would, and by *we*, I really meant my kids. I could weather a breakup, but their tender hearts suffered when yet another someone they loved left them.

"I'd never intentionally hurt your daughters, West," she said.

"No one ever means to hurt the kids, but sometimes they're the ones who get hurt the worst."

"You know," Presley said, "part of what I love about you is that you're such a good father. I applaud you for considering your kids' feelings, but did you ever think that maybe instead of protecting them from getting hurt—because you *can't* protect them from everything, no matter how much you want to—that being a good father is more about helping them navigate their feelings when life throws a curveball? Isn't that what they'll need to function as adults in this world?"

"Of course they'll need that," I snapped, sitting forward. "I just won't be the cause of their hurt again if I can help it. I'm all they have, Presley. They're going to grow up knowing they can count on me to do my best by them."

"I would think showing them how to go after their own happiness would be doing your best by them."

I found my pants and pulled them on. No matter what she said, she wouldn't change my mind.

Presley stood, hooking the blanket around her like a long towel. She wandered to the window and looked out, her back to me, her gorgeous locks a messy tumble down her back.

I forced myself to stop looking at her. I just needed to get out of here and close this chapter of my life. Figure out a way to forget about this woman and move forward with my girls.

Still facing away from me, she said, "I respect that you put your kids first, West, but I'm sad. I'm sad for your girls, who won't have a chance to have another person in their life who loves them. I'm sad for you too. And I'm sad for me."

"I'm sorry, Presley," I said from my heart.

She pivoted to face me, and as she did, a single tear spilled over the rim of her eye and poured down her cheek. She swiped at it with the same fierceness she did everything with.

Fuck.

That one little tear gutted me.

The one person, after my three children, who I never wanted to hurt was Presley.

I ached to go to her, hold her, comfort her, but I was the motherfucker who'd caused it. I no longer had the right to do anything for her other than finish up the project she was paying me for.

I grabbed my shirt from the coffee table and dragged it over my head. Without looking at her again, because I couldn't stand to see her upset, I said, "I'm sorry, Presley. I really am," and I let myself out of her house.

Chapter Twenty-Six

Presley

After West walked out of my house, I stood there gazing out my windows, clinging to my blanket, staggered by the turn my life had taken in the past half hour.

Twelve hours ago, I'd felt...bubbly and lighthearted and happy as West and I spent the day together working on the shop. We got along so well, worked together seamlessly, flirted, laughed, talked. He told me all about the trip he was planning to the beach with his daughters. I told him about the coffee suppliers I'd chosen for my first quarter in business.

Days at the shop with West, when there was no one else around, were like going on a long, very good date, except we worked instead of played.

It was also like nearly twelve hours of foreplay, so by the time we'd gotten to my house, we'd both been impatient and on fire for each other.

Though I'd hesitated to commit to calling my feelings

for him the *L* word on Wednesday with the girls at the salon, by Thursday there was no way to deny it. I loved him. Today I'd relished what it felt like to spend the day with the man I loved.

Lightning zigzagged in the sky in the distance, dragging me from my thoughts for long enough to drop my blanket and pull on boxers and a soft sleep tank, even if it was doubtful I'd sleep anytime soon. My brain was spinning, trying to make sense of West Aldridge.

I picked up my phone on the off chance he'd get home to his empty house and realize what a stupid move he'd made, then headed down to the shore to watch the storm roll in.

I went out to the end of the dock, taking in the moon, still bright and shining but on the verge of being cloaked by a bank of thick clouds. I sat on the wood surface, legs bent, my hands behind me for support as I watched the dramatic sky.

What the hell was West thinking to throw away something like what we'd shared?

I understood that when kids were involved, there was a lot to consider. I appreciated that he put his kids high on the priority list. That was such a foundational part of the person he was. I'd hate for him to be any other way.

But.

How could he think it was okay to deny himself something as good as what we had? Why couldn't both he and his kids be happy? How could he think it wasn't worth it to *try?* Because I could swear he had more than just lustful feelings for me.

His daughters were precious and full of life and seemed well-adjusted, considering how turbulent the mom scene had been for them. West had told me how much his ex-girlfriend moving out had upset them, especially Nova. How he'd wake up with anywhere between one and three of them in his bed each morning for the first few weeks after she'd left.

The picture he'd painted had absolutely ripped at my heart. I never wanted those three to feel like that again. That he'd just assumed I'd eventually leave and hurt them? Without giving us a chance?

I couldn't comprehend not wanting to at least try at something that had started out so good.

I knew there would be steps to take if we were to attempt a real, nonsecret relationship. So many steps, like making the jump from secret to public, easing his kids into the idea of us without them jumping to conclusions, and continuing to get to know each other. I didn't expect or even want a marriage proposal or an invitation to move in together. That's not where we were.

He'd shut us down before we had the chance to get there, and I wanted to shake some sense into his big, stupid self.

The tip of the cloud bank covered the moon as lightning flashed like a laser-light show. I lay on my back to enjoy the display, feeling the charge in the air as the wind picked up.

I stayed there for another twenty minutes, watching the weather change around me, feeling Mother Nature's drama in my heart, because my own life felt like a storm had come along and ripped the hell out of everything that made sense.

When the first raindrops hit me, I headed inside. The house felt like a mausoleum. A giant, empty, lonely mausoleum instead of a home. I strode to the utility room and opened the door, unleashing my tiny beasts. Call me a bad cat mom to let them out of bed at nearly midnight, but I needed company and comfort.

What I needed even more was girlfriend time and a bottle of wine.

I'd never experienced a breakup before, and I wasn't sure this could officially qualify as one since we'd only had a secret fling that started out with the intention of being short-term. My emotions were real though, so for me, this was a breakup. A heartbreak. And I longed for the support and commiseration of a girlfriend.

The clock on my new kitchen stove said ten till midnight.

I tried not to think about how much time West and I would still have left in this night together had I not mentioned moving to my bed or staying all night. The loss hurt too much.

I couldn't call Chloe and disrupt her whole house at this hour. No way would I bother seven-months-pregnant Rowan. But Magnolia had mentioned she was an insomniac.

With Chai, the lightest-colored kitten, in my arm, I pulled up Magnolia on my message app while Latte and Mocha scampered at my feet.

> Presley: Any chance you're awake?

The dots that showed she was typing appeared instantly. I'd never been so relieved to see those dots as I was now.

> Magnolia: But of course. What's up?
> Everything okay?

I sucked in a long, shaky breath. Magnolia didn't know about West and me. No one did except the three from the salon.

> Presley: It's a long story. Is it too late for a glass of wine?

> Magnolia: Not too late at all. What do you have in mind?

> Presley: I've got this big house, a few bottles of wine, and boy troubles.

> Magnolia: Send me your address. I'll be right over.

———

I'd planned to meet West at eight Sunday morning as usual to finish up the last construction details on the shop. Though there was a part of me that was tempted to skip it and let him labor through the final details himself, Magnolia and I had decided that wasn't how it was going to go down.

This was *my* shop, and I wasn't going to skip out on the work, nor was I going to let West think he'd broken me.

He'd broken my heart, yes. I'd spent hours last night bawling my eyes out as I spilled the story to Magnolia. But he couldn't dampen my determination or my anticipation for The Bean Counter.

"You've got the hungover-but-hot look down," Magnolia said as we walked down the sidewalk from the Dragonfly Diner toward my shop.

"Likewise, my friend." We'd both showered and thrown our hair up, then put on just enough mascara to look not dead. "I don't know how to thank you, Magnolia. You're going so far above and beyond for me..." My voice caught, but I pushed the tears down. Not today. I wasn't crying any more today.

Magnolia shrugged. "I'm glad you texted. No one should have to go through boy troubles—or any troubles—alone."

"That goes both ways."

I might have been doubtful of her when I first moved to town, but all doubts were gone. Whatever she'd done in the past, however she'd been before, now she was solid.

Solid was driving to my house at midnight in a downpour. Solid was sharing two bottles of wine and listening to me blubber about my very short story called West Aldridge while three pint-sized kittens crawled all over us. It was having a sleepover where we slept for no more than a few hours because of the wine and the talking. It was getting up extra early to hit the diner for breakfast, and it was Magnolia's offer to help me in the shop all day for moral support so I wouldn't have to be alone with West.

I'd already promised to spend at least as much time helping her with her business next door, but that was only the start of how grateful I was.

"Okay," Magnolia said, looping our arms together as we neared my shop door. It was quarter after eight, so chances were good West was inside already. The paper was still up, so I couldn't be sure. "Remember what we talked about," she continued. "You're calm. You're cool. This is business as usual. He might be hot, but he's stupid."

I laughed in spite of my dread. "I love you."

She leaned her head onto my shoulder. "Love you too. You. Got. This."

I opened the door to the shop, raised my chin just enough to remind me I was the boss of this place, and led Magnolia in. "Morning," I said in the blandest, most matter-of-fact tone without so much as a glance in West's direction, even though I was fully aware he was working to my right.

"Hello, West," Magnolia said in the most perfect "you've hurt my friend so we're now enemies" tone.

There was a slight pause before he said, "Hey," but I didn't stop to look at him.

Magnolia and I breezed back to my office, leaving him in the front room.

As she came all the way inside, she held up a hand for a high five, grinning. "You did great," she whispered. "Did you see how flustered he was?"

I shook my head. "I didn't look at him."

She pressed her lips together and nodded. "He's shook."

Donning my imaginary armor, I shrugged and said, "His problem."

"That's my girl." Magnolia glanced around. "Let's get started. What are we doing first?"

"We need to do all the doorknobs and most of the drawer and cabinet pulls in the kitchen. I think there's some outlet covers to finish. Little stuff like that."

"Show me how to do the pulls, and I'll do those?"

"That's a plan. Follow me."

As I led her out of the office, I once again kept my chin up. Out in the front area, West was on a ladder, working on the light fixtures. I confess I drank in his profile while his beefy arms were over his head and his shirt stretched up, revealing that trail of dark hair that led down his abdomen to the treasure in his pants.

Clenching my jaw, I averted my gaze and went into the kitchen that was a lot smaller now that all the counters and appliances were in place. There were lots of cabinets for storage. West and I had managed to install exactly two pulls last night before deciding to save them for today and then rushing to my house for...

Yeah. For the shit show that was last night.

I showed Magnolia how to attach the silver pulls on the drawers, then left her to it while I tackled the door-knobs. Back in my office, I pulled out my phone and searched for a short how-to video. This task wasn't complex, but I hadn't done it before. I had no intention of asking West.

I started with the door of the restroom closest to the front and gradually worked my way back toward my office. The three of us worked in a tense silence, each in our own spaces.

As I took the knob for my office out of the package, West sauntered into the room.

"Hey," he said in a private voice, the one he'd used with me for the past few weeks whenever we were alone and sometimes at my house when his crew couldn't hear. "How are you doing?"

My gaze snapped to his face, the intimacy of his voice making my chest hurt. I wasn't going there. He'd drawn the line last night, and I was staying fully on my side of it today and forever more.

"Just fine," I said curtly.

"Don't do that, Presley," he said in a quiet plea.

Something in me snapped. He had the nerve to plead with me?

This was his doing. He was now nothing more than my contractor.

"Are the light fixtures finished?" I asked, keeping my voice even, professional.

"Yes."

"What's left for you to work on?"

"Whatever you need me to help with. I can work on the pulls or the outlet covers."

"Magnolia and I can handle those just fine. You can go."

"If you let me know exactly where you want the shelves in the self-serve area, I could—"

"Just go, West. I'll pay you for a full day today. Send me the final invoice. I'll take care of it quickly. I'll give you good reviews wherever you need me to. Just...please, go."

He studied me with those astute green eyes, searching, as if waiting to see if I'd relent or soften.

I wouldn't.

After so many seconds ticked by, he nodded once. "Okay. I'll pick up my tools and ladder Tuesday evening."

I turned away from him and went back to my task as if he wasn't standing there.

He hesitated for one last moment, as if giving me a chance to...what? What the actual hell did he expect me to do right now? Beg him to give me another chance? Profess my undying love...again?

Too late. My love was pissed now, soon to be fading fast, I hoped.

I kept at the doorknob, my body tensed, my back to the rest of the shop.

He called out a goodbye to Magnolia, then walked out the front door.

I took a step back from the office door, tossing my screwdriver down and closing my eyes as I let the facade fall.

Magnolia came in and pulled me into a hug. We stood there like that while time ticked silently by, with me bracing against the emotional pain and her just holding on.

"I know that had to be hard, but you did so good," she said. "I want to be as strong as you when I grow up."

That made me grin. "I don't feel very strong."

"But you act strong, and sometimes that's what counts. It's just me here now, hon. I can lock the front door, and you can cry your eyes out or punch things if you want."

I straightened and shook my head. After sucking in a shaky breath, I said, "There will be no more tears shed over stupid boys today."

"Is it too soon to start up one of your brand-spanking-new coffee machines and make us some awesome java?"

"Brilliant idea." I marched out to the counter where my shiny, expensive machines were and busied myself brewing the first two coffees from The Bean Counter.

But just because there weren't tears didn't mean I didn't hurt like hell.

Chapter Twenty-Seven

Two weeks later

West

Everything was coming up roses, or whatever the damn saying was.

Today was Monday, my first day back at work after the weeklong trip we'd squeezed in. I'd just dropped off all three of the girls for their first day of school—Nova in her second year of preschool and the twins in second grade—so I was a few minutes late for work. Levi expected it. I drove toward the office for a post-vacation meeting with him.

My hard work on Presley's home renovation project had paid off. I'd gotten the promotion the week after it was finished. Better yet, so had Nick.

Levi had made us both foremen, saying he needed leadership as the projects kept coming in, and he'd committed to growing the company. We now had two full-time crews and were booked through the end of the calendar year. With the promotion came a healthy raise that I was thankful as hell for.

Presley was true to her word. I'd received the remaining balance on her coffee shop within three days of emailing her the invoice. As planned, I'd used the money for our first-ever family vacation.

Instead of choosing one of the places the girls were lobbying for—Colorado, the Grand Canyon, and Chicago—I'd chosen a neutral location they'd all love. We'd road-tripped to the Florida panhandle and spent six days on the beach. We nearly had to rent a trailer to haul back all the shells the girls collected, not to mention the souvenirs.

Witnessing their first experience with the ocean was something I'd never forget. Their sheer joy, their wonder at its vastness, their shrieks as they dipped their toes into the saltwater... Worth every minute of *Are we there yet, Daddy?*

We'd gone on a dolphin tour and a sunset cruise. We'd eaten at beachside restaurants and taken picnics to the beach. We'd swum at the hotel pool every day and built sandcastles on the shore. The girls had thanked me countless times for taking them.

I couldn't have asked for a better experience for our first trip as a family of four.

As many good memories as we'd chalked up though, I could fully acknowledge that my heart had only been fifty percent in it. Just admitting that to myself made me want to punch things.

I parked at Dawson Construction and headed inside, forcing the scowl off my face. The girls had accused me of *being sad* for the past two weeks, an accusation that bowled me over because I'd thought I was hiding my inner bullshit from the world.

Kids picked up on all the shit you didn't want them to.

"There he is," Levi said as I walked into the office. "Welcome back, West. You were missed."

"Didn't much care for covering my crew, huh?"

"I'd gotten used to bouncing between the two crews, running sales calls, and filling in wherever you all needed. How'd we do this with half the employees before?"

"We had half the work then. Everything go okay?"

"Couple weather delays. Both crews are behind schedule."

"Sounds about right."

"Your guys are trying to get the roof on the Adler addition before the next round of storms. They started thirty minutes early today."

"Good to know. Supposed to be clear till tomorrow night?"

"That's what they're saying," he answered as he stood at his desk, gathering papers and picking up his tablet. "Hey, the coffee shop opened today. You want to head there and get a cup of joe while we discuss business?"

Damn. I'd seen on the Tattler app that today was Presley's soft opening, but my plan had been to stay far away from The Bean Counter.

"I'm not so sure I'd be welcome there," I said on a defeated exhale. It killed me to admit that out loud, but if I didn't put it out there today, I suspected it'd keep coming up.

Levi, who wore a Dawson Construction ball cap as he did close to three hundred sixty-five days a year, looked up from his desk and tilted his head at me. "What the hell, Aldridge?"

I sat down heavily, figuring it was time to come clean. I wasn't worried about the job aspect. I just did not want to revisit how much I'd fucked up in my personal life.

My boss watched me closely as he approached the round meeting table and sat across from me. "I suspected you had something going on with her," he said.

"Not the night of the wedding. It started after that."

"Not gonna lie," Levi said with a half grin. "I can see how that could happen. She's quite a force of nature and looks good while she's at it."

Levi was nearing forty, heterosexual, single, and had eyes, so his observation didn't surprise me.

I merely nodded, unable to find it in me to smile back.

His grin disappeared as he watched me. "Your face tells me it wasn't just a night or two of fun."

"It was supposed to be a night or two of fun."

"She hurt you in the end?"

I scoffed, not making eye contact. "You ready to get this meeting over with?"

"Not quite yet." He leaned his elbows on the table, his attention fully on me. "You were a grouchy son of a bitch the week before your trip, even after you found out about the promotion and the raise. I'm finally putting two and two together."

I scowled. He wasn't the only one who'd told me I was being a dick that week. Plus the *sad* label from my daughters. I knew it was true, but I couldn't seem to pull myself out of it.

"I fucked up. *I* hurt *her*," I said. "She wanted more but I said no."

He studied me so intently it was all I could do not to explode.

"Because of your girls," he guessed. He knew my story. All the guys who'd worked here last year when April moved out knew my story. Understood my regret for getting my daughters hurt. "Except you're hung up on her."

I narrowed my eyes at him. The dude was spot on, but it sucked extra to hear it out loud. "I thought I could walk away and be okay with it."

He blew out a breath. "Relationships are hard enough when it's just two people trying to figure it out. You throw in three kids..." He shook his head. "Exponentially complicated. I don't have any kids, and I sure as hell don't have a gleaming track record with relationships, but I know my brother, Max, had a hard time letting Harper in because he was worried about his son."

"They seem to be doing okay," I said, remembering how happy Danny had been at Max and Harper's reception.

"But you don't think it would be okay to invite Presley into your daughters' lives?"

I braced my elbows on the table and ran my hands over my face, feeling so damn tired, as if I hadn't slept for a month. "My history with relationships says inviting her into our life would get my daughters hurt again in the end."

"How do you figure? Because April didn't work out?"

"April. Flora. I rushed in with both of them, and you know where it got me."

"I also knew April and Flora well enough to say with confidence there were reasons they didn't stick, and those reasons weren't because of you."

"How do you figure?"

He tilted his head again, the expression on his face looking like I was clueless. "Flora didn't fit in here. Never even *tried* to fit in here. She was never going to be happy in Dragonfly Lake."

"That should've changed when she got pregnant."

"But it didn't. That's on her, not you," Levi said. "I saw how hard you tried to make it work with her, West. You weren't the weak link. She just wasn't the right woman for you."

I snorted. "You're damn right about that."

"April was all wrong too."

"You think?" I said sarcastically. "I rushed in with both of them for different reasons." I shook my head, wondering if the regret, especially over April, would ever wear off. The only thing I couldn't regret was my three daughters, so as much of a mistake as it was to hold on to Flora for too long, it gave me the best parts of my life. "I make poor decisions with women." I shrugged, even though I didn't feel at all nonchalant about it.

"Is Presley a poor decision?" he asked. "Is she the same as the other two?"

"She's nothing like Flora or April," I said quickly. When I noticed how he was eyeing me, like he was waiting for shit to get through to my brain, I got his point. "You think I was just with the wrong people before."

"I know you were with the wrong people before," he said with a laugh. "You know it too."

That much was true.

"Question is," he went on, "is Presley right, and you're missing it because of your baggage?"

"I wouldn't know how to tell if she's right."

"I'm no expert, but it seems like you have deep feelings for her."

I glanced at my watch, noting how late it was getting.

My boss wasn't the first person I'd choose to discuss this with, but then I wasn't really a fan of discussing it with anyone. And yet I was sick to death of all the shit circling in my head with only me to try to make sense of it.

"Presley and I were supposed to be a simple fling," I said. "A one-time fling, if I'm being honest. Long story short, it didn't work out that way. We spent a lot of time together working on her shop. My girls didn't know we were more than friends, but they started getting attached to her anyway, so I ended it."

"Seems like you're not done with it though," he said insightfully.

"Seems like I'm a slow motherfucker who took a bit to realize what I feel for Presley is the real thing."

"You love her?"

"Pretty sure I do. Too fucking bad I figured that out after I hurt her."

"What'd you do?"

I told him how she'd said she loved me, and I'd responded by ending it. To protect my daughters.

"Your daughters who love her," he clarified.

I nodded.

"And she likes your girls too?"

Another nod.

"And you've caught feelings. And she loves you. West, what the fuck are you doing?"

"I know, man," I bit out. "I know."

He was saying all the shit that'd been coalescing in my head for the past few days.

The truth was, my feelings for Presley *were* different.

I'd been with Flora on and off for more than four years. When she'd finally left for good, my only concern was our daughters. My heart didn't get broken. It was more like I could finally breathe.

April? It'd been past time for our relationship to end. Had I not been a father, I probably would've ended it months earlier than we did.

With Presley?

Fuck. My girls didn't know anything had changed.

They were unharmed by the end of Presley and me. But me? I was fucking wrecked.

"Like I told you, I fucked up, and I don't know what to do about it."

"Fight for her. Try to get her to take you back."

"I'm not sure if she'll do that. She was pretty angry last time I saw her."

"You ever seen a chick flick?" he asked. "This is where they do the grovel."

I leaned forward and pressed my fingers into my temples. That last Sunday in Presley's shop, she wouldn't even answer a simple how-you-doing question. And dragging Magnolia along for the day? Yeah, I'd gotten the message loud and clear.

"Max's grovel was big and public," Levi continued.

"I was there. Public declaration in the diner at the height of the breakfast rush." It'd taken serious balls, but it had worked. "Our situation isn't the same though."

Levi shrugged. "Different grovel might be called for."

I didn't know the first thing about the different ways to grovel. All I knew was...I needed to try something. I could no longer lie to myself and say we were better off without her, because we weren't.

Presley was too important to me to not give this my best shot.

Chapter Twenty-Eight

Presley

My official grand opening day was Saturday, five days after the soft opening.

Planned by Magnolia, the day included hourly raffles to benefit the animal shelter, free reusable travel mugs with The Bean Counter logo, good for unlimited discounted fill-ups, and a photo backdrop tied to a social media giveaway.

By eight a.m., we'd sold out of our entire selection of savory breads, bagels, and English muffins.

By noon, we'd raised over five hundred dollars for the shelter.

By two p.m., my mind was blown, and my mood was elated, enthusiastic, and excited.

It seemed this town agreed with me on the need for good coffee, and that's what we served them.

We consisted of me and my three employees. Glenda Thomas was the fire chief's wife. She'd been a stay-at-home-mom of their son, but now that he was out of the house, she'd needed something to do with her time and wanted an extra income source.

Hadley Ballantine, the second youngest of the Ballantine family, had recently moved back home after college and a job in her field that she'd hated. She and Glenda were hoping for full-time hours at the shop.

My part-timer was Dalton Kaye, who was a senior in high school this fall and needed money for college.

We were open seven days a week, from six a.m. to three p.m., subject to change as I figured out what the heck I was doing. For now, the only food we offered was the bread, much of which was baked by our own Glenda. We'd received numerous requests for lunch options, so I hoped to figure that out in the next month or two.

"People are loving the latte flights," Hadley said as we scrambled to restock during a lull.

"And the bread," I said, making sure Glenda heard me.

"I could use a loaf of that bacon and onion bread right about now," Dalton said as he wiped one of the counters clean.

"Or the cornbread poppers," Hadley added.

"I don't even know what I'd pick. All your flavors are incredible, Glenda." I stacked more travel mugs in their spot.

Glenda laughed. "I never dreamed I'd find such a good fit for my baking addiction. I'm so happy you did this, Presley. This town needed it. *I* needed it."

"One more hour," Magnolia said from the other side of the counter. Though she wasn't an employee, she'd been here all day, overseeing the grand-opening pieces of it as well as manning The Bean Counter's social media. "I sent out a 'last chance for the raffles and free mugs' message a few minutes ago, so we'll probably see one more stream."

I went around the counter and gave her a big side hug, one of several today because I was so happy. "You're amazing, and I owe you so many favors it isn't funny. I hope you're keeping a tally."

"I'm doing no such thing," she said. "This is publicity for my business too." She gestured to the Moments by Magnolia brochures and business cards next to the raffles. There weren't many left.

"It feels like the entire town has been through here today," Hadley said.

"Plus half of Runner," Magnolia added.

Judging by the coffee we'd gone through, I could safely say we'd sold several hundred servings. I'd met so many people my head was swimming with names.

The one person you wanted to see most didn't show.

I'd had no reason to think he would, but it hadn't prevented me from wanting to lay eyes on West anyway. I hadn't seen him since that Sunday I'd been so cold to him. I knew he'd taken the girls on their trip last week, but I was surprised we hadn't run into each other.

I noticed the napkin dispenser was empty, so I headed to the storage room to grab another sleeve. I went through the kitchen, noting it was in a lovely state of disarray that spoke to how busy we'd been for the past eight hours. We'd likely be here for a couple more hours, putting the place back together, but I wasn't complaining.

Flipping the light on in the storage room, I skimmed the labels on the shipping boxes, trying to remember where the napkins were. Once I located them, I grabbed two sleeves. When I turned back around, I startled at the sight of West standing in the storage-room doorway, holding a large vase of flowers, his eyes locked on me, looking so familiar and gorgeous and...unsure.

"Oh," I said, pressing my free hand to my chest. "West. Hi."

"Hi, Presley. These are for you." He held the vase out.

I stepped closer, set the napkin sleeves down, and took the vase. "Thank you." My heart hammered, and I reeled, trying not to drink in the sight of him like a girl who was dying of thirst. "They're beautiful."

"They're masquerading as grand-opening flowers."

"Masquerading?" I sniffed the bouquet, more as something to do than because I wanted to smell the flowers. I wasn't thinking straight, too busy trying to figure out why he was here. Was it just to deliver flowers to a shop he'd built out?

"To everyone else, they look appropriate for a grand-opening gift," he said, stepping farther into the room, out of view of anyone in the front room or kitchen. "But they're actually to say I'm sorry."

My gaze popped up to meet his as my heart sped off in yet another direction like a runaway horse.

West swallowed as he peered down at me, those green eyes so intent. "I'm sorry, Presley. I ran scared."

"You don't need to apologize."

"I hurt you."

"I'm doing okay, West." I frowned, utterly confused. "I'm not angry anymore."

"I tried to tell myself I did the right thing. That I'd get over it." He shook his head and chuckled quietly. "I was fooling myself. Protecting myself. I used my children as an excuse, but the truth is, you make me feel so much. It scared the hell out of me. Because getting more deeply involved with you would be different than the two women who broke my babies' hearts. With you, *my* heart is in danger too."

He took the vase back and set it on a nearby shelf, which left nothing between us and made me fidgety.

He held out his hands, palms up, like an invitation. I hesitated for several seconds, looked from his strong hands up to the sincere expression on his handsome face, then slowly pressed my palms against his. He grasped them, then wove our fingers together.

"I've been a miserable bastard for three weeks," he continued. "Just ask my daughters or my coworkers or even my mom. Because I screwed up astronomically with you."

"What are you trying to say, West?"

"I'm in love with you, Presley. Crazy in love. Stupid in love. I want to be with you. I want to make us work. I told my daughters I had feelings for you, and I wanted to date you, like for real date. In public. Not in secret."

I stood there, staring up at him, my mind staggering to catch up, to understand, to believe. "You love me?" A smile was beginning to tug at my lips.

"I do."

"You told the girls that?"

He nodded. "I did, but I explained that didn't automatically mean we were gonna get married, because that's where their minds go. I told them people need to date and really get to know each other and see whether it would work to be a family."

I stepped a little closer, feeling light enough that I might actually lift off the ground like a helium-filled balloon. This man loved me? "Tell me again."

"I love you, Presley."

I breathed in his scent, feasted my eyes on his familiar, beloved face, sliding my hands up his solid chest and settling them at the back of his neck. "I love you too, West."

The next thing I knew, his arms were around me,

pulling me in tight to him, and his lips were all over mine. That familiar taste of him, feel of him... It intoxicated me, made me dizzy in the best possible way.

We both pulled back at the same time, breathing hard. Then we laughed.

"God, I've missed you," he said.

"Same."

"I drove hundreds of miles away on a trip that should've been nothing but magic, but all I could think about was you."

"Yeah?"

"I don't know how you got under my skin and into my heart so completely and so quickly, but you did. I don't want to live without you anymore, Presley."

I gazed into his eyes. "I had a really super-good day, but I have to say, you're blowing it out of the water."

"Congratulations, by the way. This place looks incredible. You, Presley Holiday, are inspiring and amazing and exactly the kind of woman I want my daughters exposed to."

"That's a giant compliment."

"Yes, ma'am."

I flicked his chest at the *ma'am*. "So where do we go from here?"

"Ah. Come with me." He took my hand and pulled me toward the kitchen, then out to the front room.

Magnolia looked between West and me, noted our entwined hands, and sent me a knowing smile. "You found her, I see," she said to West.

"Yes, I did, and thank God for that," he muttered as he kept walking out from behind the counter.

That's when I noticed Nova, Sienna, and Scarlet at the

raffle table with Hadley, each of them apparently writing their names on tickets to put in the kids' drawing.

"Miss Presley!" Scarlet abandoned her entry and ran over to us.

She threw her arms around my legs, and a crazy, happy laugh burst out of me.

"Hey, girls. It's great to see my favorite smart-girl brigade," I said.

Nova was next for hugs. Sienna painstakingly finished her raffle ticket, stuck it in the box, and turned to us with a wide smile.

"Miss Presley, your coffee shop looks beautiful," Sienna exclaimed.

I hugged her, aware that everyone in the place was watching us, but if West didn't care, then I didn't care. Judging by the gorgeous smile on his face as he watched us, he was not bothered one bit.

"Girls, do you remember what you're supposed to say?" he prompted.

With deliberateness and fanfare, they lined up, side by side.

"Miss Presley, would you please," Scarlet said.

"Do us the honor," Sienna added.

"Go on a date with us!" Nova yelled.

Everyone laughed, including West and me.

"That was supposed to be a question instead of a command," he said as I met his gaze, both of us grinning wide. "We'd like to take you to dinner for a family date."

"I would love to go on a date with all of you," I said. I bent down for a four-way hug with the girls, pulling them into me, inhaling the scent of little girls who'd apparently drunk our kids' version of a latte flight. "You finish up your raffle entries while I hug your dad, if that's okay."

"It's more than okay," Scarlet told me earnestly.

I turned to West and hugged him, several people cheering us on.

"Family date first," he said into my ear so no one else could hear. "And after that, we'll steal some adult time, I promise."

I nodded, overcome with elation. The day had gone as well as a grand opening could possibly go, and then it'd gotten twenty times better when West walked back into my life. "That sounds like a perfect date," I said as we ended the hug.

"Then we'll take it one day at a time," he said. "Together."

Epilogue

Two months later

Presley

"Happy birthday, my love," I said once I could put words together in the right order. "Seems like I got a present too even though it's not my special day."

West let out a low, satisfied growl. "I can't think of a better way to start the day, birthday or not."

He was on top of me, still inside me, in my bed in the master bedroom of my beautifully remodeled home.

Waking up together was a rare, cherished treat, as was spending a full night together.

His mom had invited Sienna, Nova, and Scarlet to Nashville for the weekend, promising them a movie at the theater yesterday and a trip to an orchard today. Whether she'd admitted it or not, I was pretty sure the real reason was to give West and me time together to celebrate.

We'd celebrated on and off all night.

That was the easy, no-brainer part. I hoped the gift I'd gotten him would go over okay.

My idea had seemed perfect—fitting and funny and heart-tugging all at once—when I'd come up with it. As usual I'd acted on it right away, but ever since putting it into motion, I'd had some low-key worries that it would send the wrong message.

Tamping down on that, I pulled his head to me and kissed him, taking my time and making sure he knew how loved he was.

"I'm a lucky man," he said in his gravelly morning voice. "Be right back."

He rolled out of bed and went into the bathroom. As soon as he closed the door, I gathered my nerve, hurried to my closet, dragged his large gift out, and propped it up against the bed. Nervous, I pulled my robe on, sat on the mattress next to the gift, and waited.

The door opened, and he emerged, a grin on his handsome face and not a stitch of clothing on his gorgeous body. He'd made me scream his name not fifteen minutes ago, but I already felt a stirring of desire deep inside me as I watched him walk toward me, his eyes lighting up at the wrapped present.

"What's this?" he asked.

I took in a quiet, steeling breath. "Something for the birthday boy."

"Can I unwrap it now?"

"Of course. Unless you'd rather wait till after kayaking." We'd planned an early-morning outing.

He laughed like a kid, shaking his head. "Hell no. Let's do this."

Also like a kid, West tore into the wrapping paper while I bit my lip, my gaze locked on his face.

As soon as the painting was revealed, his eyes crinkled with a grin, then they popped open in disbelief. "Holy shit balls, Presley."

I swallowed, encouraged by that initial reaction but not at ease yet.

"What did you do?" he asked, still smiling, the smile still reaching his eyes. "Who made this?"

"I commissioned Shawna Jenkins. She used the photos we took at the Honeysuckle Festival."

Using the llama photos as a guide, Shawna had painted the five of us—West, me, and the girls—plus Betty and Esmerelda. The main difference between the photos and this painting was that, in this, West and I stood side by side between the llamas, with Nova in my arms and Scarlet and Sienna in front of us. Like a family instead of two near-strangers on opposite ends with three girls drawing us together.

He let out a laughing howl as he stepped back to take it all in. "This is incredible, Pres." He held his hand out to me, his eyes still taking in the details. "We look like a family."

I took his hand, stood, and moved next to him. "You guys are my family, but I want to make sure this doesn't come across as pressure to make any changes. I know the girls are key, and we're taking it slow. I'm okay with that."

"You are?" His smile faded and his brow furrowed.

"As long as I have a piece of you, West, I can be patient. It's you I want. Not necessarily a husband. Not until you're ready." I wound my hands to the back of his neck, went up on my toes, and pressed a kiss to his lips.

He caught me, pulled me up against him, and took the kiss deeper, reassuring me he'd received the painting in the spirit it was intended.

"Thank you, Presley," he said eventually. "I fucking love it."

"Thank goodness."

"You were truly worried?"

"Maybe a little bit. I know I can come across like a loose cannon, but I hear you, West. I understand you want to go slow and why."

West

I pressed another kiss to my gorgeous, understanding Presley, acknowledged my own worries, then went to the overnight bag where I'd packed a change of clothes. I riffled through it until I found the ring box that contained the biggest, prettiest ring I could afford.

I wasn't too worried about the size. It wasn't the largest stone, but it wasn't puny either, and I knew Presley well enough to understand she wasn't about showiness. She might value her investment accounts, but it was about security, not ego or showing off. That was one of the many reasons I loved her so damn much.

As I took a moment with my back to her, the velvet box in my hand, I gathered my nerve, closed my eyes momentarily, and hoped she'd meant she wanted me as her husband when I was ready.

Because I was ready.

With the box enclosed in my hand, I straightened, faced her, met her curious gaze.

I stepped up to her and laced the fingers of my empty hand with hers. "Did you mean what you said? About wanting me in whatever way I can give you?"

"Absolutely." She smiled, her eyes sparkling with love and affection.

Man, this woman was so fucking beautiful and good and had the best heart. I didn't know what I'd done to deserve her, but I was thankful every single day.

"I want to give you everything, Presley. Every corner of my heart, every bit of my love, every day for the rest of my life. I want to share all the joy and challenges and laughter and good coffee this life can throw at us. I want to be a family with you. I want you to be the mother figure my daughters look up to, take comfort from, and learn from, because you're the most incredible role model for love, inspiration, and badassery." Still naked as the day I was born, I went down on one knee, thinking maybe I should've pulled on some pants first, but screw it. I was baring myself to her in every possible way. I flipped the box open, plucked the princess cut diamond ring out, and held it up with fingers that shook. "Presley Holiday, will you marry me?"

If I thought her face showed happiness before, it glowed with joy now, her eyes going big and sparkly, and everything in me felt as if it clicked into place. The normally unflappable love of my life blinked, and tears flowed down her cheeks as she nodded. "Yes, I'll marry you, my burly, badass, teddy bear of a man. Yes to all of it."

I stood, tossed the empty box to the bed, and held her left hand between us. Breathing in deeply, I tried to steady myself as I gently slid the ring on her finger.

She held up her hand and studied the ring. "I love it, West. I love you."

I drew her against me, her robe flapping open so we were skin to skin, my erection pressing into her abdomen insistently. I kissed her thoroughly, passionately, fervently, then pulled back enough to gaze into her soulful blue eyes. "I love you so much, Presley."

She peered back at me as she reached down and closed

her fingers around my shaft. "That's never been more evident," she said with a wicked grin.

I backed her toward the bed, lowered her onto it cross-wise, and climbed over her. Overcome with need and love, I wasted no time entering her, closing my eyes at the heavenly feel of her until it hit me. "Shit. Forgot protection."

"I don't mind," she said.

"What if I get you pregnant?"

"I don't mind," she repeated, her voice breathy as she arched up into me and clamped her legs around me, pulling me in so deep we truly felt like we fused to become one. "I love the girls so much, and I wouldn't mind making a baby with you. If you're up for more."

"With you? I'm up for just about anything."

I made love to her slowly, unhurried for as long as I could manage, reminding myself we had the rest of our lives together and there was no need to rush. That there would only be one first time with my fiancée and to make it last. Being inside her with no barriers was the most incredible feeling. Knowing she'd agreed to spend her entire life with me? It blew my fucking mind that I could be so lucky.

When Presley was close to shattering, I braced myself over her as my body moved of its own accord, climbing, reaching. I nipped at the lobe of her ear and said, "You're mine forever, Presley Holiday."

Her orgasm gripped her, her body contracting around my dick, and at the same moment she called out my name, I came hard and spilled my seed into her. For several long seconds, we were suspended together in a place where time stopped and the world possibly ceased to spin on its axis. My breath stuck, my brain stopped, and everything centered on the intense, earth-shattering ecstasy we gave each other.

Eventually I came back into my senses, registering the gorgeous smile on my fiancée's face first, then noticing the cool air on my bare ass. As my breath slowed, I managed to brace myself on my forearms so I could fully take in the beauty of this woman, with flushed cheeks, swollen lips, and a dreamy look in her eyes.

I kissed her, a slow, loving exploration of her luscious lips. Then I rolled to my side, taking her with me.

"I want to marry you as soon as humanly possible," I told her.

"I'm so up for that."

Propping myself up on my elbow, I traced her lower lip with my finger. "Last night at the dads' group, Luke told us he's opening up his barn for events to help support the farm."

"Yeah?"

"I immediately pictured us getting married there. I want to support him, but also I'm not the kind of guy who fits in at a fancy, expensive hotel ballroom. If you're set on that kind of thing, we can discuss it—"

"I'm not set on a fancy anything, West," she interrupted. "I love the idea of some kind of classy but rustic setting. Oh! What about Christmastime? Lots of evergreens? Lights? Maybe white and silver with the green?"

"Think we can put together a wedding by Christmas?"

"I happen to know an excellent planner."

I grinned. "Magnolia would be perfect. She could pull it off, don't you think?"

"I know she could." She ran her finger slowly down the middle of my chest then back up, looking pensive. "What would you think of a Christmas Eve wedding?"

"I'd fucking love it, and so would the girls."

"Three of the most adorable flower girls," Presley said,

her eyes sparkling. "In gorgeous silver dresses with lots of sparkles."

I rumbled out a laugh. "You so completely get them."

She nodded, an affectionate smile on her lips. Then the smile dropped. "One problem. Can Magnolia work with Luke? There's...something between them. Like bad blood."

"It's Christmas and a wedding. She's hungry for business, and he's trying to save his farm. Surely they can pull it off."

"She's a professional," Presley said, then she shook her head, as if shaking off the problem for now. "I can't wait to marry you, West. Christmas Eve in Luke's barn. It's a date."

"And then I want you in my bed every night for the rest of our lives."

She tilted her head and bit her lip.

"What?" I asked, frowning.

"I'm with you about the rest of our lives and the sleeping together every night but..."

"But what?"

"I want you in *my* bed. Or we can buy a new bed. I don't care. But...will you and the girls move in here with me?"

I laughed. This was what she was worried about? Could the girls and I manage to live in this big, comfortable family home on the shore? My princesses would be over the damn moon about it. But I couldn't let her think it was that easy. "You don't like my house?"

"Your house is perfect...for the four of you. But there's no place for all the kayaks. Plus three kittens..."

"And your shoes."

"And my shoes. Do you think you could feel at home here?"

I rolled on top of her, bracing myself on my arms again,

and kissed her, my heart feeling light, elated, and full of hope and optimism. "I can be at home wherever you are, my love. You're my home, Presley. I belong with you."

"And I belong with you." She pressed a quick kiss to my lips. "But just so you know... I would've sold my shoes for you."

"And I would've built a shoe shed in the yard for you."

We laughed and we kissed, and I couldn't wait to spend the rest of our lives doing that every single day.

Bonus Epilogue

June, the next year

Presley

I hoped my white lie about an emergency at The Bean Counter didn't jinx me.

I had enough co-conspirators that I should be able to pull it off, but I didn't like lying to my husband, even when it was to ultimately give him the surprise of a lifetime.

Two surprises actually.

West and the girls were in Nashville on this bright, sunny Father's Day with his mom and Thomas, who were turning out to be wonderful grandparents. They'd gone to brunch at a steakhouse Thomas and West loved. Boys' choice, as the girls had decreed. I was supposed to be with them, in theory, except for this staffing "emergency" at the shop.

As I made my way up from the shore toward the house, my phone vibrated with a text message.

West: How's it going?

Presley: Glenda's coming in to save the day, but she has to shower first. I'm hoping I'll get out of here in another forty-five minutes. How's your brunch?

West: Tasty, but I wish my wife was here.

I laughed and warmed at the message.

Presley: Me too. I'll get you a good present to make up for it though.

West: You haven't shopped yet?!!

He added a laughing emoji, telling me he was teasing.

I'd shopped. In fact I'd Shopped with a capital S, and I couldn't wait to unveil his present.

Presley: Are you ordering dessert?

West: No. We all overdid it on the buffet. I've never seen these girls eat so much, even Sienna.

Presley: How soon are you leaving?

West: Waiting on the bill now. We'll see you in a little over an hour.

Presley: I'll hopefully be home waiting for you.

I'd definitely be home waiting for him. I already was.

As far as West knew, and the girls, for that matter, I was supposed to be with the family for brunch. I did hate missing it, as his parents and the girls were my family now and meant the world to me, but this was all going to plan.

His mom and stepdad were in on it.

My employees were in on it.

Jagger and his brother were in on it.

There were a lot of moving parts to this surprise. I sat down in the living room, antsy with anticipation but determined to rest while I waited for my family to come home.

———

West

As I pulled into our driveway, it hit me again, like it did every single time I came home, how damn lucky I was.

Three beautiful daughters who were thriving with Presley as a mother figure.

A hot, sexy wife who was the most unstoppable person I'd ever met, hands down.

A mom and stepdad who were living their best life—the life my mom always deserved and could never quite pull off until Thomas had come along, fallen in love with her, and built a life with her that'd allowed them both to retire and *live*.

A job I enjoyed that paid even better now that I was a foreman.

And this house... I'd never dared to imagine living some-where like this, but I couldn't picture Presley living anywhere else. This was the kind of home I'd dreamed of giving my girls, not because it had four times as much square footage as our tiny duplex. Not because all three girls could have their own bedrooms if they chose—though the twins had decided to continue bunking together. Not even because of the view from the master bed where I woke up with the love of my life every morning.

Take all the features away, and we had what was most important—a family home filled with laughter, acceptance, patience, emotions—sometimes heated ones, sure—and love. So much fucking love.

"Pressy's home!" Nova said as we pulled next to Presley's SUV in the garage. Pressy was the nickname Nova had started using once Presley and I started dating openly, and the twins had adopted the same name for her. "We can go kayaking!"

"It's a great day for a boat ride," Scarlet said.

"We have to wear sunscreen," Sienna said.

"And take bottled waters," Nova declared.

Kayaking was something we did as a family every week when the weather was decent. The girls were getting good at it, requiring fewer saves. It was a pastime we all enjoyed, and it was a way for my wife to slow down and relax. Well, as much as a person could relax with three high-energy girls.

I cut the engine and followed my daughters into the house, Nova and Scarlet deep into the debate as to whether they'd wear swimsuits for today's float. As I walked into the kitchen, Presley sat up on the sectional in the living room, looking sleepy.

My wife was not a napper.

"Are you okay?" I asked.

"Yeah," Presley said, smiling, looking gorgeous with her

messy bun lopsided and off-center, further hinting at sleep. Chai hopped up to the back cushion next to her, equally drowsy. "I came in and sat down for a few minutes, and I guess I fell asleep."

I walked over to her, pulled her up to me, and kissed her, peering into her blue eyes. "Everything's okay at the shop?"

"Yes," she said cheerfully. "Glenda got there in time for the post-church rush so Hadley didn't have to face that alone."

"Glenda and her husband didn't have plans for Father's Day?"

"They're meeting their sons tonight for dinner," she said.

Latte scampered after Mocha through the main floor and up the stairs.

"Silly kittens," Nova said. "Pressy, are you ready for kayaks?"

"Of course I am. How was brunch?"

"The best!" Nova shouted.

"Papa loved his presents as much as Daddy did," Sienna said.

The girls had showered me with their gifts first thing this morning—a "girl dad" hat from Scarlet, a T-shirt that said "World's Best Dad" from Sienna, and socks with photos of the three kittens on them from Nova, which made me laugh. Nova had her own ideas and wasn't easily swayed. I loved that about her, and I loved my cat socks as much as the hat and shirt.

Presley took her hair down and redid it so it wasn't falling to the side. "Grab the supplies and let's go down to the boathouse to get the kayaks out."

"I've got the bag," Scarlet said, heaving the oversized

beach bag where we kept towels, sunglasses, and sunscreen to her little shoulder.

"I'll get five waters!" Nova ran to the fridge.

"Who has to go to the bathroom first?" I asked. A race to the bathrooms ensued, with all three girls hitting a different one.

Presley pulled me in for a longer, private kiss. "Sorry again that I missed brunch. I'll make it up to you tonight."

I growled, wishing my mom and Thomas would've kept the girls for a few hours so I could spend my Father's Day making love to my wife. "I'll be there."

Once everyone had relieved themselves, the five of us headed down the walkway, the three girls leading the way, Presley and I holding hands as we trailed a few steps behind them. Presley set a quick pace for us, making me wonder what the hurry was, but that thought was interrupted as Scarlet popped back out of the boathouse with eyes as big as the moon and her mouth gaping open.

Excited hollers came from within the boathouse, where Nova and Sienna already were.

"What...?" Scarlet said, looking from me to Presley and back as we reached the door.

Nova's head appeared in the doorway next. "There's a boat!"

"There's a what?" Presley asked.

"There should be four boats," I said as I went inside.

I froze right there at the top of the stairs.

There was a fucking boat.

"Presley?" I said, my gaze locked on the sparkling blue and white watercraft.

"Yes, dear?" she said in a falsely high, innocent voice.

"What did you do?"

She came up beside me and peered down at the full-size, ten-person jet boat, her mouth stretching in a wide grin. "Happy Father's Day, West."

A laugh rolled out of me. "Are you serious? Is this... What did you do, wife of mine?"

She pressed her lips together, then said, "I went shopping."

"Is this ours?" Sienna asked in hushed wonder. She was kneeling on the deck next to the boat, taking it in.

I was semi-aware of Nova jumping up and down once I made it down the stairs.

"Daddy! Daddy! We got a boat!" our youngest yelled.

Presley joined me on the deck, then nudged me toward the boat. "Go check it out. I hope you like it."

That drew out another laugh. "Like it? Are you kidding me?" I stepped to the side, then hopped onboard. "Holy..."

This thing was a beauty.

I ducked under the boat arch, which had life jackets hanging from it, to get to the captain's chair. I sat in it and took in the dashboard, too stunned for words.

We'd talked a little about getting a boat but decided the kayaks were all we needed for now. Or so I'd thought.

We'd also talked about extravagant purchases and how Presley wouldn't spend too much on gifts. She and I kept our finances separate by my request. I made a good, honest living, particularly after my promotion, and I didn't need anyone thinking I was after her money. She'd insisted on opening college accounts for each girl, and I'd relented gratefully, but for the most part, we split our living expenses. We were a team.

Except when my wife went out and spent tens of thousands of dollars on a Father's Day present.

"You shouldn't have," I said halfheartedly, as she watched me from the deck of the boathouse with the most beautiful, loving expression on her face. "But I'm damn glad you did. This is incredible, Pres."

Presley

My big, burly husband looked like a little boy on Christmas morning as he ran his hands over every inch of the dash, the captain's chair, the sides, everything he laid his eyes on. Everything except the one thing I wanted him to notice.

"Can we come on the boat, Daddy?" Nova asked, hopping from one foot to the other close to the edge of the deck.

I hadn't confided in the girls, knowing it would be too big of a secret that could easily pop out in excitement.

I went to Nova and held her hand as she stepped aboard, then did the same for Scarlet, who was singing something about boats that I assumed she was ad-libbing. Sienna was still kneeling, taking it all in.

"You want to go aboard?" I asked our middle girl.

Sienna sprung up, nodding, and I helped her in. I stayed on the deck, watching the four people I loved to pieces as they explored the admittedly beautiful boat.

"How?" West asked, taking his eyes off his present long enough to meet my gaze. "How did you pull this off? You were at the shop all mor— You weren't at the shop."

"I wasn't at the shop."

"Was Preston not really sick?" my husband asked of the alleged emergency.

"Preston was never supposed to work today. Hadley opened and Glenda was always scheduled to come in," I confessed. "They were in on it just in case you checked in at the shop."

"And my mom and Thomas?" he asked.

"In on it."

He chuckled and shook his head. "So you were, what? How'd you get the boat in the water? How'd you get it in the boathouse, for that matter? You been taking boat lessons behind my back?"

"No lessons yet," I said with a laugh. "I figure we have a guy who knows how to drive."

"That's you, Daddy!" Nova yelled.

"That's me." West let out a happy howl that filled me with joy. He so deserved that happiness. "You can do pretty much whatever you set out to do, but pulling this into the boathouse without boat-driving lessons..."

"The boat was delivered to Jagger at the marina. He and Cade brought it over after you left this morning."

"So Jagger's in on it too," West said. "I'm..." He shook his head yet again. "You got me good. I wasn't expecting anything like this."

"And we get new life jackets," Scarlet said, and my pulse sped up.

"Tie-dye ones!" Nova shouted.

"Why are there six instead of five, Pressy?" Sienna, the quiet observer, asked.

Nova went directly under the arch and pointed up at each life jacket, which I'd carefully tied for effect. She pointed at the rainbow one, then the others as she went down the list. "One for me. One for Daddy. One for Pressy. One for Scarlet. One for Sienna. And a cute little baby one."

West's gaze locked with mine at that instant. He watched me intently, as if looking for confirmation. I couldn't keep anything in, my emotions likely written all over my face in the form of a big, joyful smile.

"A little baby one," I said. "For when the baby in my tummy's born."

West hopped out of the boat in less than a second and took both my hands, peering down at me with eyes that sparkled as they sought out confirmation. His brows shot up in question, and there was so much emotion in his eyes that it made my own emotions jam up in my throat. I merely nodded.

He pulled me into his arms and spun us slowly around, pulling another laugh out of me.

I was halfway conscious of the girls shouting in happiness and group-hugging in the boat. Next thing I knew, West's lips were on mine.

As he lowered me back to the deck, he said, "Really? We're having a baby?"

I nodded. "My doctor confirmed it Friday. It nearly killed me to keep it a secret until today." As the girls continued to celebrate loudly, I added so only he could hear, "Maybe I should've waited for a private moment without the girls, but I"—I shrugged, feeling slightly worried all of a sudden—"couldn't."

"We're a family," he said. "We'll celebrate together. If, God forbid, anything goes wrong, we'll weather that together too."

"That's how we do it," I said, relaxing into him.

The girls had bounced into the bow, claiming their favorite seats as they debated whether they'd get a brother or a sister.

"I love you, West. Happy Father's Day," I said.

With damp eyes and a wide grin, he pressed his forehead to mine. "I love you too, Presley Aldridge. This is the best Father's Day ever."

"You like your present?"

"I love both of my presents. Five minutes ago I would've told you you couldn't top the boat, but you topped the boat, love."

Playing dumb, I said, "With the tie-dye life jackets?"

He let out a hearty laugh, sliding both arms around me and pulling me against him again. "The tie-dye life jackets are perfect for our loud, *growing* family." He shook his head. "A few months ago, I was so determined to stay single. Then you came along and out-stubborned me, out-determined me, and wore me down until I smartened up and embraced the life of my dreams." He paused and swallowed, visibly overcome. "Thank you, Presley."

"The pleasure, dear husband, is all mine."

Note from the Author

Thanks for reading *Single-Minded*! I hope you loved West and Presley.

Next up is *Single Wish*, Luke and Magnolia's story.

If you missed the Henry Brothers series, you can dive into book one, *Unraveled*! Find out how a marriage of convenience can test even the best of friends!

Note from the Author

Find *Unraveled* in ebook, audiobook, and paperback in my author store at amyknuppbooks.com!

———

If you liked *Single-Minded,* I hope you'll consider leaving a review for it. Reviews help other readers find books and can be as short (or long) as you feel comfortable with. Just a couple sentences is all it takes. I appreciate all honest reviews.

———

Single-Minded is part of the Single Dads of Dragonfly Lake series, which includes:

- Singled Out
- Single All the Way
- Single Chance
- Single-Minded
- Single Wish
- Single Desire

Also by Amy Knupp

<u>Single Dads of Dragonfly Lake</u>

Singled Out

Single All the Way

Single Chance

Single-Minded

Single Wish

Single Desire

<u>Henry Brothers Series</u>

Untold (prequel)

Unraveled

Unsung

Undone

Unexpected

Or binge the Henry Brothers in audio:

Henry Brothers Audiobooks

<u>North Brothers Series</u>

True North

True Colors

True Blue

True Harmony

True Hero

North Brothers Box Sets:

North Brothers Books 1-3

North Brothers Books 4-5

North Brothers: The Complete Series

Or binge the North Brothers in audio:

North Brothers Audiobooks

<u>Hale Street Series</u>:

Sweet Spot

Sweet Dreams

Soft Spot

One and Only

Last First Kiss

Heartstrings

<u>Hale Street Box Sets</u>:

Meet Me at Clayborne's

Clayborne's After Hours

It Happened on Hale Street

<u>Island Fire Series</u>:

Playing with Fire

Heat of the Night

Fully Involved

Firestorm

Afterburn

Up in Flames

Flash Point

Fire Within

Impulse

Slow Burn

Island Fire Box Sets:

Sparked (books 1-3)

Ignited (books 4-6)

Enflamed (books 7-10)

OR

Island Fire: The Complete Series

<u>Themed Bundles</u>

<u>Single Dad</u>

Opposites Attract

Grumpy-Sunshine

Cinnamon Roll Heroes

Childhood Crush

Forbidden Love

Friends to Lovers

Coming Home

Musicians

Second Chance

Workplace Romance

Heroines Finding Their Path

About the Author

Amy Knupp is a *USA Today* Best-Selling author of contemporary romance. She loves words and grammar and meaty, engrossing stories with complex characters.

Amy lives in Wisconsin with her husband and has two adult children, two cats, and a box turtle. She graduated from the University of Kansas with degrees in French and journalism. In her spare time, she enjoys traveling, breaking up cat fights, watching college hoops, and annoying her family by correcting their grammar.

For more information:
https://www.amyknuppbooks.com

Single-Minded

Single Dads of Dragonfly Lake

Amy Knupp

Chapter One

West

My three chattery reasons for living, my daughters—Scarlet, Sienna, and Nova—were even more animated than usual this morning as they ate their breakfast.

Maybe it was because today was the first day of summer break, and their favorite babysitter, seventeen-year-old Allison, would be their full-time companion for the next two and a half months.

Maybe they were feeding off my emotional state. I tried to hide it, but this was a big day for me too. I couldn't deny I was shaky inside with exhilaration and determination.

"Can we go swimming every day, Allie?" four-year-old Nova asked.

"We'll go swimming a lot if you want to," the babysitter said, taking the fourth chair at the table.

Allison had shown up right on time at seven thirty, her eyes bright and eager for her first day of her summer job. I trusted Allison. She was the most responsible seventeen-year-old I'd ever met and loved my girls. But this was new. Full-time was a lot. My girls were a lot.

"One day at a time, Nova," I told my youngest as I filled my travel mug with coffee.

"I want to do *all...the...things!*" she said in a burst of exuberance that almost always made me grin.

"Right now the thing you need to do is eat your breakfast," I told her, dumping ice cubes into my five-gallon water cooler I took to the jobsite every day, wherever we were working.

"I'm done, but Sienna's not," Nova said.

I glanced over my shoulder. Nova's and Scarlet's plates were indeed empty. Sienna's had a half-eaten piece of toast and both her sausage links, which were pushed to the farthest side of her plate.

"What's wrong with your food, Sienna?" I asked.

"Sausage is just...ew, Daddy," Sienna said, wrinkling her nose.

"You ate it yesterday," I said.

She stared at her plate, nostrils flaring, head shaking, as her sisters looked on.

"It's just sausage, Si-Si," Nova preached.

Sienna picked up her toast instead and took a dainty bite.

"I'll take your sausage," Scarlet, Sienna's fraternal twin, offered enthusiastically.

Sienna shoved her plate to her sister and continued to eat her toast.

I shrugged and considered it settled, then glanced at the time. Twenty till eight. Time for me to boogie. I turned to Allison.

"There's plenty in the fridge for lunch for all of you. If you go to the beach, don't forget the arm floats for Nova."

"A Novel Place is having story time at eleven, so I thought I'd take them," Allison said, and I swear if I could double her wages, I would.

"They'll love it," I said. I took my wallet out and gave her a couple of bills when the girls weren't looking. "Get them each one book," I told her quietly.

Money was tight, as usual, but books were one thing I stretched to make work.

Money would be less tight if I landed Davis Morten's position at work.

My phone buzzed with a text message. I pulled it out of my pocket to see my boss's name.

Levi: Running late. Plumbing emergency at my mom's. Start without me.

West: I got it covered. Take care of your mom.

Levi: You sure? You good with this?

West: 100% sure.

"I gotta roll," I told Allison and my girls. "Love you, squirrels," I said to my daughters, rounding the kitchen table and kissing each in turn.

"Love you, Daddy!" they all said.

I grabbed my lunch from the fridge, my day's worth of beverages, and my work bag.

"Be good for Allison," I called on my way out the door. "Allison, call if you need anything."

"We'll be fine," the babysitter assured me.

I headed out into the morning sunshine. The weather was already promising to be sweltering by afternoon. I was thankful to be starting a weeks-long indoor project. A cush job, as Nick Carlisle, the lead of the other crew and my competition for Davis's job, had pointed out last week. I'd happily take it, as he was overseeing a boathouse, deck, and gazebo build.

I climbed into my SUV, my mind switching from little-girl mode to work.

Levi Dawson, the owner and head contractor, had turned things upside down at work last week, or rather Davis's retirement announcement had. Levi's method of replacing the fifty-something workhorse was smart as hell. He'd pitted me versus Nick Carlisle, as we had seniority and the most experience. For the next two to three months, we'd each lead a crew on separate projects. At the end of the summer, he'd make one of us the foreman directly under him for good.

That was going to be me if I had anything to say about it.

The project I was heading up would likely take close to two months, maybe more, depending on any supply delays. Apparently it was a big-ass project, and the homeowner was paying big-ass bucks to have it squeezed into a cancellation slot.

I checked the address for the job and noted it was on Honeysuckle Road, out by my buddy Max's house, if I wasn't mistaken. I pointed the SUV that way.

As Levi was the one to meet with potential clients and bid out projects, I didn't know much about this one other than what the plans told me. It was a main floor gut of a big house directly on the shore. That tracked with being a neighbor of Max, who'd played in the NFL a few years back and had the lakeside house to show for it.

Since Levi had planned to meet the homeowner and me

first thing this morning to go over the project in detail, I didn't even know the homeowner's first name. She was apparently new to town, obviously had some cash, and I couldn't help but picture a hoity-toity widow in her sixties. None of that mattered to me. I just hoped she was easygoing, not a clientzilla, because I intended to rock the hell out of the project.

As I drove through downtown Dragonfly Lake, a text message sounded through the SUV's Bluetooth system. My ex-wife's name popped up on the display.

"Happy fucking Monday," I muttered to myself.

I didn't hear from Flora often, which pissed me off on the girls' behalf but was a blessing as far as my peace level was concerned. There was nothing peaceful about Flora.

I had the Bluetooth system read her message to me.

> Flora: We'll be in the area tomorrow. Want to take the girls to an early dinner before Gil's show. Can we pick them up at three?

"God dammit." I pounded the steering wheel. "Three isn't fucking dinner; it's the middle of the afternoon." The girls would need a fourth meal before bedtime if they ate at three.

Flora's appearances were few and far between. As much as I questioned whether she was a positive part of the girls' lives, she *was* their mother. I kept hoping she'd get her shit and her priorities together and be someone they could look up to, but that seemed to be more and more of a pipe dream.

I dictated my response.

> West: Do I have a choice?

Flora: Don't be like that.

West: Honest question. Do I have a choice between three tomorrow or maybe you could fit them in the next day and spend more time with them?

Flora: We have to be in Omaha the next day.

Of course they did.

In other words, my only choice was either to let the girls spend a tiny slot of time with their mom or make them miss out altogether. It was a shitty choice, but when I'd gotten full-time custody, I'd agreed Flora could visit her daughters whenever she wanted to. Back then, I'd hoped she'd be a regular presence in their lives instead of a special event whenever she and her guitarist boyfriend happened to be close enough to stop by for a few minutes.

West: I'll be working at three.

Flora: I can get them at daycare.

West: They have a full-time babysitter at our place. Where do you plan to take them?

Flora: Gil wants Dragonfly Diner. We'll go there.

I clenched my back teeth together. She put her boyfriend's desires over our girls'. Every. Single. Time.

You'd think I'd be used to it by now, but she continually disappointed me. That was Flora though. She'd been fun when we first met in the army. She'd gotten pregnant before we'd even thought whether we could make it long-term, but did that stop us from trying? Hell no. If I had a dollar for every bad decision I'd made where relationships were concerned, I could retire.

> West: Pick them up at my place. Have them home by five.

> Flora: We'll be done before that. Gil needs to be in Nashville by six.

Fucking fantastic.

I didn't respond. I had nothing else to say, at least nothing civil or productive.

I drove by Max's house and verified his house number was two lots down from my target.

When I spotted the right numbers on a mailbox, my brows went up. Ms. Holiday's house was cottage-style, but that term was misleading because *cottage* made you think small. There was nothing small about this place.

The exterior was white siding with gray stonework. The structure was an L-shape, one side a connected three-car garage with a bonus room above it, complete with a cupola. On the garage.

Definitely seven figures, I thought as I pulled up along the curb and killed the engine. I could see why Levi claimed this was gonna be a showpiece.

As I climbed out of the truck, I got another text message.

> Flora: Tell the girls I'll see them tomorrow.

"Go to hell," I said under my breath, my irritation flooding right back in. Flora had that effect on me.

I pulled my tool belt out and put it on, catching myself in a scowl.

The bitch of it was, while Flora annoyed me with everything out of her mouth—or her fingertips in this case—I was more pissed at myself when it came to her. She was Exhibit A in the case of me rushing in with a woman.

When we'd met, we'd been all about lust and cutting loose. We'd had fun together. Just before I was discharged, we found out she was three months pregnant. Flora's discharge was two months after mine.

I'd known she wasn't ready to settle down, but I also knew everything changed when babies came into the mix. I convinced her to give us a chance and move to Dragonfly Lake with me.

Looking back, I could see she was never going to be content in a small town. She likely wouldn't be happy in a big city either. What Flora apparently preferred was roaming, living on the road, and avoiding responsibility.

I should've seen that early on. When we'd started having problems, before the twins were even born, I should've faced that and let her go. Instead we were on and off for years, long enough for Nova to be conceived. My youngest daughter was the sole reason I couldn't regret being a stubborn dumbass who didn't know when to throw in the towel.

As I walked up the driveway, I fought to shove my irritation away. This job was important. My chance to prove myself. To prove that, while I was shit at relationships, I had value when it came to my career.

I rang the doorbell and eventually heard someone approaching inside. I stood taller and forced my mind away from my ex, toward exceeding expectations on this project.

When the door opened and I laid eyes on the client, my heart skipped a beat.

Holy shit balls.

Ms. Holiday was not a sixty-year-old widow.

I'd seen this woman before. I'd noticed her at Chance and Rowan's party a couple of weeks ago before I'd had to run out for a kid emergency. How the hell could I *not* notice her?

She was beautiful, with piercing blue eyes beneath long lashes, unadorned lips that curved into a sexy-without-trying smile, and an air about her that spoke of money and class, in spite of her casual outfit of cutoff denim shorts that revealed gorgeous legs, a sleeveless top with a halter neckline that showed off sexy, delicate shoulders, and blinged-out flip-flops my daughters would drool over.

Ah, hell.

I cleared my throat and felt like an old-time cartoon character with stars dancing around my head but fuck that.

"Morning," I said. "I'm West Aldridge from Dawson Construction."

"I know." Her smile turned knowing in a way that made my blood race. She held out her delicate-looking hand and surprised me with the firmness of her shake when I took it. "I'm Presley Holiday."

My blood raced like it was *not* supposed to race on a job. Or preferably ever.

"Come on in, West."

I followed her inside, cussing inwardly and steeling myself against the effect this woman had on me in the first five seconds of meeting her.

Chapter Two

Presley

West Aldridge at close range had even more impact on me than he had across a crowded patio three weeks ago at Rowan and Chance's party.

Those stunning green eyes were kind and attentive. His square jaw was solid, strong, and made all the more masculine by his beard. When we'd shaken hands, his was large and undoubtedly powerful, yet his touch had been restrained, almost gentle. As we'd made physical contact, my heart had fluttered in my chest.

I was so not the flutters-from-a-guy type.

As I stepped back to let him into my home, I took him in as a whole. He wore a black tee that revealed biceps I wasn't going to get out of my head anytime soon. His muscular legs were thick beneath cargo pants. And that tool belt...

I hadn't realized I was into guys with beards and tool belts until now.

"Levi had an emergency," West said as he looked

around at my new home. "He might join us later, but we'll start without him."

"I'm sure you and I can handle it just fine," I said, allowing my lips to curve into a flirty smile.

"Once you show me around, I won't need to bother you." His tone wasn't unkind, just businesslike. No grin in return. Not at all flirty.

Okay. I could read a guy. Business it was then. He'd be here for who knew how many weeks. Getting along was key. Which of course meant crossing any lines into flirtation would be a bad idea.

I was down with that. This eye candy might've been part of the reason I'd called Dawson Construction in the first place but only a small part. Multiple recommendations for Levi's company from my friends and their friends weighed a lot more heavily than the instant attraction I'd had to West at that party.

That kind of reaction to a man wasn't normal for me, but then nothing in my life had been normal for the past three weeks. I'd jumped straight off the cliff of normal when I'd walked out on my career.

"I'm assuming you have the plans from Levi?" I asked.

"Yes, ma'am." He held up a thick contractor's portfolio, but I almost didn't notice as I tried to swallow the *ma'am*.

I was thirty-five years old. I'd put West close to my age, maybe a couple of years younger. There was no need for him to *ma'am* me. But maybe that was just him being polite.

"We're gutting this whole level," he said. "Opening it up. New kitchen, new master suite, powder room, utility room, new everything, plus finishing the bonus room above the garage."

"Yes." I stepped from the foyer into the hall. "There's the formal dining room." I pointed at the mostly enclosed room, then to the opposite side. "Living room, obviously." We walked down the short hall to the kitchen doorway. "Powder and utility are that way. Kitchen's here."

He glanced to the powder room, then followed me into the kitchen. "We got some eighties going on here with the walled-off rooms, huh?"

"So much eighties," I said. "I fell in love with the lot and the view. The house is okay but..."

"We'll make it better. Nice breakfast nook. We're updating the glass there, right?"

He wasn't referring to his notes, so I could tell he'd studied the plans.

"Right," I said of the sunroom-style alcove. "Make it look like today instead of yesteryear."

He eyed the kitchen, taking in relevant details, nodded, then said, "And the master?"

I led him through the living room to the empty master suite that looked out on the lake, just like the breakfast nook and the living room.

"That's quite a view," he said, glancing toward the lake before stepping in the opposite direction, past the closets, and looking into the bathroom. "Are you not living here?"

"I am. I moved in on Saturday, but knowing you guys were starting today, I have everything either on the second floor or in storage."

He nodded. "It's gonna be loud. No way around it. You don't work from home, do you?"

"I...don't work." I forced a smile, trying to cover how much that was messing with my head.

I could see him trying to puzzle that out. No job. Big house. Expensive remodeling project.

"I was an investment banker until three weeks ago," I explained.

His brows shot up. "But now you're not?"

"Now I'm not. I loved the job...until I didn't. It was long hours, high stress, starting to become toxic. My boss was a condescending, sexist jackass."

"Sounds like leaving was a good decision then," he said as he checked something in his portfolio.

"Yeah." Even I could hear the lack of conviction in my answer, but that wasn't accurate. Leaving my job *was* the right decision. I nodded and tried again. "It definitely was. I'm just trying to figure out what to do with myself."

"You don't have something lined up?" His brow furrowed as if that didn't compute.

"No." I let out a little laugh, hoping that hid how I was freaking out pretty much full-time. "This remodeling project is it."

When I'd left my job, I'd been fueled by multiple things: concerning news from my doctor, ongoing insistence by my BFF, Chloe, that my job wasn't worth the stress and lack of respect from my boss, and chronic resentment at said boss. Walking out, seeing his stunned expression, had rocketed me to a natural high that had lasted for days.

"Levi said you purchased this place earlier in the spring?" West said.

I nodded. "It's funny how things work out. I bought it on a whim when I was still working and living in Nashville. Had no idea what I'd do with it. Rent it out, use it for a weekend place... When I quit my job, all I could think about was getting away, out of the city. Far away from everything. Starting over."

Recovering.

Getting healthy.

Learning to relax.

That was turning out to be quite the challenge.

"Gonna be rough for a few weeks," West said, "with a work crew here every day, making a racket."

"I figure I'll spend time outside, floating on the lake, reading, gardening."

"You garden?" He didn't hide his surprise.

With a self-conscious grin, I admitted, "Not yet. It's supposed to be soothing. Meditative. I bought some flowers to plant."

Please, let it be meditative. Let me get swept away by it, taken out of my head.

My head wasn't a good place right now.

For the first two and a half weeks after I'd quit, I'd kept busy by getting my Nashville condo ready to sell. I moved things to storage, painted, made some minor repairs, had the flooring replaced. I hired a staging company. I put it on the market a week ago and got a good offer right away. Then this past Saturday, I made the move to Dragonfly Lake.

Once the movers had left and I was alone in my new place, I expected to feel invigorated, excited, joyful. I'd done it. I'd taken a huge step toward changing my frantic, unhealthy life.

Instead, I'd been jittery, unable to sit still, nearly panic-stricken at the emptiness that stretched out in front of me.

My single-minded purpose since grad school had been to earn a shit ton of money, then invest it and turn it into a double shit ton. Quadruple. Tenfold.

By working my fool ass off, plus having spot-on gut instincts and general good luck, I'd accomplished a bigger net worth than I'd thought possible. When most people would think, *I've made my nest egg; I'm good,* I became determined to do it again. Build it into more. Climb higher.

"I'm gonna take a closer look at the kitchen," West said,

closing his portfolio and leaving the bedroom, dragging me out of my musing.

I followed him. "I was under the impression there'd be a whole crew here. I bought a dozen donuts for you guys," I said, gesturing to the box on the counter as I reentered the kitchen.

West was eyeing the windows in the sunroom, then turned his attention to me.

"Paul, Nathan, and Fritz will be here shortly to get started with demo. Some days it'll be the four of us. Some days it'll be more. Just depends on the day and the tasks. You didn't have to get us anything, but thank you."

"I would've gotten coffee too, but I don't love the bakery's one-size-fits-all pot of java. I haven't figured out the best place to get coffee in town. What's your favorite?"

He paused as if he hadn't thought about it before. "I just make some at home. I don't know of a good coffee source in town."

"You're kidding me." This town might be small, but its people still needed good coffee.

"No, ma'am."

Ma'am again.

"Can I ask you a personal question?"

"You can ask," he said.

"How old are you?"

"Thirty-one."

I filed that away. "I'm only four years older. You don't need to call me *ma'am*."

With a tilt of his head, he said, "Are you not from the South? It's a way to be polite."

"Be less polite. Pretty please? Just call me Presley."

"Yes, ma—" He stopped himself, laughed. "Presley. I'll do my best.

"And please eat some donuts." I opened the box and held it out. "Save me from myself."

He grinned, and my God, my heart... I swear it fluttered again. It didn't make sense how much this guy's smile affected me.

"You got a sweet tooth?" he asked as he took a single glazed donut from me.

"If it's bad for me, I crave it. Sugar, wine, coffee, you name it."

"The guys'll take some of these off your hands when they get here. I'm going to poke around a little deeper, see what we're up against."

"Anything I can do to help?"

"No, ma— Dammit," he said quietly. "Presley. I'll just do my thing, and you can do yours."

"Okay," I said, as if I had any idea what my thing was. "I'm going to eat a donut out on the patio, then maybe plant flowers."

After that, I had no clue, but I needed to figure it out. It was that or lose my mind.

Chapter Three

Presley

Sunrise on the lake was a thing of beauty, and I had a front-row seat to it. Every day for the rest of my life, if I wanted it.

I'd woken up at quarter till five, even though I had no reason to be awake until West and his crew arrived. Old habits died hard.

New habits were going to take a bit.

Like sleeping. Relaxing. Plus filling my waking hours with...something.

I'd texted Chloe, my best friend since business school, and asked her if she could get away for breakfast at the Dragonfly Diner.

Breakfast was *something*. It would fill an hour.

Baby steps.

Just after I was seated at a booth along the front windows with a view of the heart of town, Chloe came in, glanced around, greeted Patrick—one of the servers—by name, and headed toward me.

I stood and hugged her.

"God, it's good to see you," I said.

Chloe laughed. "I just saw you Saturday. Because you live in town now," she said with pronounced enthusiasm.

"I'm still getting used to that," I said as we slid into opposite sides of the booth.

"Good morning, ladies." Patrick came up to our table with a coffeepot. "Do we want coffee?"

Chloe flipped her mug over. I eyed the pot, knew it would be mediocre, and turned my mug upright anyway.

"Yes, please," I said in case my face had revealed my thoughts about standard diner coffee. Normally I liked my coffee black, but that was when it was the good stuff and I wanted to savor the true flavor. "Could we get real cream too?"

"You bet, sugar. Do you need some time with the menu?" Patrick asked as he poured.

Chloe looked at me in question.

"Those waffles..." I said.

"Dragonfly Dust," Chloe said.

"Those. Please."

"That's really why you moved to town, isn't it?" Chloe said.

"Definitely a perk," I said.

"Oh, new resident?" Patrick asked. "Welcome to Dragonfly Lake. The waffles are a marvelous reason to move here. What can I get you, Chloe?"

She hesitated.

"You want the waffles," I said, knowing my friend's sugar tooth.

"We're celebrating your move. I want the waffles."

"You got it." Patrick hurried off to another table.

The place was filling up fast, despite it being barely six thirty.

I eyed my mug, knowing the java was subpar. I'd had it before. With a sigh, I glanced around for Patrick to see if the cream was on its way. The bowl of artificial creamers on the table... No.

"You're such a snob," Chloe said, laughing.

"I like good coffee."

"Bronson's spoiled you."

"I miss Bronson's."

The indie artisan coffee shop was across the street from my condo in Nashville. Chloe had lived two floors below mine until she and Holden hooked up, and Bronson's had been our daily routine for years. I'd kept it up even after she moved out. Bronson's specialized in craft-brewed coffee. Once you started drinking the high-quality stuff on the daily, it was impossible to go back to standard fare.

"Is there really not one place to get"—I lowered my voice—"even halfway decent coffee in this town? Like, even somewhere off the square? Anywhere?"

She tilted her head and shot me a look that said, *Sorry but no.* "You have money. Go online and buy the nicest home coffeemaker you can find."

"I'm on it. At least the waffles are going to be amazing."

"Nothing compares," Chloe said as Patrick delivered an individual-sized cream pitcher.

"Your waffles just came up," he said. "I'll be right back."

We thanked him, and I poured cream into my coffee.

"Where's Sutton this morning?" I asked as we waited. "I figured you'd bring her with you."

"Holden's taking her to Quincy's at her usual time. It's hard to pivot with a one-year-old. She was just waking up when I left."

"I didn't think about that when I invited you out. I'm confusing Mom Chloe with Single Chloe. Sorry about that. It's okay to tell me no."

"I didn't want to tell you no. Holden can handle it just fine today. You sounded a little...desperate in your text."

"You can't hear a text."

"You know what I mean. Something about the *please tell me you can save me from myself and meet me for breakfast.*"

"Ah," I said. "I might've felt a little desperate."

Patrick returned with our waffles, saving me from having to say more.

"You're amazing," I told the server who was probably in his late forties.

"All I do is deliver," he said dramatically. "These waffles speak for themselves."

Dragonfly Dust Waffles were thick Belgian waffles that had blue, green, and purple sprinkles in the batter. On top was a generous tower of homemade whipped cream and more sprinkles, these in the shape of tiny dragonflies in the same colors. They were a thing of culinary beauty, a treasure at this unassuming diner. Almost enough to make up for the blah brew in my cup.

Once Patrick left us, I poured pure maple syrup on my sugar-laden waffles and took my first bite. The sensory pleasure of sweetness on my tongue was instant.

"Between this and donuts from Sugar, I might become diabetic before I hit thirty-six," I said.

Chloe laughed. "They do have eggs here."

I made a face that showed my opinion of eggs, particularly as I dipped my next bite into the thick, fluffy whipped cream.

"So what's up with the desperation?" Chloe asked.

My waffle-induced endorphin rush faded. I chewed and stared at my food, organizing my thoughts.

"Things sort of caught up with me over the weekend," I said. "I finally got all the moving details and real estate stuff taken care of. I've been consumed by that for the three weeks since I quit, you know?"

"You basically overhauled everything in your life in three weeks," Chloe said empathetically, nailing the issue like only my best friend could. "And now you have time to think."

"What have I done, Chloe? Like, I threw away more than a decade's worth of career. All my life goals were tied up in that job. Now suddenly I have this blank slate, and I don't know what to do with it."

"You said you don't want to go back to investment banking, right?"

I let the idea roll around in my head while I ate another bite. The thought of starting a new position with a different company doing what I'd done since grad school... There was a part of me that missed the challenge, the thrill of success, the sense of accomplishment, but... "Honestly? It sounds exhausting."

"I've thought you were nearing burnout for the last year or two."

"You might be right. I didn't see it while I was in it. I didn't have time to see it."

"You didn't have time to do anything but work, eat carryout, and hit Bronson's every day."

"Fact. I thrived on it for so long..."

"But you're human, and that job required a super-human effort always. Plus your boss..."

I made a face. "Toad."

Rob Landers was the one part of my career I'd detested.

He was twenty years older than me, had been in the industry forever, had been good at the job in his day, but he sucked as a manager. Throw three parts barely veiled misogyny into the mix, and I'd been at a slow boil for the past few years.

From the day he'd become a partner and been put in charge of my division, my love for the job had slowly leaked out of me. The final straw came when I'd expressed interest in becoming a partner. He'd assured me I had no chance, even though I was the youngest VP in the firm's history and had the numbers to back up my competency.

Normally when someone told me I couldn't do something, I put my head down and proved them wrong, but between years of friction with Landers and other old-schoolers in the industry, the extreme demand of the career itself both in terms of time and stress, and my doctor's advice, his condescension had snapped something in me. I think I'd been working toward making changes in my life on some level for months. He merely fast-forwarded me.

"You were a badass superhuman investment banker for more than a decade. You gave it everything," Chloe said with admiration in her tone. "But I don't know how much longer you could've sustained that, even without the toad. You haven't had a life since undergrad."

She didn't lie. To succeed at that career, you had to eat, sleep, and breathe it. To succeed as a woman, you had to give up the sleep part and basically hustle for eighteen hours a day.

"It's time for you to have a life," she continued. "Maybe meet a guy, fall in love, start a family."

I scoffed. "Should I take cooking lessons first so I can be a good housewife?"

Chloe laughed. "I'm getting you an apron for your birthday."

"You know me better than that."

"I know you're not the relationship type or the 'stay at home and look at the lake all day' type."

"And I've been at home looking at the lake for two days straight now."

"Thus the desperation."

"I'm losing my mind." I dared a drink of coffee, then chased it with a bite of waffle.

"Didn't the remodelers start yesterday?"

"They did. Demolition is loud. I spent most of the day outside. I even planted flowers."

Her brows went up as if she couldn't believe it.

"Twenty pots," I told her. "I set them around the deck and along the steps going down to the water. They're gorgeous, but next time I'm hiring a landscaper."

"Gardening is supposed to be relaxing. Therapeutic."

"I'm not the right girl for that. It turns out I don't like dirt."

Chloe laughed. "That's an important thing to learn about yourself, I guess. Cross landscaper off the list of possible new careers." She took a bite, chewed, swallowed. "So demo. Remodeling. Have you seen West yet?"

I tried to hold back a smile, but the thought of him made that difficult. "Eight a.m. yesterday, he was the one at my door."

Chloe's brows rose. "Not Levi?"

"Levi had an emergency of some kind, so it was just West at first, then three of the other guys joined him with all the equipment."

"And?"

"They demoed half the main floor down to studs. The kitchen is today."

"Yay, demo," she said dryly. "You know what I really want to hear about. Or rather who."

I finished the food in my mouth. "I'm unreasonably attracted to him," I said in as unbothered a voice as I could manage. Inside, I was bothered just thinking about him. "That guy-in-a-tool-belt thing? It's for real."

"Yeah," she said, making it a two-syllable word with the tone of *du-uhh*.

"He's not my type," I said. "Just like you said at the party."

When I'd spotted West Aldridge at Rowan and Chance's gender-reveal party, something had happened to me. There was almost an actual click of lust locking into place. I'd never experienced anything like it before. Not on that level.

"And yet?" Chloe prompted.

I shook my head. "He made it clear we're business only."

She tilted her head. "Understandable. Your project is big. He'll probably be in your house for weeks."

I couldn't deny the way my blood heated at that thought. "I might've had a handyman-nailing-me fantasy or two last night," I said, grinning. "Another reason I need something to occupy my mind and my hours. In his mind, I'm his client and nothing else."

"Rowan said he's all about his little girls and doesn't do relationships."

"I wouldn't want a relationship, just a mutual relieving of tension. A satisfaction of curiosity. I doubt we have anything in common."

Chloe shrugged. "I'm sure you'll get to know more about him if he's spending eight hours a day in your home."

"Possibly," I said, though I wasn't so sure. We'd talked a few times yesterday, but it was only about the project. That and I'd given him the garage code so they could get in whether I was home or not. "Ideally I won't be sitting around at home all day every day."

"Which brings us back to, what do you want to do with the rest of your life?"

I shoved the last big bite of waffle into my mouth, hoping the sugar rush would compensate for the unpleasantness her question aroused.

"I used to like that you were so direct," I grumped once my food was gone.

"You still like that I'm direct." Chloe pointed at me with her fork. "Sitting around, planting flowers isn't doing it for you. What would? A part-time job somewhere like the boutique? A gym membership and a personal trainer?"

"No and no," I said easily, though I should definitely consider the trainer.

"What about finance stuff? Could you open a personal financial-services business?"

I had the background for that, but advising individuals on saving and investing sounded like torture. Some people were made for nurturing, hand-holding, and teaching, which would be a lot of what a small-town financial-services business would entail, but that wasn't me.

I'd gone into finance to make big money. I didn't care if people judged me for that. It was who I was, who my background had made me, and I wasn't going to apologize for it. But I was going to be honest with myself about what called to me.

I made a gagging sound as I automatically reached for my mug, then stopped myself from taking a drink.

Chloe laughed. "Okay, so we know what you don't like. What *do* you like?"

"Coffee," I said, staring at the butterscotch-colored, diluted joe in my mug. "*Good* coffee."

"So you said," she said indulgently. "Talk to Monty, the owner here. Suggest some better coffee."

My mind was off and running in a different direction. "What if I opened my own coffee shop instead?"

Anyone else might not've taken me seriously, but my business-school bestie took the baton and went. "You've got the money, the coffee knowledge, and the business background."

I sat up straighter, my sad mug forgotten, and met Chloe's gaze. Without words, we shared the understanding that this could be exactly what I did for my next career.

"Wow," she said.

"Wow. I need to think through everything, but I haven't felt sparked like this since I quit. Since before I quit."

Patrick slid the bill tray onto our table and kept on going, as if he sensed there was something big going on with our discussion, and he didn't want to interrupt.

Distractedly I pulled out my card and set it down to cover the bill.

Chloe took her purse out, but I waved her away.

"I've got this one. You can get the next time. Chloe!" Excitement zipped through me at the coffee shop prospect.

Our eyes met again, and my brows shot up. It was all I could do to sit still.

"I have to get to work, but tell me what I can do," she said. "I can help you research or taste test or whatever."

I laughed, because this was sort of crazy and yet sort of awesome.

"I'll definitely keep you posted."

By the time I walked out the diner door, I was absolutely buzzing with possibilities.

Chapter Four

West

Day two of the Holiday project was nearing an end, and I had yet to see Presley.

Which was just fine with me.

The guys and I had made good progress on the demo and hoped to finish gutting the main floor tomorrow.

Though ripping out cabinets, yanking up flooring, and pulling down drywall was damn hard work, this job, at least today, nearly felt like cheating in the battle with Nick, my competitor for the foreman position. Presley had cranked up the AC considerably yesterday when she'd noticed my guys sweating, so the temp was close to thirty degrees cooler than the other crew's outdoor project in the Tennessee sun.

Nick was also dealing with a disruptive homeowner on their jobsite. Mr. Castille, a retired teacher, was apparently questioning everything they did and how they did it. Nick had to take time out to explain every step, which had to be exhausting and would likely put the project behind schedule soon, if it hadn't already.